GRACELAND EXPRESS

By

Marie Vernon

Graceland Express
1st Printing

© Copyright 2011
by Marie Vernon
St. Augustine, FL 32080

Cataloging-in-publication data for this book is available from The Library of Congress.
ISBN: 978-0-9827019-7-3

Marie Vernon
Author

For information write:

Dementi Milestone Publishing, Inc.
Manakin-Sabot, VA 23103

www.dementimilestonepublishing.com

Cover Illustration & Design by: Kelly Brown and Anthony Sclavi of Brio Books

Manuscript design by Dianne Dementi.
diannedementi@yahoo.com

Printed in the USA

DEDICATION

This book is dedicated to the millions of fans who keep the memory of Elvis Presley burning brightly.

ACKNOWLEDGEMENTS

My sincere thanks to the friends, family and fellow writers who have urged me on in writing this book. To Mary Cahill and other members of the Baltimore Writers' Alliance (now the Baltimore Chapter of the Maryland Writers' Association) thanks for spurring (nagging?) me to get aboard the Graceland Express. My appreciation goes to the many editors and writing instructors whose insights and inspiration have helped me persevere in my writing career; most notably the late Sister Maura Eichner, SSND, and Frederic Morton, author of *The Rothschilds*, who, at Johns Hopkins University, unknowingly set me on the path to fiction writing. Thanks to editor Jessica Page Morrell, author of *Thanks But This Isn't for Us*, for her help and encouragement.

Special thanks to daughter Holly Feist for reading the manuscript and offering valuable insights. For their critiques of the story during many late night sessions, I owe thanks to a number of St. Augustine writers including Claire Sloan, Drew Sappington, Ray Feliciano, C.J. Godwin, and Jim James.

Thanks to author Arliss Ryan for steering me through the jungle of website design and to web designer Dan Hubley for his expert help with the site. Thanks to Anthony Sclavi and artist Kelly Brown of Brio Books for a great job of translating our cover concept into reality. To Wayne and Dianne Dementi and the staff of Dementi Milestone Publishing, thanks for making the journey to publication a joyful and productive one.

Finally, saving the most important for last, I thank my husband, McCay Vernon, for his love and support. The wonderful example he sets and his unique talent for bringing out the best in others have made each day of our lives together a fulfilling adventure. Mac, you are the best!

INTRODUCTION

Graceland Express is a lighthearted crime caper filled with adventures, romance and hilarious mishaps, but it also offers meaningful insights into the tremendous vitality of the Elvis legend and the attraction of Graceland for fans all over the world.

Vangie O'Toole is an Elvis fan whose dream of going to Graceland with the Elvis-4-Ever Fan Club seems hopeless. She's stuck in her job at the Kmart and is the sole caretaker for her paranoid mother who is convinced Gypsies will kidnap her if she's left alone. Vangie's brother, Floyd, is no help—he's in Miami, mixed up with a drug gang and planning to double-cross them. Vangie wishes the Elvis who lives in her closet could solve her problems, but he's only a mannequin in an Elvis costume.

The inspiration for this story came from a newspaper interview with a passionate Elvis fan. Although I had a strong appreciation of Elvis's music, I knew little about his fans and approached the interview with some reservations, not sure what sort of person devotes her time and energies to the memory of a performer no longer alive.

It soon became obvious that Betty Lou Watts, the woman I interviewed, had a strong sense of Elvis's influence in every aspect of her daily life. Her home was decorated entirely with Elvis memorabilia, Elvis's music and films were her preferred entertainment, and her free time was devoted to her fan club activities, including Elvis's legacy of charitable work for those in need. In the end, I came away from the interview thoroughly impressed by Miss Watts's sincerity and her genuine sense of connection with Elvis.

In an attempt to better understand the amazing vitality of the Elvis's legacy, I dug deeper, trying to discover what inspires such loyalty among his fans. Part of the answer, of course, was Elvis's unique voice and his innovative song styling. The physicality he brought to his performances changed the American music scene forever and introduced generations to newer, more visceral rhythms. Whether crooning a love song or grooving on rock and roll, the effect was always undeniably Elvis.

Another factor that drew fans to Elvis, women in particular, was his appearance. He was tall and muscular with a well-built physique. An expressive mouth and soulful eyes gave his face sensitivity and, at the same time, an undeniable sensuality. In his later appearances, the costumes he wore helped to exude a sense of power and drama.

However attractive those aspects of Elvis might be, what most strongly accounts for his fans' lasting fascination is the fact that his life story contains all the elements of the American legend, both the good and the bad. The bell curve his career followed demonstrates both the glory that can be attained through sheer talent and, at the same time, reveals the price fame demands. The majority of Elvis's fans do not come from the rich and the famous, but from working class people who can identify with his struggles, live vicariously through his triumphs, and grieve at the ultimate failure to outrun the fame that became his enemy.

From the little Mississippi boy in overalls, his father in jail, and his mother struggling to survive, to the young truck driver pursuing his dream, to the man who willingly left wealth and prestige behind to serve this country, to the husband and father glorying in success, to the celebrity betrayed by some he trusted, to the ultimate shocking end, the tale is one no novelist could invent.

Little wonder then that Graceland has become the American Mecca, the place that holds the dream together, where people like the fictional Vangie O'Toole of this book can still gather, both to reestablish a sense of connection to their idol, but, more importantly, to confirm the bond that will always hold them together as Elvis fans.

Marie Vernon
St. Augustine, Florida, June 2011

NOTICE TO ALL CLUB MEMBERS

IN ORDER TO RESERVE THE BUS FOR OUR

GRACELAND TRIP TO HONOR

THE TENTH ANNIVERSARY OF ELVIS'S PASSING,

ALL DEPOSITS MUST BE IN BY NO LATER THAN

JULY 3, 1987

BE SURE TO GIVE YOUR DEPOSIT MONEY

TO THE CLUB TREASURER BY THAT DATE.

NO REFUNDS!!!

REMEMBER THAT THE FEE DOES NOT INCLUDE THE

MEMPHIS CITY TOUR WHICH IS EXTRA FOR THOSE

WISHING TO TAKE IT.

BRENDA SUE HIGGS, PRESIDENT

ELVIS-4-EVER FAN CLUB

1. "That's All Right, Mama"

Palm trees.. Waves suff-suffing against the sand. Hula music in the background. They are side by side on a sun-drenched beach. He leans in closer, begins to croon, his voice smooth as moonlight...

A sound as jarring as the backup warning on a dump truck, a harsh, garbled *OOOO...AAAYYY...EEE...*followed by a prolonged *EEEEEECH* splintered the morning quiet. Vangie O'Toole sat straight up in bed, squinting among the blurred shadows of her room. By the grudging dawn light that crept through the room's only window, she could just make out the tall figure standing in the alcove that had once been her closet. His face glowed dim and mysterious under the blue Christmas lights that surrounded his niche while the mirrors that lined the closet wall behind him reflected infinite images of the sequined eagle that adorned the back of his costume.

The screeches continued. Vangie reached toward the nightstand and groped for the off button on the tape player. The wire that led to the speaker in Elvis's chest must have come loose when she changed his costume. She'd fix it later, but for now all she wanted was to duck beneath the covers and onto the warm beach of her dreams. The intrusion of morning sounds made that impossible. Through the open window came the muted roar of distant interstate traffic, the mournful wail of a boat's whistle down the bay, and insistent bang and clatter from the rail yards. Closer to hand, car and truck doors slammed and reluctant motors revved to life. Like Baltimore's other working class neighborhoods, Dundalk was beginning another workday. Any hope for a few extra moments in her dream world gone, Vangie emerged from beneath the covers.

Soon as she raised her head, another sound caught her attention, a scraping and banging from downstairs, furniture being shifted about, little clinks and clanks of knickknacks getting moved from one place to another. Mama was rearranging.

All thoughts of sleep vanished, Vangie threw back the sheet. "A bad sign," she told Elvis as she swung her feet to the floor. In the half-light it was easy to imagine the mannequin's painted eyebrow lifted in sympathy. She snatched her robe from the chair next to her dresser and hurried toward the bathroom.

With the plastic shower curtain pulled closed, Vangie ducked as the water dribbling from the nozzle alternated from tepid to scalding. She adjusted the faucet, then stood under the lethargic spray, eyes closed. Of late, things had seemed to be going okay, but now Mama was rearranging, a sure sign she was having premonitions again. What could be setting her off this time? Last night Mama hadn't seemed at all upset at the hint that she, Vangie, might be going to Graceland with the fan club.

A sinking feeling settled in Vangie's chest—come August 16th, the fan club would be there at Graceland, and once again, she'd be left behind. The other times she was unable to go hadn't seemed so bad, but this time was special, the tenth anniversary of Elvis's death. Fans from all over the world, as far away as Finland and Japan would be there, and here she'd be, stuck as always in Dundalk. It wasn't fair.

The bar of soap slipped from Vangie's hand and she stooped to retrieve it. One good thing, Mama's premonitions most often turned out to be no more reliable than those tabloid stories about how some guy in Indiana had spotted alien spaceships sucking electricity out of high-tension wires. With Mama it was usually Gypsies, Mama insisting Gypsies had broken into their home, Mama prowling about all night so Gypsies couldn't steal her souvenir ashtray of the 1939 New York World's Fair.

The water began to run cold. Vangie stepped out and hurried to dry herself. The sooner she got downstairs the better. If Mama's premonitions weren't cut off in a hurry she could end up crying and distraught, insisting that Gypsies were coming to kidnap her. Ever since Dad died, the episodes had gotten worse and more unpredictable. Once, just once, it would be nice if every plan didn't have to revolve around Mama's illness. Once, just once, it would be nice to feel the way other twenty-seven year olds felt—free to live her life without worrying that any least little upset, the smallest variation in routine, could set Mama off and send her back to the hospital.

Vangie slid back the shower curtain, pulled a towel off the rack and stepped out onto the bathmat. Wrapped in the towel, she checked her hair in the mirror. Yesterday Darla Wisnewski had told her she ought to try that that new Super Sun-In Rinse to bring out her highlights. Trouble was, there was no guarantee she even had highlights. Hair an indeterminate shade between blond and brown wasn't in the same league with Darla's dye-enhanced locks, this week a shade known as Magically Magenta. Vangie applied face lotion. At least she had nice skin, but that and what Larry Kroger had once called her "amber-colored" eyes weren't likely to knock guys out, not even if she piled on Darla's Midnight Madness lipstick, Rose Riot blusher, and Definitely Daring eyeliner. As for the little stream of freckles across her nose—she could do without them. Twenty-seven was a little old for cute.

Still, a person couldn't help wanting to be able to afford stuff like cosmetics and maybe some new clothes once in a while. That cute blouse in J. C. Penny's window. She leaned over to towel-dry her hair. No use wasting time with wishful thinking—at the end of the month the bill for the roof repairs would come due.

Back in her room, Vangie debated for a moment between the green skirt and the blue one, then with a quick eeny-meeny settled on the blue. "Doesn't make much difference," she told the Elvis mannequin. "The Kmart smock looks like a pup tent no matter what I've got on underneath."

She perched on the edge of the bed and began pulling on the unstylish but comfortable shoes that would see her through what was bound to be an exhausting day. "With the Sizzling Summer Sell-Out going full blast," she told Elvis, "the minute the doors open the customers will be storming in. All day long they'll be battling over the carts, bullying their way through the aisles, snatching up the sale leaders, and arguing over places in the checkout line."

Elvis's mouth seemed to give a sympathetic little twist.

She slid her foot into the other shoe. "I'm keeping my fingers crossed that Dennis shows up on time—or shows up at all. The way he's been hitting the bottle since he and Fran broke up, that's probably too much to hope for."

Again, Elvis's expression was sympathetic.

She stuffed the badge that read *Vangie O'Toole, Assistant Manager* into her purse, picked up the bag that held her textbooks, then blew Elvis a quick goodbye kiss. He glowered sexily back at her from beneath his pompadoured wig.

Downstairs, Mama was seated at the kitchen table, her sparrow-like body perched on the very edge of her chair, gravity scarcely holding her in place. Another bad sign. Vangie got out the milk and Cheerios and took the facing chair. Hoping to derail Mama's mind from whatever ominous track it had switched to this time, she offered, "We're getting in a big shipment of window fans today. Thought I might get a new one for your room. That old one kept me awake last night—it sounds like a 747 taking off from BWI."

Mama stared into space as she slid the Priscilla and Elvis salt -and-pepper shakers from one side of the crocheted napkin holder to the other. "They used to call it Friendship Airport which was a lot nicer sounding," she said. "Don't see any reason they should have changed." Then, without pause, she added, "Floyd's on his way home. I feel it plain as anything."

Vangie's hand gave a convulsive jerk and the stream of milk she was pouring sloshed onto the tabletop. She jumped up and grabbed a paper towel from the holder by the sink and dabbed at the mess. "Mama," she said, "it's been over three years since we've laid eyes on Floyd. It's not likely he'll show up here in Dundalk now." She didn't add, *and for that we should be thankful.*

Mama paid no attention. Eyes closed, she tilted her head toward the ceiling as if the chrome light fixture was sending down a vision…Our Lady of Florescence. "It's not just your brother that's coming, either," she said. "Two dark men and one light one. They'll be following after."

Mama's prediction came at Vangie like a wild pitch at Memorial Stadium and left a sinking feeling inside her chest. The Floyd thing was even worse than Gypsies, a no-win either way. If Floyd should show up—please, God, keep him far away—there was always trouble. Money stolen from her purse. Things disappearing around the neighborhood. Last time there'd been police trouble. On the other hand, if he didn't come, Mama might keep getting more and more agitated. Sometimes it got so bad that even the medicine didn't help, and then it was the hospital again.

Vangie mopped the spilled milk from the tabletop…at least Formica was hard to ruin. By the time she finished, her Cheerios had inflated into soggy little doughnuts. Seating herself, she picked up her spoon and shoved the cereal flotilla from one side of the bowl to the other. Why, of all days, did Mama have to start now—the Kmart's Sizzlin' Summer Sale in full swing, three new cashiers to break in, and Dennis probably too hung-over to manage getting out of bed, let alone managing the store. All day long it would be "Void on Number Two, Vangie!" "How do I ring up a rebate, Vangie?" "Where do I shelve these whats-its, Vangie?" And that didn't even take into account cranky customers and careless stock boys.

A quick glance at the front page of the *Baltimore Star* Mama had shoved to one side showed streams of traffic heading for the Bay Bridge. "Thousands Seek Escape from Record Heat," the headline announced. Another scorcher in downtown. Here in Dundalk, it would be worse. Already the tepid air oozing through the back screen door was thick with metallic fumes from the steel mill.

Still, problems at work and the miserable heat were the least of her worries at the moment. All the months of planning for the trip to Graceland could collapse in minutes under the weight of Mama's out-of-the-blue premonition. The best hope was that, like warts, that weird notion would disappear on its own. With luck, tonight she'd come home from work to find that Mama had forgotten all about Floyd and the dark and light men.

"Gotta go, Mama." Vangie snatched her purse off the countertop, slung the strap of her book bag over her shoulder and bent to give her mother a quick kiss. "If I run, I can just catch my bus."

Mama followed Vangie to the door. "First Floyd and then two dark men and one light one," she stated in matter-of-fact tones. "I see them clear as anything."

2. "Playing for Keeps"

Floyd O'Toole planted his elbows on the railing of the apartment's balcony and exhaled a column of cigarette smoke. It hung for a moment before fading into the sludgepot of smog and fumes that made Miami's summer air thick enough to slice. From the open window of a nearby apartment the shrill voices of a couple arguing rose above the incessant blare of a radio. Below, sounds of traffic blended with the crash and clatter of metal on metal that rose from the garbage truck rumbling its way down the street.

Floyd pitched the stub of his Lucky Strike over the railing. One more day and he could kiss this lousy low-rent neighborhood goodbye. Hell, with 250,000 beautiful greenbacks in his pocket, he could buy Miami...half of Little Havana, at least.

Dolores, seated behind him on one of the Wal-Mart plastic chairs, had started slapping her sandal against the concrete again, *tap...tap...taping* like to drive a person nuts. The broad's antsiness was beginning to get to him.

"I'm tellin' you, Floyd," Dolores whined, "it ain't gonna work. I shouldn't of never—"

Floyd swung around to face her. "Look, Babe, nothing's gonna go wrong. Me and Lieutenant Arena got this thing down pat. Soon as the mules get there, Arena and his cops break in and grab the stuff. Then they ice the rest of Cenicero's gang…except for me."

Little worry lines traced themselves across Dolores's forehead. "So while all that's going down, you're gonna make off with the dough?"

"I got it all scoped out."

He did, too…hoped he did. While the guys in the front room checked out the stuff to make sure it hadn't been cut, he and Jose would be waiting in the back room with the pay off money. All he had to do once Arena's cops got there was to take out Jose, grab the cash, jump in the rental car he had stashed down the alley and hit the road. *Adios amigos.*

"I dunno, Floyd," Dolores whined. "Even for four Gs I shouldn't of let you talk me into this. Last night, Cenicero was…I don't know…different. Kinda like he suspicioned or something."

He reached to give her chin an encouraging nudge. "Trust me, Babe, Cinecero ain't got a clue. By the time the fireworks are over, you and me'll be long gone."

Floyd turned back to stare over the railing. A helluva lot better if he hadn't needed to cut Dolores in on the deal, but with Cenicero being so close-mouthed, she'd been his only hope of dragging out of the boss when and where the deal would go down. Broad hadn't come cheap, either. Took every cent he'd gotten from the Vegas job. She might not have gone along even then, only she suspected Cenicero was about to dump her for the bimbo he'd picked up on his last trip to the Bahamas.

Behind him, the chair scraped as Dolores stood and began pacing up and down. He sloped her a cautious look. The purplish bruise under her left eye was a beaut, the flesh around the socket still puffy and swollen. Cenicero's trademark. But that was for the good. The damage the boss's fist had done to her face had got Dolores really steamed, pissed off enough so she'd been willing to come on board with his scheme.

She halted beside him, flung her half-smoked cigarette over the railing and watched the blazing stub sift downward to the street. "You ask me, Floyd, you shoulda just took your regular split, let it go at that."

Floyd snorted. "Look, Doll, I been Cenicero's errand boy three, four years now, and what've I got to show for it? A couple of silk suits, a little tequila money, but no real pay off. Even that moron Gecko with his voodoo charms and mumbo-jumbo superstitions gets a bigger cut than me, and he's not even in on the drop. Well, as of now, I'm through playing the flunky. July 4th, 1987 is gonna go down in history as the date Mister Floyd O'Toole cleared himself a cool 250 grand!" He circled Dolores's shoulders with his arm and let his fingers make a little excursion in the direction of her breast.

She shrugged off his arm. "I shouldn't never let you talk me into this. They don't call Cenicero 'The Ashtray' for nothin'. If he gets wind of what's going on, you and me are toast."

"Hey, sweetheart, I wasn't born yesterday, you know. Cenicero ain't never gonna get wise. All we gotta do is stay cool for one more day."

Dolores shook her head. "I still don't like this double-cross you're pulling. Why can't you just split the dough and the dope with Lieutenant Arena the way you and him planned?"

"Fat chance. Ain't a damned thing to keep the crooked cop from offing me along with the rest of the guys. You can bet he's already got it figured that a one-way split's a heap more profitable than a two-way one."

"Yeah, but screwing a cop…."

"Once I cut out of there with the dough, ain't nothing Arena can do about it. Besides, the lieutenant and his boys get to keep the coke. By the time that happy dust gets back to the station house you can bet at least half of it will have 'disappeared.'"

She sniffed. "Yeah, but what about Cenicero? He ain't disappearing."

"Before he ever figures out what's happened, I'll be…" he quickly corrected himself, "*we'll* be long gone. Besides, with Jose and Miguel out of the way, the only one of Cenicero's Costa Rican cane chewers left will be Gecko, and he's so stupid he can't find his own pecker in the dark."

Dolores flopped back into the chair and lit another cigarette while Floyd swung back to stare out over the rooftops. Too bad he couldn't take Dolores with him like he'd promised. She was a decent enough broad, even if it sometimes seemed like her gears were stuck in neutral. But hell, she'd be okay—Dolores had been on her own since she was twelve and her old lady put her out on the street. No excess baggage for him. Angelina was waiting in New York. Now there was a broad with class. Having a Mafioso for a dad might cause a few problems but she'd never end up shopping in Kmart. Once he had his hands on the dough all he had to do was go up there, collect Angelina, and next stop Mexico, the good life.

He pulled the pack from his pocket, took out a fresh smoke and lit it. Yessir, there'd be plenty to celebrate this Fourth of July. Only one more day and he was home free. Never have to take any more crap off that Spic, Cenicero. Never have go running back to Dundalk with his tail between his legs. Maybe, though, he'd stop by there on his way to New York, show Mama and Vangie how flush he was…yeah, maybe even take them a little something. For Vangie, anything with Elvis's mug on it would do. And for Mama? Hell, ought to get her a Uzi so she could scare off those Gypsies she was always claiming were coming to get her. Anyhow, with all that dough in hand, Mama and Vangie would see he'd made the big time, that he wasn't about to wind up behind the wheel of a stinking garbage truck like his old man.

3. "Help Me Make it Through the Night"

Floyd cringed as another THA-ROOMP! of fireworks sounded from the little park at the end of Casaverde. The gut-jarring explosions and banshee shrieks of the rockets had him so wired he couldn't think straight. In between bursts of red and green, the room was dim as the inside of a dumpster and smelled worse. The stink of dead mice and mildew and rotten food and a pile of something over in the corner that it didn't pay to think about had his sinuses draining like a swamp, and thick, ropy snot kept choking off his windpipe.

What in the name of sweet hell was he doing here in the back room of this trashed out bungalow, playing Russian roulette with a drug boss and a crooked cop? The plan he'd scoped out didn't look so easy now, what with Jose gripping the briefcase with the 250 Gs like he was grafted to it. Taking out Jose was the tricky part. The Spic might be short and stocky, but he was mean as a bullwhip and tough as a combat boot. "Cenicero's Crocodile," they called him. One wrong move and Jose would whack him quick as he'd stomp one of those cockroaches scuttling across the filthy floor.

Floyd slid a cautious hand into his pocket and felt the reassuring touch of the pistol butt. That part at least had worked out—Cenicero had made sure he wasn't carrying, but thanks to Dolores's inside dope about the drop site, he'd been able to sneak in ahead of time and stash the gun, so Jose had no way to know he was packing. If only he could breathe. With his sleeve he tried to stem the flood of mucus pouring down over his upper lip.

"*Idioto!*" Jose snarled. "Your sniffle, snort, honk gonna give us away before the guys in the front room got a chance to check the merchandise."

"Can't help it." Floyd hissed back at him. "From the time I was a kid, mold and dust and animal hair been poison to me."

Jose didn't say anything, but even in the dim light Floyd could feel his beady-eyed glare. Well the Spic could glare all he liked. After tonight, Jose was history, same as the rest of Cenicero's gang.

Either that or one Floyd O'Toole would be wearing cement overshoes. Wrong—Cenicero wouldn't go that easy on a double-crosser. More likely he'd end up as the main dish at a barbecue. Maybe Dolores was right. Actually, he'd had it pretty damned good working for Cenicero. Tooling around Miami in the boss's Masserati sure as hell beat driving a garbage truck like the old man had done all his life. If Mama had her way, that's what he'd be doing right now. "Oh, Floyd, it's a good, steady job.

A paycheck every Friday." Like, sure, he was gonna schlep around in a green jumpsuit picking up other people's shit.

He'd tried going legit once, but even that had been a bummer. Loading trucks in Herb Polaris's warehouse up there in Jersey, in a lifetime he wouldn't have pulled down the kind of cash sitting inside that briefcase. After tonight he could buy his own Masserati. Leather seats. All the fancy gadgets.

Maybe once the heat cooled off and it was safe to come back to the states, he'd tool on up to Jersey, invite Herb Polaris to take a little ride, show off his new wheels. "Looks like you hit it big, O'Toole," Herb would say. Yeah, that's what he'd do. Polaris was one of the few guys who'd ever given him a break, treated him decent. Herb and that cat of his, Konstanze. Take her for a ride, too.

At the impact of another crunching explosion, Floyd glanced toward the open window, its glass and sash long since gone the way of the room's plumbing and light fixtures. He watched a rocket spread a fiery umbrella across the night sky, then sag into shapeless sprinkles of light. Fireworks. When he was a kid back in Dundalk, Dad always took the family to Patterson Park every Fourth of July. People sprawled on blankets across the hillsides, little kids rolling on the grass, oooh-ing and aaah-ing with each new burst of light. Vangie scared of the noise, huddled on Dad's lap, hands over her ears. This one time—he must have been about seven or eight then—this fat little kid was running through the crowd, firing off his Lone Ranger cap pistol. God, but he wanted that pistol. He could imagine exactly how it would be to whip the gun out of its holster, feel the slick metal butt heavy in his hand, hear the satisfying *Ka-pow! Ka-pow! Ka-pow!* as he pulled the trigger.

That night his wish had come true. A skyrocket misfired, zig-zagged along the ground instead of taking off skyward. Mothers screamed for their kids. People ran, ducked, rolled, did anything they could to get out of the way. The sizzling rocket made a crazy pattern across the grass, and, for a moment, seemed to head straight for where he and Vangie and Dad and Mama were sitting. Then it veered and took off after Little Fatso with the gun. The kid raced squealing up the hill, trying to outrun it, but he looked back over his shoulder and tripped just as the rocket caught up with him and exploded.

Chaos. The fat kid rolling on the grass, his shirt in flames. Firemen running up the hill with extinguishers, spraying the kid with foam. The ambulance screeching in through the park gates. Medics loading the kid onto a stretcher, racing off toward Hopkins, sirens howling.

Floyd grinned to himself. That had been his lucky night. With all the commotion nobody noticed him sneak up and pocket the cap pistol. Nobody, that is, except Vangie, and he'd convinced her that he was going to take care of the gun until he could find the kid and give it back to him. She even bought his story about how he'd asked around and found out where the kid lived and how the kid's hands were so burned he couldn't shoot, so he told Floyd he could keep the pistol.

Vangie. Tell her anything and she believed it. Wasn't that she was dumb, just that she thought because she told the truth everybody else did. Which, come to think of it, was pretty stupid in itself.

All that business was years ago. Penny-ante stuff, stealing a kid's pistol. So maybe he'd been nothing but a teen-aged punk when he lit out from Dundalk. So maybe he'd botched a few deals in the past, but now—on this Fourth of July night—he was about to hit it lucky. The world would see that Floyd O'Toole was no small-time loser, that he was sharp enough to outsmart Cenicero and his Costa Rican mob and a bunch of stupid-assed Miami Police Department narcs besides.

Another explosive THA-ROOOMP jarred the house. Any second now the guys with the dope would show up, Arena and his cop crew right behind them. Floyd reached to adjust the weight of the gun and mentally rehearsed his move. Wait until the drug guys were inside the front room. Then, the minute Lieutenant Arena's cops hit, pull the gun out, aim, fire. But what if he missed? His gut began to heave like little green lizards were doing the rumba in there. Maybe this whole thing was a mistake. Maybe….

Just then Jose reared back and held up his hand. "*Silencio.*"

Floyd held his breath and listened. First came the sound of feet shuffling across the gritty pavement, then the signal. Three taps, two more taps, then three more. Show time. The lizards in Floyd's gut went into a Tarantella.

After a heart-stopping second or so of silence came the rattle of bolts being slid back and the front door scraping open. Low voices mumbled in the other room. Floyd slipped his right hand into his pocket and wrapped trembling fingers around the gun butt. Timing was everything.

He crouched low, his every sense focused on the sounds coming from the front room. The fiery torture inside his sinuses began to escalate. He shoved his free wrist hard against his nostrils. A sneeze now could blow the whole deal. He tried to stifle the threatened eruption but it was no use—he couldn't hold it.

The multi-megaton sneeze came ripping out, feeling like it had blasted a crater in the top of his skull. At the sound, all hell broke loose from the front room—shouts, gunshots, wood splintering, furniture crashing to the floor.

Jose leaped to his feet and went for his gun. Having to hang on to the briefcase made him awkward. Floyd tried to pull his gun from his pocket but it caught on the fabric and flew from his hand. No hope of retrieving it in time. He grabbed the metal chair he'd been sitting on and swung wildly at where he judged Jose's skull to be. For once, luck was with him. A thunk like a baseball bat hitting a ripe melon, and Jose crumbled into an elephantine heap.

Drenched with sweat and gasping for breath, Floyd heaved Jose's bulk to one side and jerked free the briefcase. He clutched it to his chest and made a dive for the window at the same moment Arena's vice cops came crashing through the door.

4. "Shoppin' Around"

Vangie was in the stockroom checking out a shipment of beach towels when one of the stock boys hoisted a bottle of Old Crow from a carton of size large ladies' panties. "Wouldn't you think the boss would at least hide his stuff some place where it won't leave half the ladies' drawers smelling like booze." he asked.

Vangie sighed. With the outside temperature at ninety degrees, the brass due later in the day, and the sale in full swing, she didn't need more grief. "Best not to say anything about this, Larry," she told him. "After all, we can't be sure who put it there."

Flo was punching in, sliding her time card into the slot. She folded toothpick arms over her scrawny chest and gave Vangie The Flo Look. "Yeah, Hon, and my number's gonna come up in the lottery this week. Five'll get you ten Dennis don't even show up for work today."

"He's only twenty minutes late," Vangie told her. "It's probably the traffic."

"Get real, Hon. He's fallen off the wagon big time. If you hadn't seen to it the sale merchandise got shelved, it would still be in the back room, and the flyers would've gone out two weeks after the sale was over." With that, Flo went marching off, her lips pressed thin as a ninety-eight-cent pair of panty-hose.

Vangie, having lost count on the beach towels, started over. Flo was right, of course. Ever since the new marketing director had changed all the procedures, Dennis was like a little wind-up car that could only go in circles. Except that his engine ran on booze. She checked the rest of the items on the list then hurried to the front of the store where Darla Wisnewski was manning the service booth alone.

"Sheez," Darla exclaimed, "the blue-lighters are sure in a fighting mood today. When Register Three messed up that order a coupla minutes ago, I thought the woman was gonna' climb the counter and yank Terri's hair out. Not that I'd blame her—that's the third time already today Terri's screwed up."

"Terri just needs a little more time…"

"Oh, come on, Vang. You know that when Dennis hired those "i" girls – Brandi, Terri, Traci—all he checked was their young, bouncy boobs. Speaking of which, our beloved manager's still nowhere in sight."

"Probably held up in traffic," Vangie offered without much conviction.

• Shoppin' Around •

"Or hung over." Darla turned to take care of an overweight woman who heaved a pair of jeans up onto the counter like it was someone else's fault that there wasn't room in a size fourteen for her size eighteen rear end.

The phone shrilled. When Vangie picked it up a female voice screeched in her ear that the new barbecue grill she'd just bought had ruined twelve dollars worth of New York strips and completely singed her husband's hair and eyebrows. "Now he looks just like Mr. T," she yelled.

Vangie assured the woman the Kmart would supply a replacement grill with no delivery charge. Brandi on Register Nine had her fourth void for the day.

At her break, Vangie headed for the back room where Flo and Darla were already gathered in the cramped space set aside for employees, Darla, seated on one of the plastic outdoor chairs—$4.99 on special this week only.

"What did you do this weekend?" Vangie asked, knowing Darla was always eager to relate her latest romantic episode.

"Charlie Higgins came by my place," Darla licked at the raspberry colored goo oozing from her jelly doughnut. "We drove over to Patterson Park and watched the fireworks."

Flo snorted. "Isn't Charlie the guy that just last week, you said was worthless as a slug in a Coke machine?"

Darla lifted both shoulders in a what-can-I-say gesture. "Yeah, well, Charlie's got this hot new car. A red Datsun roadster. After the fireworks were done we went for a ride out in the country."

Vangie sank into a chair. "That sounds nice. Dundalk was one gigantic oven all weekend."

"Yeah, well, the ride didn't cool Charlie down much. All the time we were parked, he wanted me to reach in his pocket, see if he had some Lifesavers. 'Charlie,' I told him, 'the only Lifesaver you got in there sure ain't the kind *I'm* lookin' for.' Except for that car the guy's a total dork."

"Woods are full of dorks," Flo said, "but I can tell you one thing—if a guy like that cute Mr. Jenkins, the one who was coming on to Vangie at the Customer Service Booth this morning, if a guy like him ever gave me a tumble, I'd say yes in a New York minute. I couldn't believe it, you brushing him off like that."

Vangie shrugged. She knew well enough the guy Flo was talking about. Curly brown hair, blue eyes, good smile, age about thirty-one or thirty-two. "Since Missy's mom left us, I've pulled some real goofs," he'd admitted. "Thought I should get her tights the same size as her dresses. Guess it doesn't work that way."

He'd seemed nice. Sort of hung around a while, like he was waiting for her to say something more. But she'd been down that road before. Mama would spot Mr. Jenkins in a minute. Like with Danny Carstairs. A real bad episode when she and Danny announced they were engaged. The hospital for Mama that time. Then months of holding Danny off with promises and maybes until he finally gave up, called it quits. It didn't take a brick falling on her head to know how Mama would react to Mr. Jenkins.

Back at Customer Service, Brandi was having her fifth void and Earlene on Register Seven was signaling for change. While she was counting out rolls of quarters and dimes, Vangie felt a nudge from Darla's elbow. "Check out the snack display." Darla pointed to Aisle Six. "Looks like you-know-who just slipped a package of Nabisco Fig Newtons inside his shirt."

Vangie looked. Mr. Finley. "I'll take care of it."

She snatched up the rolls of change and hurried toward the registers, dodging between loaded carts and wandering toddlers, all the while keeping an eye out for Mr. Finley. He was steering toward Opal's register. Every checkout was jammed with customers, so she had plenty of time to get there before the old man was close enough to hear the instructions she whispered to Opal.

Opal, two hundred fifty pounds of fine black attitude, managed to say more with a single roll of her eyes than the folks on TV could pack into an hour-long talk show. "Girl, that's the second time this week." she snorted. "You oughtn't let that old geezer keep on that way."

"His check's probably late again. Besides, he never takes anything he doesn't really need."

Opal shoved her register drawer shut with a hip swivel. "Well, it's out of your pocket. It was me, I'd turn him in."

Back at the Customer Service booth, Darla gave Vangie a look just as hairy as the one she'd gotten from Opal. "Look," Vangie told her, "life's tough for Mr. Finley. He's got a sick wife—her medicine costs a fortune. The two of them barely scrape by...."

Darla blew that off with a flip of her shoulder. "Well, you ask me, he's using you for a patsy. Ain't that what Social Services is for, to take care of people like them?"

Vangie told herself Darla wasn't really as hard-hearted as she sounded, just young. She still thought real-life problems were the kind she read about in *The Inquirer.* "I sure do feel bad for poor Liz Taylor." Darla said one time. "The woman must be scared to wake up in the morning for fear she's got some new disease."

At eleven, they spotted Dennis scurrying into his office, shirtsleeves rolled up as if he'd been hustling about the store all along.

"You know what he puts me in mind of? " Darla said. "That White Rabbit, the one in Alice in Wonderland that was always in a hurry, only he never got no place. You mentioned to Dennis yet that you need those extra days off in August?"

"Not yet." Vangie pointed out the restrooms to a customer with a three-year old in tow who was jumping up and down and holding his crotch. "Thought I'd wait 'til the sale's over before I bug him about it." Actually, if Mama's premonitions got worse, there'd be no point in asking for time off.

When things quieted down for a few minutes, Vangie left the Service booth to check out the rest of the store. Eyes and ears open, she passed along each aisle. Ceiling fans sounded an off-beat *Whap, whap* above the electrical department. A damp, mustiness oozed outward from the Garden Shop. The popcorn machine at the snack counter repeated a steady *bip, bip, bip,* and the tires stacked along one aisle in Automotive gave off a sharp rubbery tang.

She noted an empty shelf here, a disorderly display there. She steered a customer toward the mini-blinds, reminded a stock boy to remove the handcart he'd been using, and retrieved an empty candy wrapper from a towel display. Even the district manager said she was good at her job. So why was it that lately the Kmart's aisles felt like a maze where she'd lost her way? She was a few months short of twenty-eight, but did she still want be "Vangie O'Toole, Assistant Manager" when she was thirty-eight?…forty-eight?

Worst scenario, she'd end up like Flo, her hopes dried up along with her collagen. Or like Opal, nursing aching feet and a tired back, stuffing herself with sweets so that she could forget the pain in her body. Maybe it was those 'i' girls—Terri, Brandi, Judi—who were the smart ones, just marking time, determined that the minute they latched onto Mr. Right—or Mr. Almost-Right—it was adios, Kmart.

At least, thanks to urging from her old high school math teacher, she had a goal that would be her escape from all that. Or so she hoped. Sometimes the degree in accounting she was studying for seemed farther away rather than closer. Miss McDowell's words, "You were always so good in math, Vangie— it would be a crime for you to waste that talent," kept her inspired, but Miss McDowell had no idea what it was like taking night and weekend classes, holding down this job, taking care of Mama and, and always knowing they were only one paycheck away from the poorhouse.

Lost in those thoughts, Vangie rounded the corner from Sporting Goods into Toys and nearly collided with Dennis, clutching a thick stack of invoices. "Vangie, you gotta help me," he puffed. "These new registers got everything screwed up again. According to this, the ladies' shoe department sold 29 snow shovels last week and half the toy sales are listed under Infants Wear."

"Dennis, the store's swamped with customers. We're knocking ourselves out just to keep up with the sale. I don't see how...."

"I know, I know." Dennis ran shaky fingers through what was left of his hair. "I meant to get on this stuff before, but what with the sale and everything, I couldn't get around to it."

Dennis's dragon breath gave ample evidence of why he was behind in his work...as if there'd been any doubt. One part of Vangie wanted to tell him where he could stuff his screwed-up numbers, but seeing his little White Rabbit eyes—today they were traced with red vein lines—she hadn't the heart to refuse.

She hurried back to the front and pulled Flo off the register to help with Customer Service. Flo gave her a frown. "Cripes, Vangie, when are you gonna quit knocking yourself out covering for that asshole?"

"Dennis can't help it," Vangie said. "The divorce and everything…"

"Sure. So he drowns his 'problems' in booze while you get stuck doing your own job and most of his besides."

"I was Vangie I'd file a complaint," Darla said. "Like with that Equal Opportunity thing."

"Get real, Hon," Flo said as she handed a customer her refund. "They might talk that shit over in Washington, but in real life it's balls over brains any day."

Once Vangie was settled in Dennis's office with the door closed, it wasn't so bad. A treat to shut herself up for an hour or so, to log on to the sweet rock and roll of calculations. But the telephone on the desk reminded Vangie that she hadn't checked in with Mama yet. She dialed their home number. The phone got picked up after the second ring, but there was no sound on the other end.

"Mama? Mama are you there?"

No answer.

"Mama, it's me. Vangie. Can you hear me?"

A hoarse whisper came over the wire: "What was your daddy's mother's maiden name?"

"Mama, it was Medairy. Frances Louise Medairy."

Mama said in a perfectly normal voice, "Oh, it's you, Vangie. I was just about to fix myself a bite of lunch."

Vangie let out the breath she'd been holding. Maybe the worst was over. Maybe she wouldn't go home tonight and find Mama huddled inside her closet, hugging Dad's old uniform and crying to herself. Maybe Mama wouldn't start in again about

Floyd, how, if Floyd would only come home, everything would be all right.

Mama didn't realize how lucky they were that Floyd stayed a thousand miles away in Miami.

5. "Suspicious Minds"

Floyd stumbled along the road shoulder, the Tamiami Trail's sizzling macadam stretching endlessly before him. His head throbbed like a jungle drum, mosquitoes had chewed holes in his ankles, and the sun was broiling him like a Burger King special. With cautious fingers, he explored a lump the size of a coconut on top of his scalp. His hand came away streaked with half-dried blood.

Lousy bastard in the U-Haul that cut him off never even stopped. Other cars whizzed right on by, too, like he was some street bum they were afraid was gonna hold them up, or something. Nothing else to do but leave the rental car upended in the drainage ditch, start walking.

He'd had it. If he couldn't persuade the Indian to sell his truck, he was done for. Tomorrow morning they'd find his body sprawled in the middle of the trail, deader than one of these squashed armadillos that littered the roadside every few yards. He swallowed hard, trying to lubricate a throat that felt like the lint trap in a clothes dryer. "Look," he told the Indian, "I can pay for the goddam pick-up. Give you twice what any dealer would for a heap like that."

"Don't need to sell no truck." With that, the Indian turned his back and walked away.

Floyd stared after him—like money didn't mean anything to this guy who lived in sagging trailer with half a dozen black-haired kids and a pack of mangy dogs running around the yard. Still, he couldn't blame the Indian for being suspicious of him, he must look like crap. The frames of his Armani shades—a cool two hundred in Miami—had gotten twisted in the accident. Not to mention the silk shirt that set him back another two C's. Pocket half ripped off. And his pants were streaked with filthy black mud from where he'd crawled out of the ditch.

Money. A couple of C's would change the Indian's mind. Floyd pulled two hundred dollar bills out of the duffle bag and waved them at the Indian. "How 'bout giving me a ride, then?" he called. "Just take me some place where I can get a bus or a rental car? There's gotta be a town around here someplace."

The Indian halted by the trailer's rusted steps to drill him with another suspicious stare. "Miami fifty miles that way." He pointed east along the two-lane strip of highway. "Nothing the other direction but Everglades City."

Miami was definitely out. But the other should be okay. Any place that called itself a city ought to have a car rental agency. "Okay. Just take me far as Everglades City."

"Cost you three hundred."

The damned aborigine had him by the balls. He handed over the three C's and climbed in. The Indian started the truck and headed it west on the Tamiami Trail.

Twenty miles later, except for a couple of chickee huts and a ranger station, they hadn't passed so much as a gas station. Nothing ahead or behind but godforsaken wilderness. Spooky damned place, the Everglades, gray moss hanging from the cypresses, buzzards wheeling round and round, sky with all the blue bleached out of it. Made a person dizzy, heat mirages dancing off the macadam, the horizon always melting farther and farther away.

Everglades City. Maybe the Indian was bullshitting him. Maybe that was a mirage, too. Maybe there was no such place. A major mistake, letting Geronimo see that the duffle bag was full of cash. Greedy sonuvabitch—milking him for three hundred.

Floyd leaned forward to peer through the bug-streaked windshield. "How much longer to this Everglades City? We nearly there?"

No answer. Couldn't tell a thing by the Indian's face, either. Guy with a deadpan mug like that could put a knife through a person's heart, take his money, dump his body out there in the swamp, all without batting an eyelid.

He had to stop thinking like that. Just hang on till they got to Everglades City. Rent another car there, or hop a bus, whatever. Head for New York. Pick up Angelina. Then Mexico. Might be better to go someplace a lot farther from Cenicero, but Angelina had this thing for movie stars, was set on Mexico, that Acapulco, place where all the actors went to screw around.

***

The sign said *Welcome to Everglades City*, only there wasn't any town. The Indian dumped him at ratty looking combination gas station/convenience store/restaurant. From the convenience store's dust-streaked window Floyd could see nine-tenths of the place, and the other tenth wasn't worth looking at either. All the town amounted to was a roach-haven motel, a bait and tackle shop, and a dozen or so rundown houses with siding held together by mildew.

The cold beer, the one good thing Everglades City had to offer, tasted like salvation. Half to himself and half to the creepy-looking guy behind the counter, Floyd muttered, "Whoever named this lousy burg Everglades City must've sniffed too much glue."

The guy paused in refilling the beer cooler to shoot Floyd a look from beneath the greasy lock of hair straggling down over his forehead. "We had a big hotel here onct, but it burnt down years ago. Fellow that brought the railroad down the west coast thought this was gonna be the next Miami." His snicker showed off the gap where a front teeth were was missing.

"So where's the bus station?"

The man dried his hands on his filthy apron and pointed in a direction Floyd guessed would be north. "Naples."

"How far's that."

"Ummmm...thirty, thirty-five miles up the Trail."

"Any taxis in this town."

The man's grin gave another glimpse of his tooth gap. "Nah. You wanna go someplace, try standing out by the bridge and hitching. How'd you get here anyhow?"

Even though he was now a hundred miles and what felt like half a century from Miami, Floyd wasn't about to discuss where he came from or how he got there. "Uh...car broke down. Hitched a ride." He slid off the stool to retrieve the Miami Herald somebody had left on one of the scarred tables.

The headline on the front page hit him with a thousand-volt charge. "Exotic Dancer Dies in Apartment Blaze." He didn't need to read the print beneath the picture of a burned-out apartment to know the dancer's name. Dolores. Floyd felt the sweat freeze on his body. Arson Suspected. Cenicero's signature, loud and clear.

NOTICE TO ALL CLUB MEMBERS

IF YOU HAVE NOT TURNED IN YOUR

DEPOSIT FOR THE TRIP, TONIGHT'S

MEETING IS YOUR LAST CHANCE.

ALSO, AT THIS MEETING WE WILL DECIDE ON

FINAL TRIP DETAILS INCLUDING

AN APPROPRIATE FLORAL TRIBUTE.

7 P.M. SHARP.

BRENDA SUE HIGGS, PRESIDENT

ELVIS-4-EVER FAN CLUB

6. "A House That Has Everything"

The automatic door swished Vangie and Darla from the Kmart's air-conditioning to the heat-soaked parking lot. They crossed the street in mid-block under a streamer of red, white and blue bunting left over from the firemen's parade, now drooping limp and flutterless. The late afternoon procession of weary, bag-laden shoppers moved in slow motion through the smog-thick air.

At the bus stop Vangie and Darla took their place in line behind a woman pushing twins in a double stroller, each of them licking half of a double orange Popsicle, most of it melting and running down their hands and arms. As they waited, Darla asked, "So you think the girls in your club will like me? I mean, I ain't never been into this Elvis stuff before."

Vangie switched the strap of her book bag to the opposite shoulder. "Sure. At the last meeting I told them how you've started collecting his records, and that you've rented the video of *Blue Hawaii* five times."

"Yeah. I mean, the things that guy was able to do with his bod."

The five-fifteen bus grumbled its way to the curb. "Yo, Vangie," the driver, a grizzled black man with a weary grin greeted her as she climbed aboard.

"Hey, Martin. How's the back?"

"Not bad, Baby, not bad. Hurts like hell, but still movin', still groovin'. Two empties back there. You gals better grab 'em quick, give your feets a rest." He hissed the door shut, then jerked the bus out into traffic, ignoring horn blasts from the cars behind.

Darla sighed as they plopped into the last two empty seats. "Ya' know it's funny," she said, "long as we've known each other, I ain't never been to your house before. Never even met your mother.

"Yes, well. Mama's a little odd about strangers coming into the house. Luckily she liked Elvis, so she figures anybody that's in the fan club is okay."

"So the fan club always meets at your house?" Darla said.

"Twice a month," Vangie slid the bag with her books to the floor next to her feet. "Years ago when Floyd and I were little, Dad fixed up our basement for a playroom. Now it makes a great place for the club to keep our Elvis memorabilia."

"This Floyd – he's your brother?"

Vangie nodded.

"Funny. Like I ain't never heard you mention him before."

"I guess his name just never came up."

Dad had always told her that if you couldn't say something good about a person then don't say anything at all. The best thing a person could say about Floyd was that he stayed far away. In fact, if there was any chance of Floyd showing up, she'd go put up a billboard somewhere down Interstate 95—FLOYD GO BACK. DUNDALK IS CLOSED.

More people crowded onto the bus at the next several stops. The aisles were soon packed with riders hanging to the overhead bars, bumping and swaying each time the bus swerved. Vangie leaned over to fish a textbook from her bag.

Darla checked out the book's title. *Accounting Procedures, III.* "Don't tell me you work on that stuff on the bus, too."

"Got to," Vangie told her. "If I let the assignments pile up two days in a row it takes two weeks to catch up."

"Well, you got more guts than I do if you can hit the books after working all day." Darla flipped open the *People* magazine she'd picked up before leaving the store.

Vangie tried to focus on the page in front of her, but little strands of worry kept dragging her back to the day's work. *Did I ring up that last rebate on the right key? Did I remember to tell Dennis about the lay-away on the lawn mower? Did I write down the confirmation number on that big credit card charge?*

Determined to focus on her assignment, she flipped to the next page and read, *Federally exempt interest dividends attributable to municipal obligations....*

Darla interrupted, shoving her magazine in front of Vangie. "Looka here." The magazine was open to a full-page color photo of a slender woman with olive skin, reddish-blond hair, and eyes the color of crème de menthe. She was posed against one of a wide veranda's white columns. A tall, gray-haired man wearing a red jacket, jodhpurs, and polished boots stood next to her. The caption under the photo read Much-*Married India Marlowe Trades Hollywood Glitz for Role as Baltimore's Lady Bountiful.*

"Remember I told you how last night Charlie wanted to get out of the city so we drove out to Greenspring Valley?" Darla said.

Vangie shrugged, not sure what connection Darla was trying to make.

"So we're driving through the valley, out there where there are horse farms all over the place and white board fences that go on for miles. We passed this humongous mansion perched by itself high up on a hill and Charlie said that's where India Marlowe lives. I thought he was putting me on, but he's right. This picture's the very same place."

Vangie scanned through the article.

Although rumor has it she doesn't know a farthingale from a check-rein, movie star India Marlowe has wasted no time elbowing her way into new hubby Daniel Dulaney Stowell's horsey set.

"Weird, ain't it?" Darla said, "why a big movie star like India Marlowe would be living here in Maryland instead of out in Hollywood." The next part of the article explained that.

Marlowe recently announced she is taking a hiatus from her film career, saying she 'refuses to lower her standards for the sleazy roles the studios are offering these days.' Rumor has it that offers, 'sleazy' or otherwise, have not exactly been pouring in since she walked off the set of her last picture after being handed second billing behind hotter-than-hot juvie star, Kevin Tiles.

"I just read about that Tiles kid in *The Star*," Darla said. "He was so nasty to work with that half the film crew quit."

Vangie read on.

Whatever the reason for her exodus from Tinseltown, the oft-wedded Miss Marlowe (five trips to the altar if you include both times with the beer baron, but who's counting?), says she intends to participate actively in the social life of Greenspring Valley. Miss Marlowe's first social coup is her role as honorary chairperson of the Valley's most prestigious charitable bash, the annual fund-raising drive for The Children's Oncology Unit of St. Ignatius Hospital in Baltimore.

At that last line, Vangie straightened in surprise. "Saint Ignatius – that's the hospital where our Elvis-4-Ever Fan Club does volunteer work with the kids in the cancer unit."

Darla grimaced. "Ain't it a downer being around sick kids? I mean, cancer."

Vangie hesitated. It wasn't easy to explain to someone like Darla why the best hours of the week were the Thursday evenings and Sunday afternoons she spent with the kids at St. Ignatius – Donny, Tandora, Betsy the Brat, even. "It can be tough," she said, "especially with the ones who aren't getting better. But once in a while one of them makes it even after the doctors have given up. Then it's all worthwhile."

Darla's moon-round face, usually a sort of blank, showed a glimmer of comprehension. "Must be a little like seeing a horrible wreck," she said "then finding out afterwards that nobody got hurt."

"A lot like that."

Darla's attention had already returned to the article, the raspberry nail of her index finger tracing slowly from syllable to syllable. Vangie couldn't help thinking that if it had been Darla Miss McDowell had handed *A Tale of Two Cities*, she'd be reading it clear into the next century.

A few moments later Darla remarked, "Says here that the fund-raiser's going to be a big dinner and auction on August 7th at the Baltimore Civic Center and that India Marlowe's getting a lot of other Hollywood stars to donate stuff."

Darla's comment didn't require a response. For the balance of the ride she would be caught up in India Marlowe's latest project, Burt Reynolds' nude photos in *The Enquirer*, and fantasizing about Paul Hogan as *Crocodile Dundee*.

Vangie settled deeper into her seat and closed her eyes. Under the bus's lurch and sway rhythm, she gradually slid into a soft, floating state, halfway between oblivion and awareness. After tonight's meeting, there'd be no turning back, she would have paid her deposit money for the trip. No refunds, the treasurer said.

They'd be rolling down US 81, GRACELAND EXPRESS spelled out in lighted letters across the front of the silver Greyhound coach, Elvis's music spilling hot and silky from the overhead speakers -- "Heartbreak Hotel"... "Lawdy, Miss Clawdy"... "Crying in the Chapel"...

Several sudden jolts disrupted Vangie's daydream, but she willed herself back into the half-drowsing state where all things seemed possible—*Dennis would give her those days off in August for the trip to Graceland... Mama's episode would be forgotten by the time she got home...Tandora's latest round of chemotherapy would be the last... And maybe Mr. Jenkins....*

The bus had spewed out most of its passengers by the time it reached Shirley Street. Vangie stepped down onto the pavement, Darla following, and waved goodbye to the driver. For a moment she saw her street as Darla must be seeing it—cloned story-and-a half post-World-War-II bungalows skulking behind skimpy lawns, the only distinction between them the colors of their wavy asbestos siding, either dingy yellow, an algae-like green, or the faded peach of the home she and Mama shared. "Number 2744 is ours," she told Darla. "The one with the shiny ball in the yard and those plaster ducks and the dwarfs? Mama's crazy about lawn ornaments."

They started down the street, but before they'd taken ten steps Vangie realized something was wrong. Mama was standing on the narrow slab of concrete that served as a front stoop, leaning forward, one hand cupped over her forehead like the carved figurehead on an old-time sailing ship. Vangie grabbed Darla's arm to hurry her along. "Mama, what happened?" she called soon as they were close enough for Mama to hear.

"They've been at it again, changing things around." Mama cried. "Not more than ten minutes at most was I gone, just next door to see Mabel's night-blooming cereus."

Vangie flinched, feeling as if a fist had been jammed into her midriff, even as she struggled to keep her voice calm and reassuring. "Mama, are you sure?"

"'Course I'm sure. I knew it was them soon as I saw what they'd done."

***

Vangie's eyes swept the room, taking inventory. Mama had long since turned their home into a museum of discards, fringed Victorian lampshades, evergreen-scented pillows embroidered with "For you I Pine and Balsam," a lava lamp from the sixties, an Eames chair knockoff, a plastic hassock from the forties, an uncomfortable wood-framed love seat covered in a tapestry design that was the Depression Thirties notion of elegance, a table with cattle-horn legs, furniture, vases, pictures, and ornaments in every style from every era.

"It all looks the same, Mama," Vangie told her. "I can't see where anything's missing or moved."

Lotte beckoned toward the far wall. "Just you take a look at that picture, the one hanging over the settee. You'll soon see what they been up to."

The picture showed three women dancing in a circle around the columns on a Greek patio wearing flimsy little chiffon scarves draped around their hips, the kind the Kmart sold for $1.59 in ladies' accessories. "I don't see…it looks exactly the same," Vangie said.

"Ha. It *is* the same. The picture, that is."

"Then what?..."

"The frame. They've switched the frame on me."

Vangie pretended to examine it more closely. Sometimes if she went along with these weird notions, that was enough to satisfy Mama. "I can't tell any difference," she said. "Are you sure the frame's been changed?"

"'Course I'm sure." Lotte poked her forefinger at the frame. "The gold's much yellower than on the old one. Not even chipped in the same places."

Darla's mouth gaped wide enough to reveal her wad of gum. "Mrs. O'Toole, you mean to say somebody came in your house, and took a picture out of one frame, and then put it back in another? Like if they want to steal something, why not just take the whole picture?"

"That's what makes them so devilish clever," Lotte told her. "They mostly never take things outright, just switch what you got for things that *look* almost the same. They're sharp, they are."

Darla stared dumbfounded. "Who'd want to do a weird thing like that?"

"Gypsies, that's who. The frame was gold. Gypsies love anything that's gold."

Darla shot Vangie a questioning look. "Gypsies come into your house and take stuff?"

Lotte gave Vangie no time to answer. "Oh, yes." she assured Darla. "There's hardly a single piece Vangie's Dad brought home off the route the Gypsies haven't carried off. You take this very rug we're standing on, a real Oriental. Came from this big house out in Greenspring Valley. Hardly any wear on it except for one charred spot where it must have been put too close to a fireplace. They came one day and took the real rug, left this one in its place. Looks exactly the same, right down to the burnt spot."

Darla stared down at the rug's intricate pattern. "So what makes you think it's different?"

Mama pointed to an overstuffed chair covered in a salmon, red and lime-green floral pattern. "That armchair used to set with both its front legs on the rug. Now it barely comes to the edge of the fringe."

"Ain't there no way you can stop them? Like maybe call the police?"

"Doesn't do a bit of good." Mama said. "Oh, sure, Gypsies are scared to death at the sight of a uniform, but time the police get here they're long gone. That's what was so good about when Vangie's Dad was alive. He was a Sanitary Engineer, you know, had that embroidered right above the pocket on his uniform, *Albert O'Toole, Sanitary Engineer.* 'Hap,' everybody called him, even though his real name was Albert. With a man in uniform close by, my stuff was safe. Now he's gone, they've got so bold they walk right into the house in broad daylight. That picture frame is just a warning. My only hope is that Floyd will get here before they come to carry me off."

7. "I've Got a Thing About You, Baby"

Vangie flipped on the basement's overhead lights.

"Holy Jeez!" Darla exclaimed, "I never seen nothing like this!" Her surprised glance spun from one side of the room to the other, taking in the display cases and shelves loaded with Elvis mementos, the pictures and posters that nearly covered every inch of the club room walls. "Every which where I turn there's another Elvis looking at me!"

Vangie pointed out the glass case that contained the club's special mementos, a piece of denim taken directly from a pair of jeans Elvis actually wore, a fiber of crimson carpeting from Graceland, and an autographed photo of Elvis's father, Vernon Presley.

"*Hol-ee!*" Darla whispered as Vangie gently removed a plastic box with six strands of Indian-dark hair inside. "Blows my mind to think these actually came straight off of Elvis's head!"

The tour finished, Darla helped Vangie arrange chairs for the meeting in a semicircle facing the card table at the front of the room. Darla, struggling to unfold one of the chairs, nodded toward a door in the paneling on the far side of the room. "What's in there?"

Vangie shifted the card table to the left. "Years ago, that used to be our coal bin. Later on, after we switched to natural gas, Dad set up his workbench in there. But it hasn't been used for years. Too damp and musty."

Vangie pointed out the two doors on the other side of the room. "The one on the right is the laundry room, and next to it is a powder room. Dad did the whole job with plumbing fixtures that people on his route threw away. In fact, he paneled this entire basement with lumber they threw out at a construction site over in Woodlawn."

Darla popped her gum in approval. "Your dad sounds like one handy guy."

Vangie nodded, but speaking of her Dad reminded her once again how much she missed him. Not just his help in keeping Mama calm, but for herself. Dad would have understood how much the trip to Graceland meant to her.

Around seven, the club members began to filter in. "That's Donna Ports, wearing the t-shirt with Elvis's picture across the front," Vangie said. "Pearl Makinskey is the older woman with the cat's eye glasses." She also introduced Darla to the club secretary and the treasurer, a skinny woman wearing a red beaded top and white slacks.

"Don't you have any guys in your club?" Darla wanted to know.

The treasurer tapped Darla's arm, her bangle bracelets clattering like wind chimes. "Hon, Elvis is all the man we need in this club!"

The other woman tilted her head, careful not to strain the lacquer holding her beehive of peach-colored hair in place. "Well, I can tell you, my Steve is downright jealous of Elvis! Ain't a *real* man good enough?' That's ol' Stevie's whine every time I leave the house to come to a meeting."

"It's great, though." Another woman gave a little wiggle that shook the fringes on her white leather jacket with rhinestones spelling out "ELVIS LIVES" across the back. "Blows the guys ever-lovin' minds that we girls get turned on by Elvis."

Pearl Makinsky, the elderly woman Vangie had introduced earlier, gave Darla's arm a shy little pat. "You ladies are giving this little girl the wrong impression. Hon, we might joke about how Elvis turns us on, but there's a lot more than that to being a fan."

"Yeah," one of the others said, "but try explaining that to people that don't understand. I was telling the girls at work how our club members busted their butts raising money for the kids at the hospital, and this snotty secretary pipes in, 'So you girls really believe that Elvis is alive and driving a truck in Tennessee?'"

The women standing nearby gave disdainful snorts.

When the last of the club members had arrived, the club president, Brenda Sue Higgs, called them to order. After a little chair scraping and seat switching, they were settled and Brenda Sue proclaimed, "Let's all bow our heads for a moment in a silent tribute to our honorary President, Elvis Aaron Presley, to whom we dedicate this meeting of the Elvis-4-Ever Fan Club." For a moment, the room was still except for the "whup-whup" of the fan as it swung back and forth.

After the secretary had read the minutes of the previous meeting, the treasurer stood to give her report. "I hope the forty-eight dollars and nineteen cents in our Flower Fund is going to be enough," she announced. "You girls have got to remember that the guitar floral arrangement is more expensive than the plain basket with the Teddy bear on the handle."

A chair scraped in the back of the room. "Sylvia, I thought we decided on the 'Crying in the Chapel' design," a voice called out. "You ask me, that's a lot more appropriate as a memorial to Elvis's death. Besides, practically all the clubs order the guitar one."

Sylvia stared at the speaker over the top of her half-glasses. "If you were at the last meeting, Eudora, you'd know that the chapel one has gone up to ninety-five dollars. After all, we haven't got a hundred and twenty members like the Pink Cadillac Fan Club over in Highlandtown. Besides, across the front of the guitar they're going to put a ribbon that reads *Elvis, We Love You 4-Ever.*"

Eudora flounced back into her seat, muttering loud enough for everyone to hear, "Well, I suppose you don't *care* if everybody that visits his grave thinks *our* arrangement looks cheap next to the fancy ones the *other* clubs send."

Brenda Sue over-ruled Eudora with a rap of her gavel. "Our next order of business is Lucille's DJ report."

A tall dark-haired woman seated in the front row stood up. "This past week we made twenty-one calls and out of that we got nine responses," she announced. "WPOC was the best: They did a "Three-In-A-Row" of Elvis numbers on Tuesday night."

Next up was Vangie's report on the work of her Special Projects Committee. "This letter came in the mail yesterday." Vangie stood and read aloud: *The Board and staff of St. Ignatius Hospital wish to express their sincere gratitude to the Elvis-4-Ever Fan Club of Dundalk, Maryland, for their generous donation of $4,143.37. The funds supplied by the club will be used to provide much needed services and supplies for the Children's Oncology Unit. Your generosity and the many hours of volunteer service your members provide throughout the year are greatly appreciated by both staff and patients.*

The members applauded as she sat down.

Brenda Sue tapped the gavel again. "In connection with that," she said, "don't forget that we've called a special meeting for next week. That's when the reporter from the *Baltimore Star* who's writing an article about our work with the hospital will be here. Her name's Lacey McLeod and she sounded really nice on the phone."

"Yeah," Eudora snorted. "Nice on the phone is one thing, but five will get you ten her article will make us sound like a bunch of kooks. It'll be the old 'Elvis on Black Velvet' story all over again!"

Eudora's comment aroused a lively discussion as to whether or not good publicity about the club's volunteer work outweighed the article's negative possibilities.

When the argument threatened to drag on, Brenda rapped for quiet. "Ladies! We have other business to attend to!" The buzz subsided, she went on, "As you all know, there's been a lot of controversy about Rosie Holiday's Elvis mural."

Vangie whispered to Darla, "Rosie owns the Don't Be Cruel Saloon over on South Street. She's got this 12- by 15-foot mural of Elvis's face painted on the outside of her building."

Brenda continued, "Some of Rosie's neighbors have gotten up a petition to have the bar's liquor license taken away. They say the painting makes the neighborhood look bad. They're also complaining that Rosie plays 'Are You Lonesome Tonight' on her jukebox at least twenty times every night with the volume so loud a person can hear it six blocks away."

Again Eudora jumped up. "Rosie's got a perfect right to put Elvis's face anywhere she damned well pleases!" she said. "You ask me, he's a hell of a lot prettier than those ads the whiskey and cigarette people plaster over the sides of buildings."

"You said it!" Pearl chimed in. "And I'd a lot sooner listen to Elvis singing 'Are You Lonesome Tonight' than Perry Como or Bing Crosby sounding like sick moo-calves."

"Crosby's dead," someone in the back called out. "Died ten years ago, couple of months after Elvis."

"Guess I never noticed," Pearl said. "Anyhow, neither of those fellows could hold a candle—"

Brenda Sue's gavel cut off the discussion. "Our secretary will write a letter from the club to the liquor board in support of Rosie. Be sure, Ruthann, you tell them we have 47 members, all of them voters." Brenda lifted her glasses from their resting place on her bosom and consulted her agenda. "Our next topic for discussion is our trip to Graceland."

Vangie sat silent, the knot inside her chest growing ever tighter as the group plunged into a heated discussion as to whether to opt for the Elvis Memorial Tour of Memphis or the tour of Elvis's mansion. She'd handed in her deposit money for the trip, but would she really be on the bus when it rolled up to the gates of Graceland? The others could make their plans confident they'd be going, but for her there was always Mama. Mama and the Gypsies.

Still, Mama seemed much better the last several months, well enough that the trip seemed like a real possibility. But now there was the break-in. The picture frame *looked* exactly the same. It didn't matter—if Mama got it in her head that gypsies were around, that was trouble.

***

Vangie carried the remains of the Oreos and lemonade up from the basement. Mama was at the kitchen table, working the *Star's* crossword puzzle in ink, refusing to fill in any block until she was positive she had it right. When she was finished, the puzzle would be perfect without a single smudge or empty space.

Vangie paused to stare over her mother's shoulder for a minute. How did Mama do that? Here was a woman who confused the days of the week, got lost two blocks from home, and on bad days could scarcely remember her own name. Yet words like *liaison* and *confluence* came spilling from her brain along with the names of minor movie stars and obscure authors. Anyhow, this was a good sign. Crosswords acted like a lubricant on Mama's nerves. With luck, by bedtime she'd forget about the picture frame and the Gypsies. Her mood lighter, Vangie began stowing away the refreshments.

Mama looked up from the paper. "They had this show on TV this afternoon about cross-dressers," she said, "fellows that like to dress up in their wives' underwear. You ask me, they ought to do a program about Gypsies that break into people's houses and mess with their stuff."

Vangie froze with the pitcher of lemonade halfway onto the refrigerator shelf. "Couldn't it be that the picture frame just *looks* different?"

Mama tossed her head as if that notion weren't worth considering. "It was Gypsies all right. That missing frame wasn't the only sign they've been here."

"What makes you say that?"

"Oh, different things." Lotte inked in a 'Down' row with precisely formed letters, L-U-C-I-D. "You know that lampshade with the gold fringe, the one on the end table next to the sofa?

Well, I always put it with the part of the fringe that's missing to the back. When I looked just now, it was turned a different direction."

Vangie watched over her shoulder as Lotte filled in 42 down, *cormorant,* and 37 across *cribbage* then remarked, "You ask me, the fellows that make up these things got no imagination. Every single puzzle's got at least one 'emu' or 'Aida' or 'Ute' in it.

"What's a 'Ute'?" Vangie said, hoping to derail Mama's train of thought.

"An Indian. But they could be Gypsies. They're dark, you know."

Vangie closed the refrigerator door. "Why don't I call that company that sells security systems? It's really not all that expensive, and then you'd always feel safe when I'm not here."

"You ever take a good look at the fellows that install those security systems?"

Vangie took a bite of an Oreo as she stowed the rest of them back into the bag. "I'm sure all the security people are bonded and everything," she said.

"Bonded, hah. Gypsies is what they are. What better way to check out a person's house than when they're installing those wires and whatever? No, the only way we're going to keep the Gypsies out is when Floyd comes back."

The Oreo stuck in Angie's throat. Why did it always come back to Floyd? Floyd coming home. Floyd, the one who would keep Mama safe, make everything secure again. "Mama, it's been over three years since Floyd even stopped by to see us. What makes you think he's coming back?"

Lotte ignored the question. "Floyd said he'd have a real nice surprise for me when he came. Judging by that big car he was driving last time, it'll be something really special."

8. "Teddy Bear"

The poster in the hospital elevator reminded Vangie of the article Darla had spotted in *People* magazine. The taller of the two aides standing next to her noticed it as well. "You believe that?" he said. "A big movie star like India Marlowe helping to raise money for those kids on the cancer ward?"

The man with him snorted. "Sure, she lets them use her name, but you can bet your paycheck that somebody else will be doing the scut work."

Vangie stepped off the elevator on 6B. "About time you were getting here." The duty nurse's pert dark face lit with a grin. "Tandora won't let me give her shot unless she's got one of Miss Vangie's cookies first. Said the needle won't hurt if she can eat a Snickerdoodle at the same time. I told Dr. Mossman that, and he said if you've discovered a way to make kids like shots, he's nominating you for a Nobel prize."

Vangie opened her shopping bag and pulled out a cookie tin. "Snickerdoodles all around. Mama and I baked four dozen last night."

Miss Mathews leaned forward to peer over the counter of the nurse's station. "What else you got in the magic bag today?"

"Two teddy bears and a Lisa Marie doll." Vangie took them out and set them on the counter.

"Whoo – ee. Your Elvis-4-Ever gals been busy this week." The nurse picked up the Lisa Marie doll and smoothed its skirt. "Mighty pretty. Hard to think this cute little thing lost her Daddy like that. Anyhow, we got a new little patient. Heather McNair. Real sick. Maybe one of these dolls will help."

Vangie could scarcely bear to ask the question to which she already half knew the answer. "Jennifer?"

Miss Mathews' smile disappeared. "Last night. Late."

Vangie squeezed her arms tight against her ribs to hold back the sick feeling rising inside her chest

"You okay?" Miss Mathews smoothed the doll's skirt, not looking at Vangie.

Vangie tried to nod, but could only shiver and squeeze herself tighter. Five years now she'd been volunteering at the hospital, but the death of a child was something she still hadn't learned to accept. Little kids snatched away, as if demons had carried them off, disappearing without a trace. Like Mama's Gypsies, death picked the dark of night to do its work.

"Honey, I know it's hard. This here 6B is dangerous territory. Every morning I come to work I have to steel myself all over again, knowing I might find Tandora's crib empty or

Andrew's place taken by a new kid, or see Michael's teddy bear staring up at me from an empty pillow."

"I don't see how you and the other nurses, the interns, the doctors, how you stand it," Vangie said.

"Lots of us can't. Big turnover from burn-out on this ward."

At the entrance to the ward, Vangie paused and sucked in several deep breaths. The huge room was painted in bright colors with a border of nursery rhyme figures, but fear and uncertainty lurked in its corners. Her subconscious counted the stainless steel cribs lined along one side of the room. Last week six. Now only five. Please, God, you've taken Jennifer. Let that be enough.

Luckily, a couple of the kids had visitors, parents, grandparents, brothers and sisters. Less need to feel guilty about devoting so much time to those like Donny whose mother was in jail on a cocaine charge or Buzzy whose dad disappeared after he lost his job, or Tandora, her mother and father both killed by the fighting in El Salvador.

In the second crib from the door, Tandora was asleep, her head propped high on pillows, a Lisa Marie doll clutched in her arms. Oversized Mickey Mouse ears hid her bare scalp, the beautiful, Indian-straight hair gone since the latest round of chemotherapy.

Vangie was trying to tiptoe past the crib when Tandora stirred. The child's dark eyes opened, stared blankly for a moment, then lit with recognition. "Snickerdoodles," she whispered.

In the next crib over, Heather, the new patient, began screaming as Miss Mathews and an aide tried to install an IV in her tiny veins. Vangie shuddered, imagining what it must be like for the four-year old to be in this unfamiliar place, surrounded by strangers who stuck needles into her.

Heather's mom couldn't stand it, and slipped out into the hall so the child couldn't see her crying. After the IV was in place and the nurse had finished, Vangie showed Heather the doll. "Her name's Lisa Marie. Would you like to have her for your hospital friend?"

Heather didn't answer, but she moved her head a fraction to one side so the doll could share her pillow.

Later, when Vangie left the ward, Heather's dad followed her into the hall. "Thanks," he said. "She loves the doll." The way Mr. McNair's chin trembled told her that he would like to add something more, but was afraid to speak his fears or hopes aloud.

"They'll take good care of her here," was the best comfort she could offer.

On the elevator going down, memory of the pain on Mr. McNair's face reminded Vangie of a comment Darla had made – "I don't see how you do that volunteer stuff. Ain't it a real downer?"

Why did she do it? The nurses and doctors had skills that could save kids' lives, but she had nothing like that to offer.

Even the four thousand dollars the club had raised didn't really amount to much. Lisa Marie dolls, Teddy Bears and Snickerdoodles. Toy weapons against an all-too-real enemy.

Before the elevator door opened to the lobby, she glanced again at the poster about the upcoming fund raiser. At least these kids would get lots of help from the money a big movie personality like India Marlowe would bring in.

***

The five-carat marquise-cut diamond on India Marlowe's ring finger signaled fiery indignation as the actress swept away the array of photographs her secretary had placed in front of her. Head-shots, torso-shots and full-length poses tumbled from the desktop to form a jumbled pattern against the splendor of the antique Kirghiz carpet. "A chimpanzee with a Polaroid could have taken better stills than this," India hissed.

Dina Andrews stooped, gathered up the photographs, and carried them to one of the room's tall windows. "I certainly see what you mean," the secretary said, examining each one closely. "None of these does you justice."

"Justice," India snapped. "Every damned one makes me look thirty pounds heavier and ten years older. We should never have agreed to let that local asshole handle the publicity photos."

Dina shuffled through the pack a second time, then extracted an eight-by-ten of India stretched out in a chaise longue under one of Gwynnbrook's venerable elms. "This one's not bad," she said. "The shade from the tree gives your features a kind of ethereal quality. And the backlighting is terrific. Brings out the copper highlights in your hair."

"You think so?" India took a closer look at the photo her secretary had selected. Actually, that one was rather good. Those hundreds of grueling hours in the gym had definitely paid off, the body was in superb shape, and the breasts as firm as ever thanks to Dr. Pyle's magic scalpel. As for the legs, they'd still be the envy of any twenty-year-old.

Dina confirmed that assessment. "Mel will absolutely flip when he gets a load of this one." She had no more than mentioned the agent's name when the phone rang. She reached for it, then mouthed as she handed India the receiver, "It's him."

"India, Darling!" The agent's voice came crackling across three thousand miles of continent. "Wonderful news. I just got off the horn with J.C. He thinks you'd be absolutely fabulous as the rich widow in the series. "

"So does 'absolutely fabulous' mean he's giving me the part?" The diamond sparkled impatience as India tapped her fingers against the chair's armrest.

"Angel, you know how these things go. J.C.'s still looking, but the way I see it, the part's a wrap for you."

"Mel, cut the bullshit. Are we talking contract or not?"

"India. Sweetheart. Let's not push this too fast. Remember, our game plan is for you to take a little 'time out'...re-group...build a whole new image for yourself."

India clenched her jaw in a supreme effort to keep from telling the agent what he could do with his "new image" crap.

"Dammit, Mel, I've been vegetating in this lousy Maryland backwater for six months. How long does it take for Hollywood to forget one teeny lapse?"

"Sweetheart, we mustn't forget that your 'one teeny lapse' cost the studio some really big bucks."

"Screw that. What about the millions I've made for that same damned studio?"

"Baby, you know this town. Nobody cares about last year's numbers. Now if you want to come back out here and play over-the-hill types, I can get you work. But I thought we agreed on this little hiatus, a come-back with you in a completely different style, a broad with dignity...class."

"All right. I know what we agreed: No more 'flash-the-tits' roles, from now on I'm high society all the way. Call me Grace Kelly."

"That's my girl. Now you just leave everything on this end to ol' Mel. And keep that good publicity coming. When's that big charity 'do'?"

"August. The committee's meeting here next week to plan everything."

"Great. Honorary Chairmanship. Just the thing to polish up the old image."

9. "Goin' Home"

Floyd squinted through the windshield. Ever since Richmond, traffic had been running heavy, a double line of southbound headlights coming toward them, double line of red taillights stretched out in front. Mostly eighteen-wheelers making their nighttime runs from Baltimore, Philly, Richmond, New York, or Boston. Like those hauls he and Herb Polaris used to make. Only back then he hadn't been on the lam, exhausted, filthy, and ready to kill for a decent night's sleep.

He tried to force the numbers on the dashboard clock into focus. One-fifteen. In the A.M. A crummy time to be barreling up Interstate 95, stuck in the cab of a chicken hauler's truck. But after nearly a week on the road with hardly any sleep, everything looked like crap.

Floyd started to doze, but the truck's swerve jerked him awake.

"Harbor Tunnel," the driver grunted as he braked for the tollbooth.

Toll keeper kept staring at him. Like the creep suspected something. Maybe seen the APB Arena had out on him. Floyd cringed a little lower in the seat then slumped with relief when the toll keeper handed the driver a receipt and waved them on.

Ahead, the tunnel's grungy tube burrowed downward. Spooky feeling, being under the river like this. Nothing but a few thin feet of concrete holding back those tons and tons of water overhead. Was building tunnels one of those jobs they handed to the lowest bidder?

The tunnel walls sent the growl of motors, and the hum from the big rigs' tires, sizzling through his brain. Probably quieter if the window on his side could be closed, but just his rotten luck he'd hitched a ride with a guy whose gut was filled with chili from Happy Hannah's All-You-Can-Eat Truck Stop. Enough gas in the cab by now to blow up the tunnel and half of Baltimore besides.

Not that he smelled like any rosebud himself. Never realized how tough it was going to be, putting up in sleazy, flea-bag motels, sticking to the back roads, ducking into the ditch every time a cop car passed.

The whole miserable trip like scenes from some lousy B movie. All the way through Georgia in the back of that cracker's pick-up truck along with three kids and two flea-bitten coon dogs. That scurvy-looking Overland truck driver who'd picked him up at South of the Border. Big tattoo that read "Born to Kill" and a picture of a guy having his heart ripped out by a vulture. Then there was the queer that gave him a lift into Richmond. Hand slipping off the gearshift....

Floyd rubbed at his burning eyes with the back of his fist. Ten years ago when he'd lit out for New York, he'd figured he'd be coming back home in style. Fancy wheels. Snappy threads. A hot-looking babe on his arm. Now here he was – sneaking back in the middle of the night, dead beat and smelly, stuck in the cab of a chicken carrier with Mr. Stink Pot. One major difference, though. Now there were nearly two hundred and fifty beautiful Gs—he'd only spent a few hundred so far—sitting on his lap.

Floyd shifted the duffle bag to restore circulation to his cramped leg. Damned wads of cash in there might as well be bricks for all the good it had done him so far. Couldn't even risk using a little of the dough to buy a plane ticket...couldn't take a chance of carrying it through the airport where those jerks were always watching for anyone carrying too much cash. Taking the bus wasn't safe, either. Couldn't risk being spotted by some two-bit pusher Cenicero had hanging around the stations. Even that crummy little dump of a store in South Carolina where he'd stopped to buy a soft drink had his picture plastered next to the post-office window.

One good thing at least – nobody with an IQ over twenty would think of looking for him in Dundalk. Just have to figure out a way....

If only he wasn't so flat-out tired. Eyelids felt like they had lead weights attached. Maybe close them for a minute....

Something hit Floyd in the ribs. He jumped and grabbed for the duffel bag before he realized it was only the driver poking him with an elbow. "Which exit you say you wanted to be let off at?" the guy grunted.

"Right after the tunnel," Floyd told him.

The driver rolled up on one hip to release another barrage.

Floyd held his breath and leaned toward the window.

The driver gave him another poke. "So, got yourself a hot chick here?"

"Hell, no." Floyd told him. "The babes I take out ain't the kind that don't know the difference between filet mignon and a hamburger at Mickey D's."

"What brings you here then?"

"Family. I got family here. Ma and my sister."

"So this sister of yours. She a nice girl?"

"Yeah. Nice."

Vangie. Did he dare let her in on what was going on? Nah. Too risky. She might not rat him out, but that was a chance he couldn't take. As for Ma, let her find out he was back and you'd just as well put it on the evening news. Smarter to stick to the original plan. Hide out in that old coal bin in the basement, the place where he used to stash his dope. Stay there for a few days until the heat was off. Then get in touch with Angelina in New York, scope out a plan, head for Mexico.

They were clear of the tunnel now, heading north, city lights spreading a streak of red across the horizon. Off to the right the lights of Dundalk Marine Terminal floated like a space colony on the Patapsco's black waters. The air blowing through his open window felt like it came straight from Sparrows Point's blast furnaces. More than anything else, that eau de Dundalk scent brought it all home. He'd landed right back where he started, breathing the same stink he'd breathed every day when he was growing up.

***

Two A.M. Floyd slunk through back alleys and side streets, making his way toward Shirley Avenue. As he approached the 2700 block, he hugged the dark side of the street. From what he could see, the old neighborhood hadn't changed for the better. Same shabby story-and-a-half bungalows. Same old beat-up cars and vans with construction ladders on top hulking next to the curb. Same sulphury glow from the streetlight at the end of the block making everything look shrunken and seedy.

Lucky for him, the rest of the streetlights were out. He checked once more, then ducked out from behind a pick-up truck and made a wild dash for 2744, planning to head straight for the rear of the house. He made it to the sidewalk okay, but halfway across the front lawn something snagged his foot and sent him sailing headfirst. Floyd hit the ground, and his skull cracked against what felt like concrete. The duffel bag flew from his grasp. Unable to stifle a groan, he grabbed his head in both hands, curled himself into a fetal ball, and rolled on the grass while skyrockets exploded inside his brain.

When the light show finally began to fade, he crawled about, groping for his bag but came up with nothing but handfuls of grass. Gone. The bag with all his money was gone.

Every direction he turned he kept bumping into things. It was Mama's lawn ornaments, those goddam dwarfs or ducks or whatever the hell other pieces of junk she had setting around the yard that had tripped him up.

More frantic searching, then finally his fingers touched canvas. Almost crying with relief, he snatched up the bag, staggered to his feet, and paused for a moment to listen. No reaction from inside the house. No lights flicked on at the neighbors. So far okay.

On hands and knees, he crept toward the back yard. For once his luck was good. The basement window leading into the old coal bin flipped open with scarcely a creak.

***

Vangie peered into the darkness outside her bedroom's open window. All quiet now. The sound must have come from one of the neighbor's dogs.

She slid back beneath the sheet, closed her eyes, and tried to lose herself in the music. But tonight there was no way to get comfortable. She flipped her pillow, searching for a cooler spot. More than just the heat was keeping her awake—it was the remark Flo made when they were chatting at noon. "You goin' out with that cute Mr. Jenkins if he comes back?"

She'd tried to sluff off the question. "Doubt I'll ever see him again."

"Oh, you'll see him all right. I noticed the way he always looks at you. What I want to know is will you say yes if he asks you."

"We'll see," was the best she could manage.

But Flo was as persistent as a rash. "Just tell me this," she demanded, "when was the last time you had a date?"

Luckily, the phone had rung just then so she'd been able to avoid Flo's question.

But now, alone in her bedroom, Flo's words stuck like a briar in her mind. Her last date? Probably that time in April. Coffee with Rob Harmon after Mergers and Acquisitions class.

If you could call it a date.

At the time, it had seemed harmless enough. Rob had asked if she'd like to have a bite at the coffee shop around the corner. Only nine-thirty, still time to catch the last bus to Dundalk, so she'd said yes.

He'd been nice and really easy to talk to. By the time the waitress refilled their cups, she was telling him about how Brandi kept ringing lipstick and blusher on the Housewares key because that was stuff you put on in the bathroom, and about the way Darla picked her boyfriends by the make of their cars. "Darla says guys who drive convertibles expect too much on the first date, the ones with Chevvies can't afford nice places, and she never goes out with any man who drives a van because they're sure to be married."

Rob's eyes had crinkled when he grinned. His story about the Fax mix-up that caused his boss to ship sixteen cases of beer to the nuns at St. Vincents had both of them laughing out loud. She liked it, too, the way he talked about his family. "Jacie—that's my youngest sister… fourteen going on twenty-four—she thinks a weekend without a trip to the mall is like a weekend in Purgatory."

Rob was a lot more than just talk. Even though he was working as a deliveryman for a local brewery, a person could see he was someone with solid plans for his future. "I don't care how long it takes for us to get our degrees the way we're going, taking these night and Saturday classes," he said. "When we're finished we'll have a chance for real careers."

She liked the way that "we" had made her feel. Vangie O'Toole, CPA. She could almost see those initials after her name. Working full time plus taking care of Mama wasn't the quickest route, but by the time she was thirty or thirty-one, that dream could be a reality.

The longer they talked, the more she enjoyed being with Rob. He must have liked her okay, too, otherwise why would he have invited her to the Orioles pre-season game the following Saturday? Even so, she'd hesitated. To make sure there wouldn't be a problem, she'd excused herself and called home. She told Mama she was having coffee with a friend and that she'd be a little late. Everything had seemed okay, Mama perfectly calm. When she returned to the booth she told Rob yes, she'd love to go with him to the game.

A little later, she'd glanced at her watch. "I had no idea we'd talked so long," she told him as she picked up her purse and collected her books. "I'll have to hurry to catch the ten-fifteen bus."

"No problem," he said. "I'll drive you home."

She'd hesitated. Rob lived in Timonium, on the north side of Baltimore. After taking her home he'd have to drive all the way back across town. Besides, she was a little uneasy about how he would react when he saw where she lived. Too often people from other parts of Baltimore tended to look down their noses at Dundalk. Still, Rob didn't seem at all like that sort of person, so she thanked him and said yes.

His car was a Ford coupe. "Eight years old, ninety thousand miles on her and never a problem," Rob said when she admired the car's like-new condition. Rob Harmon was obviously a person who knew how to take care of things.

They crossed the Key Bridge, leaving the lights of Baltimore behind. Ahead the stacks of Bethlehem Steel spewed out rust-colored smoke against the night sky.

"You always lived here in Dundalk?" Rob asked.

"Yes."

"Your Dad a steelworker?"

"No. Dad died almost ten years ago, right after I graduated from high school."

Aware that her father's occupation was another thing that people sometimes reacted strangely to, Vangie hesitated before adding, "At the time I was born, Dad ran the garbage collection route in this end of Baltimore County, so it made sense for us to live here."

Rob's response set her at ease. "Must have been a tough job. I've always thought our society has it all wrong—it's not the rock stars and athletes who should be pulling in the big bucks, it's guys like your Dad, the ones who keep things running for the rest of us. They should be the millionaires."

That made it easy to tell Rob how great a guy her father had been. "Later on, Dad was assigned to a route in Greenspring Valley, up north of Baltimore. You should see some of the perfectly good stuff people up there throw out. He brought home all sorts of vases and artwork and furniture, most of it still usable. That suited my mother perfectly. She's the original pack rat. Never gets rid of anything."

"So it's just you and your mother?"

"Yes. Well, no, there's Floyd. My brother. But he's been gone ever since Dad died."

Vangie hoped she hadn't sounded too bitter about Floyd. After hearing Rob tell about the good times he and his three sisters had together, it was hard not to feel angry toward a brother who'd left without a word, abandoned her and Mama when they needed him most.

She would like to have told Rob about the Elvis-4-Ever Fan Club and the kids she worked with in her volunteer job at St. Ignatius Hospital, but by then they were nearing the street where she lived. "It's the 2700 block, fifth house from the corner. The pink one with all the lawn ornaments. Like I told you, Mama's a collector."

Rob grinned. "Sounds like my old man. He's a flea market addict. A basement and a garage full of tools, most of which don't work."

As they drew closer, Vangie could see that the all houses facing each other across Shirley Street were mostly dark with only an occasional blue flicker from a TV set except for 2744. There, lights were blazing in every window, upstairs and down. *Oh, Mama…please not again.* What was it this time? A mouse skittering across the kitchen floor? The wind blowing through the leaves of the maple tree?

Rob ducked to stare through the windshield at the brightly lit house, then glanced questioningly at her. "Anything wrong, Vangie?"

"Probably Mama's jittery because I'm late."

He opened the driver's side door and started to get out. "I'll walk you in. Make sure everything's okay."

"No! I mean, that's nice of you, but I can manage. Thanks for the ride. See you in class." With that she'd leaped from the car and scooted up the walk, digging keys from her purse as she went. As she was thrusting the key into the lock, she glanced over her shoulder and saw Rob still standing beside the car.

She waved for him to leave, then into the house's narrow front hall, shouting, "Mama, it's me."

Mama, her face distraught, was standing at the head of the stairs in her nightgown, Floyd's old baseball bat clutched in her hands. "They been here again," she sobbed incoherently. "This time they've come to get me for sure."

Vangie, fighting down the sinking feeling in the pit of her stomach, had tried to soothe Mama with tea and reassurances. "There's no one here, Mama," she'd repeated over and over.. Look, I've checked the closets, the basement, everywhere. Nobody's here but us, you and me, that's all."

"They've been here. Signs. Signs everywhere."

"What signs, Mama?"

"Little things. Like that green vase on the mantel. It's been moved."

Vangie went to the mantel and picked up the vase. "Mama the vase is right where it always was. Look, you can even see the lighter ring where it rests on the wood."

But nothing she'd said during that long, long night could stem the flood of her mother's fears. Dawn turned the sky outside to gray before she was finally able to coax Mama to take her pills and go to bed, the baseball bat still clutched against her as she fell asleep.

The next morning she'd called Rob, told him the baseball game was off. Told him....

In the darkness of her bedroom she whispered aloud, half to herself, half to Elvis. What difference does it make what I told him? Whenever Mama suspects there's someone else in my life, the story's always the same.

When she and Floyd were growing up, they'd always been on the watch for signs of any "episode" that might set

Mama off, but with Dad as a buffer, they'd been protected from the worst of it. Since Dad died, Mama had become worse, much worse, always insisting that the Gypsies were coming to steal her away, that she couldn't be left alone at night, that they were everywhere, always watching and waiting. No amount of proof could persuade her otherwise.

A whisper—half imagined—came to Vangie out of the darkness. *Is this how the rest of your life is going to be?*

What choice do I have? her inner voice argued. Mama's fear of being left alone is real. Everyone else has abandoned her, her husband dead, Floyd gone. No one's left but me.

But what about your life? the Elvis voice persisted.

So I'm supposed to walk out and leave Mama all alone? Goodbye, I've got my own life to live?

No response came to that question. Vangie turned over and pounded her pillow into shape. Why ask when she already knew the answer—she couldn't abandon Mama any more than she could walk away from those kids on the cancer ward.

NOTICE TO ALL CLUB MEMBERS

REMEMBER THAT A REPORTER

AND A PHOTOGRAPHER

FROM THE *BALTIMORE STAR* WILL

BE AT TONIGHT'S MEETING.

LET'S MAKE A GOOD IMPRESSION.

DON'T FORGET TWENTY-FIVE CENTS

FOR REFRESHMENT FUND.

BRENDA SUE HIGGS, PRESIDENT

ELVIS-4-EVER FAN CLUB

10. "A Fool Such as I"

The moving van with fancy crests on its side panels and "Aragon Transfer Company" spelled out in burgundy and gold letters turned the corner into Shirley Street. Its driver, Herb Polaris, checked the street sign. 2500 block. Two more to go. "I wasn't such a sucker, I'd be heading this rig back to the Newark terminal right now," he told Konstanze. "If we drove straight through there'd still be time to give Gertie a call, have a bite of dinner, a little 'dessert' afterwards."

The cat gave him a look as easy to read as USA Today. Polaris, that feline mind of hers was saying, can the bullshit. You know you're gonna make a stab at finding him.

"Whole thing's probably a waste of time," Herb told her. "Most likely O'Toole's family moved long ago. No reason to think he'd hide out here in Dundalk. "

Konstanze's whiskers twitched. She wasn't impressed with his argument.

"Besides," he reminded her, "anybody who knows Floyd O'Toole would consider it a public service to let Cenicero barbecue the creep."

The cat's icy stare made it clear she resented his bothering her while she was listening to the Puccini tape. She turned her head away and flicked her left ear, Konstanze's way of letting him know which of them was in control. As if there was ever any doubt. Herb grinned to himself. The little hussy cost him a fortune in fancy cat food and eight-track tapes, but what would he do without her?

Cat was probably trying to tell him that at forty-eight he ought to be smarter. Here he was, fourteen hours behind the wheel without a break, the afternoon hotter than a blast furnace, and those pork chops at the I-95 Truck-In searing his gut. He had half a brain he'd give up the crazy notion of looking to save the skin of a two-bit chiseler who probably wouldn't give him so much as a "thank you" for the effort.

Halfway down the block Herb started checking out house numbers. 2744. Fifth from the corner. A mango pink one, its lawn all floozied up with ornaments, a plastic Snow White and her seven plastic dwarves, a pair of pink flamingos, a Bo Peep complete with sheep, and, in one corner a wooden cut-out of a woman's rear end as she bent over a flower bed. In the middle of this menagerie, a headless mother duck paraded three concrete fledglings around the base of a purple reflecting ball that had been knocked off its pedestal.

The driver of the battered Datsun that was tailgating him honked impatiently then scooted past, the metallic discord of his dragging muffler temporarily drowning out Puccini. "If O'Toole's hiding out here," Herb observed, "he sure as hell must miss his high-rolling Miami life-style."

A twitch of Konstanze's whiskers indicated she shared his opinion.

Seeing this neighborhood up close reminded Herb of a night some eight or so years back when he and O'Toole were rolling up I-95, transferring a load of tax-free smokes from North Carolina to New York City...giving smokers in the Big Apple an opportunity to get their cancer cheap. Just past the harbor tunnel, O'Toole had pointed out one of the overhead exit signs. "Dundalk," he said. "That's where I grew up. Ma and my sister still live there."

"You ever go back to see them?" he'd asked, just to make conversation.

O'Toole had snorted. "Hell, no. That place is dead, man. The week after my old man got his, I hit the road and never looked back. Vangie—my sister, Evangeline—she tried to talk me into staying around to help out with Ma, but I told her, 'No way, Babe...I'm cuttin' out of here toot de damn sweet. If you got good sense you'll do the same.'"

Herb shook his head as he swung his moving van into a parking spot ahead of '69 Plymouth with multicolored fenders. Floyd O'Toole was a real beauty, all right. "Scheme-of-the-Week O'Toole" the other loaders in the warehouse used to call him.

Full of hot-assed plans for hitting it rich, making it big. Too dumb to realize his half-baked scams would net him nothing but trouble.

"Big trouble, trouble with a capital T, that's what O'Toole's got a freight load of now," Herb told Konstanze. "Doesn't take an Albert Einstein to figure that when one of Cenicero's goons comes around trying to pump me about where to find somebody, that somebody's ass is grass."

Konstanze agreed with a switch of her tail.

"And God knows O'Toole's got some bad Karma coming."

Herb killed the motor, careful to turn the key only halfway—cut the music off in mid-tape and Konstanze would go into one of her royal snits. "Never had enough proof to nail him, but my gut always told me it was Floyd who set me up for that heist. If the dummy hadn't fingered the wrong truck, that load of furs would have been on its way to Canada, and I'd have been out a cool half million. Scheme had Floyd's signature written all over it, especially with him taking a powder right after it happened."

He flipped down both sun visors. "Actually," he told Konstanze, "I could have gone after the punk, if I'd wanted to. Wouldn't have been all that hard to pick up Floyd's trail—L.A., the jewelry store robbery, jail...Chicago, a bank job, jail...Miami, drug gang, jail the inevitable next stop. But sometimes it's better just to say good riddance to bad rubbish. Anyhow, considering

Cenicero's record in dealing with double-crossers, O'Toole's about to collect what's coming to him."

Konstanze cocked her head and gave him a look.

"Okay, okay. I get the message. We do owe him one." He reached over and ran his fingers down her silky back. "Hadn't been for Floyd going back into that burning warehouse...pulling you out of there...."

A delicate ripple shuddered along Konstanze's spine.

Herb checked the dashboard clock. Fourteen hours from Atlanta to Baltimore, not bad time. Late afternoon sun had him yawning, though. He stretched and shifted his legs to get more comfortable. Through the truck's side view mirrors he checked out the street. Not exactly the kind of neighborhood where a van like this fit in. Just the opposite from the big advantage it had offered last night when he drove it up to the Atlanta museum's delivery entrance and, with a little help from a greedy curator, loaded up a Mary Cassatt and a couple Matisses.

He gave another yawn, then settled down in the seat, feeling both tired and satisfied. The job last night had gone off just the way it should, precise as a Rolex, nobody hurt, everybody a little happier. The museum would collect from the insurance company, the curator could now 'retire' with his boyfriend to Majorca, and that rich bastard in Atlanta had added to his 'private collection.' And fifty grand for a single night's run would buy a lot of cat food and opera tickets.

"But it's not just the money," Herb reminded Konstanze, "It's our reputation. Important for the big-time operators to know they can rely on Aragon Transfer any time they got a special shipment."

He took pride in that. Whether it was the diGrasso mob with a load of Gucci knockoffs that needed to find their way to New York, the Danelli family wanting to turn a few fast bucks on illegal hootch, or even the CIA with a body on its hands that had turned up in the wrong place, they all knew they could call on Herb Polaris to handle the job, get the merchandise there safe and on time, no questions asked. More important, they knew they could count on him to treat them square. In twenty-some years of doing business, there wasn't a single customer he'd ever taken advantage of or cheated. Other truckers might lift a little of the merchandise or add fuel weight to a load's tonnage, but Herb Polaris played it straight. With his clientele, that was the only smart way to go.

Another stretch eased a little of the ache across his shoulders. "Course a fellow's gotta draw the line at hauling drugs," he reminded the cat. "That's a whole different ball game, one I got no intention of playing. Mess around with those bad boys and sooner or later it's 'Goodbye, Herbert.'"

Konstanze gave another little shudder.

"Too bad Floyd O'Toole hasn't figured that out," Herb said. "Only thing that loser's gonna get out of the money he lifted will be a fancy funeral. If there's anything left to bury when Cenicero gets finished with him."

Out of respect for Konstanze's delicate nature, he didn't mention what Cenicero's goon had said about how his boss took care of double-crossers: "Is not a pretty sight, Senor Polaris. Cinecero has this fondness for blowtorches applied to various sensitive parts of the anatomy. His...how you say?—*clientes*—have much time to regret crossing Cenicero before death comes to their rescue."

Herb shook his head—he sure as hell wouldn't want to be in O'Toole's shoes right now. Hot enough here in the cab with the air-conditioner off. Even though it was past four o'clock, the sun's rays were still lasering through the windshield. He reached across to crank open the window on the passenger side. Konstanze purred approval. She hated the heat.

A slight adjustment to the side-view mirror gave a perfect view of Number 2744, opposite side of the street, three doors down. Herb slumped lower in the seat, stretched his cramped legs. "We'll give it a shot for an hour or so," he said, "scope out the neighborhood, see if there's any sign of O'Toole. . If not, we say the hell with it and head on back to Newark."

***

Lacey McLeod swung the Toyota into a parking space behind the moving van with fancy lettering on its side.

Mike Dowling grabbed the dashboard as she jammed on the brakes, "Jesus, Lace, this is only a stupid little fan club meeting we're covering, not a presidential assassination."

"I know. I know..." Lacey responded absently as she jockeyed her car in next to the curb. "But I hate being late for an assignment. Besides, you know what Avery tells us...."

"Ah, yes. 'There are no 'little stories,' only 'little reporters.' I've heard that line a hundred times."

She grinned at him. "It goes for photographers, too. So grab your Leica and let's get going. The story of the year awaits."

"Dream on, Lois Lane. Next you'll be trying to convince me that a piece about the Elvis-4-Ever Fan Club is going to reap us a Pulitzer and a book contract to boot."

"Feature piece, my friend. Magazine section. Color photos, yet."

"I'll start writing my acceptance speech."

***

In the pine-paneled basement room, Lacey and Mike trailed behind the Elvis-4-Ever Fan Club's President, Brenda Sue Higgs. "Holy Jehosephat," Mike muttered under his breath. "This place sure is a shrine to the fat guy."

Lacey rolled her eyes in response. Every possible medium in which Elvis could be immortalized was here—Elvis posters, Elvis photos, amateurish paintings, exaggerated sketches, needlepoint cushions, latch-hook rugs, plaster statuettes, etched crystal.

Already Lacey could feel the meat of her article forming. Which of these images was the real Elvis? The pristine early Elvis whose polished, androgynous features could just as easily be those of a girl? The shy country boy with a knowing gleam in his eye? The Elvis of jailhouse rock with dangling forehead lock and a bulge under his tight jeans? Or was it the Las Vegas Elvis, a-glitter with spangles and sequins, the nearly-done-in Elvis of the final concerts, all jowls and soft chins, bleary eyes concealed by dark glasses, dyed sideburns jutting onto cheeks puffy as half-deflated balloons?

"This is great stuff." she whispered to Mike. "Almost too easy—a bunch of women with a yen for a dead singer."

Brenda Sue, glowing with pride, unlocked a glass case to show Lacey a square of printed silk. "This couple down in Richmond decided to get a divorce," she said, "but neither one would agree to give up their Elvis memorabilia. Finally, the judge ordered them to sell their collection and divide the money. We were fantastically lucky to get this scarf." Lacey stooped to read the hand-lettered sign Brenda Sue pointed out to her. *Thrown by Elvis Aaron Presley in person and caught by Anna Marie Dunn of Richmond, Virginia on December 3rd, 1975 at the Las Vegas Hilton Hotel, Las Vegas, Nevada.*

"And I thought my baseball card collection was hot stuff." Mike whispered. "After tonight, I'm trading in all my Cal Ripkens."

Lacey estimated the majority of the women Brenda Sue had introduced to be in their forties or early fifties. A few, like Ruth Ann and Eudora and Vangie, were closer her own age, mid-twenties to early thirties. Pearl and one or two others looked old enough to be grandmothers.

One exception was a scabby-kneed pre-teenager. "Aarona's been real crazy about Elvis ever since she was just a little bitty thing," Aarona's mother announced, shoving her offspring forward. "She's got pictures of him plastered all over the walls and ceiling of her room. Right by her bed she keeps this life-sized Elvis cutout we bought for her eighth birthday. Came straight from the lobby of a casino where he was performing. That's A-A-R-O-N-A you spell her name."

Mike posed little Aarona next to plastic bust of Elvis.

While Aarona's mother was making her pitch, one of the other women standing nearby tossed her head and flounced huffily away muttering, "You might know Willadeen would bring dear little Aarona to meet the reporter."

"That's Sylvia," Brenda Sue explained. "Her son is 'Little E.P. He does Elvis impersonations in clubs and American Legion halls and county fairs. Sylvia claims he never so much as heard of Elvis, just woke up one morning when he was four years old and started singing 'Jailhouse Rock'."

Lacey managed to keep her composure. "I get the impression there's a bit of jealousy between Sylvia and Willadeen," she said.

Brenda Sue nodded. "Luckily," she said, "when it comes to working for the good of the club, those two put their jealousy aside and pitch in. Willadeen made a beautiful quilt with scenes from Elvis's life that we raffled. And Sylvia's son donated all the proceeds from his performance at the state fair last fall."

***

"Vangie O'Toole -- that's O- apostrophe - T-O-O-L-E?" Lacey McLeod asked.

Vangie nodded and recoiled as Mike's flash went off.

Lacey consulted her notes. "Miss O'Toole, Brenda Sue tells me it was your idea to raise money for the children's cancer unit at St. Ignatius?"

"All the members pitched in," Vangie said.

"That's quite a feat, for a club with only forty-seven members to raise...." Lacey stopped to consult the memo her editor had handed her. "to raise over $4,000. How'd you manage that?"

"Everybody helped with our Elvis Fun Fair, members, their husbands and families. And fans came from as far away as Buffalo, New York, and Spartanburg, South Carolina. The Kmart employees gave over two hundred dollars. And the local Girl Scout troop raised seventy-five dollars from their bake sales."

"But isn't this a rather unusual project for an Elvis fan club?"

Vangie shook her head. "People don't realize that Elvis helped lots of people, little kids and sick people in particular. We fans just follow in his footsteps. That's our club motto—"In His Footsteps."

In his footsteps, Lacey scribbled. "And you raised that sum by selling these Elvis mementos you and the others made?"

"We cleared over nine hundred dollars on the teddy bears alone. Plus we auctioned off some souvenirs and held raffles. But the other members can tell you more about that."

Vangie's obvious sincerity gave Lacey a momentary twinge of guilt. But business was business. Sure, she'd been assigned to write about the Elvis-4-Ever Fan Club's charitable work, but the more bizarre aspects of the Elvis cult was what would really grab readers. She turned to the other women who had gathered around while she was interviewing Vangie. "So what inspires a person to become an Elvis fan?" she asked. "Why are you still attracted to Elvis even though he's been dead for ten years?"

"Well, everybody knows Elvis had this fantastic talent." Ruth Ann said. "He's the only singer that ever lived who could take a song and really shake it loose." She gave a little butt jiggle to demonstrate.

Pearl interrupted, "I don't care how good Elvis could sing. He was a nice, down-home boy who always respected his mother."

"Not to mention he was about the sexiest hunk that ever lived," Darla added slyly. "A real bed-warmer."

A middle-aged woman with dark circles under her eyes and a suspicious-looking bruise on her forearm had been standing at the edge of the group. Now she interjected shyly, "When I listen to Elvis sing about how he cares about people, I always feel like he's singing right to me."

Pearl reached to give the woman a sympathetic hug. "You're absolutely right, Gloria. Elvis really does care about us all."

Lacey felt a tug at her sleeve. She turned and found herself looking into the glistening eyes of a tiny gray-haired woman. "They've got it wrong, Hon," the woman said.

"Wrong?"

"About him."

"Elvis?"

"Yes. Him. Some of them don't like to talk about it, you see."

Lacey didn't know if it was the woman's far-away stare that was so disconcerting or the confusing conversation. "Exactly what is it they don't like to talk about?" she said.

"The Coming." The woman announced, as if that would be perfectly clear to anyone. "Like the Bible promised.'

"You mean the Second Coming?"

The woman nodded. "It was Elvis. I could tell right off."

Lacey struggled to hide her surprise. Calling Elvis the new Jesus went way beyond merely kookie. But the woman seemed so positive, so sincere, that Lacey couldn't help being intrigued. "So what convinces you Elvis was...Jesus?"

"Lots of things. You take his music, for instance. The first Jesus went around preaching at people. With Elvis, he just sang to them. Now sermons are all right for the older church-going crowd, but it was the young ones Elvis came for. Got 'em, too. Gathered them in like the Bible says about sheep into the fold."

Lacey took a moment to digest that notion. "Do you really think Jesus would get up on stage and make those...ah...motions like Elvis did?"

"Oh, indeed yes! He was showing us that a person's body is nothing to be ashamed of. Why, if they'd had rock and roll music back in the old days, you can bet that first Jesus would have shown them how to groove just like Elvis did."

Lacey's mind raced as she tried to visualize Jesus riding into Jerusalem on a Harley Davidson. Now *there* was an angle for her story.

Just then Brenda Sue called the meeting to order. "We will open our meeting tonight with Sylvia Collins reading for us the beautiful poem she's written in loving memory of Elvis."

Sylvia stood, cleared her throat importantly, then commenced, "My poem's called, 'Never Another Like Him, A Loving Tribute to Elvis Aaron Presley by his Devoted Fan, Sylvia Collins."

<u>Never Another Like Him</u>

Oh, Elvis it's been so long
Since you left us and took away your songs.
But your memory will never grow dim
Because there's never been another like him.
We've kept on so faithful and true,
'Cause we always have been 'Stuck on You.'
We want you, we need you, we love you today,
And always will cherish each word you did say.
Death cannot keep you apart from your fans,
Forever and ever we'll be in your hands.

11. "Nothingville"

India Marlowe slid farther down into the huge claw-footed tub. Maybe a long, hot soak would wash away the pissed-off feeling. Mel's bitch of a secretary was lying through her capped teeth. The agent's refusal to take her call could only mean one thing – the bastard still hadn't put a lock on the role.

It wasn't like he was plugging her for the lead in *My Fair Lady*, for Christ's sake. Why should she, India Marlowe, have to grovel just to get a lousy TV series?

The bath bubbles touched her chin, and she swiped them away with an impatient hand. Damn it all, didn't two nominations for Best Supporting Actress count for anything? So maybe she wasn't a superstar like Kim Basinger or Sigourney Weaver, but she wasn't some flash in the pan either. Not like that new crowd of anorexic look-alike bimbos who had nothing going for them beyond great hair and bouncy, young tits.

If Blake Whitney, her louse of a fourth husband, hadn't diddled away her savings with his "can't miss" investments, she wouldn't be in this bind. Matter of fact, if it weren't for Blake and that miserable brat, Kevin Tiles, marrying Daniel Dulaney Stowell might not have looked like an easy out, a chance to thumb her nose at a town that was ready to toss her aside like last week's *Variety*.

This Greenspring Valley crowd was even worse. Bitches acted like she was some trashy nobody, an outsider who'd used every trick in the book to snatch away their prize bachelor. What a laugh that was—after fifty years trapped under Mama Stowell's thumb, all it had taken to land their precious Daniel was a couple of blow jobs.

But who really got hooked? Oh, sure, Daniel was loaded. All the Stowells came loaded. But he was about as exciting as a last year's Oscar runner-up.

She missed Hollywood, dammit, missed the excitement, the insider gossip, the thrill of walking into Morton's or The Mustache Café, knowing every eye in the place was turned her way. But mostly it was the work she missed.

God knows managing Daniel's household was a nothing job. Mazie and Ruthella had made it clear from the start that they could run the house without her help. A relief, though, not having to know Spanish.

"Your job is to look pretty, be a good hostess," Daniel always said when she complained.

What a joke. Since age fifteen she'd been getting up at four or five to be at the studio for make-up, worked through weekends and holidays, stayed on her feet and on cue when every bone in her body felt like it was breaking. She'd been thrown off a horse, damned near drowned filming a shipwreck scene, worn costumes that weighed forty pounds and a wig so heavy she thought her neck would break. So now she was supposed to do nothing but sit around this musty old mausoleum and look pretty.

At least, thanks to Mister Anthony of *Ne Plus Ultra Design*, she didn't have to live with Gwynnbrook's ratty old furnishings any longer. But now that she'd jazzed the place up, given it some pizzazz, what was left?

Why hadn't anyone warned her that life among these old-line Maryland families would be an endless, bloody bore? Even their parties were about as much fun as getting embalmed. Hunt breakfasts, for God's sake, where everyone stood around arranging liaisons for their breeding mares. If they'd tried to film *Gone With the Wind* in this place, everybody in the audience would be sleeping while Atlanta burned.

Not one person here she could talk to. All these snobby valley women wanted was to drawl on about was which prep school junior would attend or who'd gotten picked for the Altar Guild at St. Johns or Sinjins or whatever they called it. That and their damned horses. And look at the way they dressed. If dull and dowdy ever came in style, this place would become the fashion capitol of America. God, what she'd give right now for a good hour of dishing the dirt with the women at Mr. Milo's Salon, or one of those wild evenings with Jamie and Lillian and Darrell and the rest of the BelAir crowd. Hell, drinks with the guys on the backlot would beat this dead fish affair.

The luncheon on Thursday would be another yawn, trying to charm a gaggle of women who thought Talbot's was high fashion. Dina would expect her to remember each of their names, what private schools their kids attended, what banks or law firms their husbands ran. Knowing Dina, she probably even had their horses' names down pat.

Dina. What a godsend to have a secretary with both looks and smarts. Thanks to Liz for teaching her that. "Some women in the industry think they can make themselves look good by having a secretary who's plain and not too bright," Liz had cued her over drinks at Prego. "But you've got to remember that you're the one the star-sniffers will be looking at, not some two hundred a week secretary. Fact is, a smart, classy secretary not only makes you look good, she can make your life a helluva lot easier. She'll keep the press happy, keep your agent happy. If you want, she'll even keep your husband happy."

India stepped out of the tub and reached for her robe. Liz had been one hundred percent right. Except for the husband part. Proof of that came when Dina picked up on the fact that Blake was embezzling from her accounts. Of course, it was always possible that Dina had squealed because Blake *quit* screwing her.

Hollywood or not, it was all the same. Turn your back for ten seconds and somebody was sure to be standing there, ready to shove a knife in it.

12. "I've Lost You"

The sound of a truck backfiring startled Herb Polaris into instant wakefulness. How long had he been asleep? Something felt wrong. He glanced around the cab.

Konstanze?

The window. He'd left the passenger side window rolled down. Still, it wasn't like Her Majesty to take off without warning. A quick search under and behind the seat. No cat. He climbed down from the cab, knelt on the gritty pavement and looked underneath the chassis. Not there, either.

No need to panic. Most likely Madam Konstanze had felt the urge to stretch, take a little walk, look the neighborhood over, relieve her royal self. She wouldn't have gone far in this heat. Dead-end street. Hardly any traffic. Plenty of daylight left. Give her a few minutes, she'd come parading back, nose in the air, lifting her paws like some Victorian dame too dainty to set her feet down on the common sidewalk.

Another half hour, six-thirty by the dashboard clock, and Konstanze still hadn't turned up. Twice he left the van to check out all the nearby streets and alleys. Cats, but no Konstanze. She didn't show up soon, he'd have to go door-to-door, hope that somebody had spotted her, maybe taken her in. Not smart to get himself noticed. That dame who parked behind him in the Toyota in need of a valve job had given him a funny look. So had the guy carrying the camera. Wonder what business those two had at the O'Toole house.

Herb was getting ready to haul himself out of the van again when there was a flurry of activity across the street. A bunch of women were going in 2744, all ages, shapes and sizes. From the looks of it, some kind of meeting must be going on. No sign, though, of Floyd, but then the hope of finding him here in Dundalk had been a long shot at best.

After most of the women were inside 2744, Herb left the cab and started checking for Konstanze at houses on the odd-numbered side of the street. He got two "Ain't seen no cat, Mister," one nobody home, one near-attack by a German Shepherd, and one *We ain't buyin' nothin'*.

He peered down the block, hoping maybe he'd spot the cat scooting between houses, but nothing. The whole thing was beginning to feel like Mozart's "The Abduction from the Seraglio." Maybe he ought to do the Belmonte role, stand outside these houses singing *Hier soll ich dich den sehen, Konstanze* -- "Here may I hope to find you, Konstanze." But then, if any evil Pasha carried off *his* Konstanze, he'd damn quick regret it. Get her riled and she turned into a regular tiger.

He crossed to the even side between his van and the Toyota. At least Konstanze's disappearing act gave him a legit excuse to talk to the people in the O'Toole house, maybe even get a clue as to whether or not Floyd had showed up there.

His knock at 2744 brought a scrawny little lady to the door. She was wearing a flower-patterned muu-muu, black orthopedic shoes and white anklets. Judging by the wrinkles and the frizzy cloud of white hair framing her pointy face, she was probably in her sixties, but age hadn't clouded the piercing blue eyes that stared suspiciously at him through the screen.

Herb yanked off his cap. "Ma'am," he said, "I wonder if you've seen anything of a cat around here this afternoon. She's dark grey, blue eyes, velvet-brown paws and she has on a white leather collar with little silver studs on it."

The woman didn't answer, just stood there, her inquisitive blue eyes raking him up and down. Herb wondered if he'd spilled something on himself or left his zipper open. He risked quick downward glance, but his tan Aragon Transfer uniform seemed to be in order.

Then, as if she'd made up her mind about him, the woman suddenly swung the door open and beckoned for him to enter. "You've come about them, haven't you? About time they sent somebody official."

He blinked. "Ma'am?"

"It's them you're looking for. I could tell right off."

"Well...yes, ma'am. I *am* looking. But it's only one...."

"Just one of them working alone this time? That would explain it, why they only switched the frame and not the picture. Probably didn't have time."

"Ma'am, I don't think you understand. It's my cat I'm looking for. Konstanze. She's a Persian...."

"Persian. Then I was right. Sure as my name's Lotte O'Toole it *was* the Gypsies that did it." She motioned toward the archway that led to what was obviously a living room. "Come on in here. Let me show you what mischief they've done."

She pointed out a picture. "See for yourself. Vangie didn't believe me that they'd been here. And that Darla girl she brought home with her just stood there with her mouth open like a toad catching flies."

None of that made any sense, but the woman's name was O'Toole, so he'd hit the right place. But what was the rest of that about? Herb rubbed his forehead in an effort to act like he knew what he was talking about. "Shame somebody came in here and tampered with your belongings," was the best he could manage. "I'll...uh...I'll be sure to report it."

Who he was going to report it to, he had no idea, but at least his assurance seemed to convince Lotte O'Toole that he was legitimately concerned. She ushered him into the kitchen, offered him coffee, explained that her daughter's Elvis fan club was meeting in the basement, and continued her litany of complaints about Gypsies breaking into her house and stealing her things.

The coffee was surprisingly good—its rich aroma soothed his empty stomach. He cast a surreptitious look around as he sipped. This was one weird setup—the house furnished like a yard sale addict's idea of heaven, the daughter an Elvis freak, a bunch of women crooning songs in the basement and, to top it off, this weirdo lady mistaking him for some kind of cop and ranting on and on about Gypsies.

Struggling to make sense of it all, Herb set his cup down carefully. "Now how was that again?" he said. "You claim that these people...."

"Not people," she said, "it's Gypsies."

"But Gypsies are people..."

"You can call them that if you want to. I guess in your line of work you got to be careful to use official terms for things."

His line of work—apparently the uniform had given her the idea he was some sort of law officer, a secret agent or something. He'd play along with that for a bit and maybe she'd spill some information on Floyd's whereabouts. "So what you're saying is that these Gypsies come into your house, steal things, and leave something in place of what they take?"

"Something that *looks* the same but always the teeniest bit different. But I already told you that. What are you going to do about it?"

"Well...what would you *like* me to do, Mrs. O'Toole?"

"Investigate. Isn't that what you people do?"

Okay, if Lotte O'Toole wanted him to investigate, he'd oblige. "So tell me, ma'am, how long has this sort of thing been going on?" Columbo would have been proud.

"What's today's date?"

"Uh...it's Tuesday...July 11th."

"Let's see, this is 1987 and Hap got killed the summer of '76...August the 3rd to be exact. "That would make it nearly eleven years."

"They've been coming and taking your things for almost eleven years?"

"Started the week after Hap went through the compactor."

"Compactor?" The word came out as a gurgle. Either he had walked through Alice's looking glass or stumbled into the middle of some weird modern play where nothing anybody said or did connected with anything else—including reality.

"On the garbage truck," Lotte said. "You see, Hap found this little radio in somebody's trash, practically new, still in its box. Tiny thing it was, small enough to put in your pocket and even came with earphones so you could carry it in your pocket and listen to music whatever you might be doing. Hap loved that thing, listened to it all the time while he was working. Always did like music, Hap did, even though with all the noise of the truck's machinery he had to turn the volume up far as it would go. Anyhow, with this gadget, he could turn it up loud as he liked and still keep right on loading. That's how it happened."

"It...?"

"The accident. Or that's what they called it. I got my own theories about that. Anyhow, the Sanitation Company claimed that this plastic picnic cooler got stuck in one of the blades of the compactor. His partner claimed he didn't see Hap climb inside to get it unjammed before he turned on the compactor. Flattened poor Hap, perforated him like a waffle."

"Jeez, what a gruesome accident."

"Accident?" Lotte O'Toole leaned across the plastic tabletop to tap Herb's chest with her bony forefinger. "Wasn't no accident whatsoever. It was Gypsies that got him. I knew it the minute I saw Hap compacted like that."

"I don't underst...."

The glance she gave him was as scornful as one of Konstanze's. "Don't you see? That's their way exactly. Always leave something just the tiniest bit different in place of what they take."

Too stunned to reply, Herb felt his eyebrows hit his hairline as the strains of "When I'm Over You" drifted up the basement stairs.

***

Floyd sat upright and clutched his reeling head in both hands to stop the spinning. Singing. Somebody was singing.

He hadn't woke up yet. Yeah, that was it...all a bad dream. He lay back down and closed his eyes against the pain.

Cenicero setting fire to Dolores's apartment, burning her up, that part was real. The crocodile with black beady eyes that grabbed his leg, pulled him off into the swamp. That must have been a dream. The chiggers he'd got from hiding in the woods whenever a cop car was in sight. The old coot with white legs sticking out of his touristy plaid shorts who'd offered him a ride then tried to get fresh with him. All of it oozed together into one endless nightmare.

With tentative fingers Floyd explored his throbbing skull. A knot the size of a baseball. That was real enough. Got that when his head collided with Mama's lawn ornament. No recollection of how he'd managed to crawl in through the basement window and climb down onto the workbench. How long had he been passed out?

Had a cat really jumped on his face or was that part of the nightmare? Not just any cat, either. Konstanze. Herb Polaris's cat. He opened one eye. The cat must be real because she was sitting right there, staring up at him. "Shoo! Beat it." he flapped his arm at her but she didn't move.

He must be dreaming again, but he was sure now he was hearing voices. They were coming through the flimsy partition that separated the coal bin from the rest of the basement. He raised his head to listen for a moment, then swung his legs over the edge of the workbench and sat upright. When the spinning stopped, he slid down from the workbench and dragged himself over to where light was shining through an eyeball-sized knothole in the paneling. A whole flock of women was out there. And Elvises, all over the place. He blinked to clear his head —must be some kind of Elvis club meeting in the basement.

The cat nudged up against his leg, but when the women began murdering another old Elvis tune, their caterwauling sent her wild and she began jumping from one wall of the coal bin to the other, whining and slapping at her ears with her paws. Floyd grabbed her and squeezed her against his chest. "I know that ain't your kind of music, but shut up, " he hissed. "You bring those women in here and I'm dead meat. What the hell you doing here anyhow?"

He checked the silver tag attached to her collar. No mistake, it really was Herb's cat. Even had that same crook in her tail where it got caught in a truck door one time.

Konstanze's being there could only mean Herb Polaris was somewhere close by. But that didn't make sense, either. Been six, seven years at least since he worked for Herb. No reason his old boss would come looking for him now. Could Cenicero have sent him? Nah, Herb Polaris would never do business with The Ashtray. But the cat? Herb was bound to be looking for her.

Konstanze started her low throaty whining again. Floyd picked her up, tried to quiet her. Immediately his nose started running. "My damned allergies," he muttered. The combination of coal dust, dampness and cat hair was a killer. All it would take to give him away was one of his industrial strength sneezes. He had to get rid of the cat. "Come on, nice kitty," he whispered, "time for you to go back wherever it was you came from."

But when he lifted Konstanze to shove her through the high window, she bristled at the indignity and leaped out of his arms with an ungodly screech. If the women hadn't hit the song's chorus just then, the yowling would have given him away for sure. "Little hussy," he snarled as he dabbed with his shirttail at the blood oozing from the claw marks that ran the length of his forearm.

Konstanze, her poise restored, ignored him to go prancing about the room. Floyd watched her delicately lift her feet and cock her head, casing the joint like she was planning to settle in. Probably best to leave her alone until the Elvis freaks cleared out.

He carried a wooden crate over to the wall and positioned himself where he could peer through the knothole at the women. Nearly four years since he'd last seen his sister, but she was still the same old Vangie. Twenty-eight, and still stuck here in Dundalk. Probably working at that same old minimum wage Kmart job. Just the thought of that kind of life was enough to make a person gag.

Vangie surprised him though when she stood up and told about raising over four grand for those kids with cancer. Blew his mind just thinking about how many of those Lisa Marie dolls and pillows embroidered with "Elvis-4-Ever" and God knows what other junk the women had turned out to come up with that kind of dough.

Those broads had to be nuts, going to all that trouble then giving away the entire haul. But then, Vangie always had been the kind of sucker to put herself out for others instead of looking out for Number One. Hadn't been for Mama being crazy like she was, Vangie might have had herself a husband by now, maybe even a coupla kids.

"I was sure smart to get out of this crummy set-up when I did," he told the cat. "Could've been me stuck here in Dundalk taking care of the old lady and she's even loonier than these Elvis babes."

He put his eye back to the hole. One of the women was reading a poem about Elvis. "Jeez," he muttered to the cat, "sure that Elvis dude had an okay voice, but is that any reason to make some kind of saint out of him? That's like calling Madonna the new Virgin Mary."

Konstanza meowed agreement.

13. "It's a Long, Lonely Highway"

Shortly before dawn, an '83 Ford Falcon with bald tires, vestiges of several paint jobs, and a missing front bumper drifted to a stop on the shoulder of Interstate 95. A chunky, brown-skinned man whose straight black hair could not conceal the purple and blue lump that protruded in the exact center of his forehead leaped from the driver's side door. He aimed a vicious kick at the car's front fender. "Gecko, you stupid sonvabitch," he screamed at the small man cowering in the passenger seat. "I tol' you we never make no Baltimore in this heap of junk."

His companion, a thin, yellow-complexioned man with a scar slashed diagonally across one cheek, cringed. "How I'm supposed to know the fockin' car won' run?" he whined. "Cenicero tell me to steal a car. He don' say I should steal no fockin' Rolls Royce."

"*Soy un hombre muerte.*" Jose Espado raised a fist to the unheeding heavens. "Better I should pull out my gun right now, shoot myself through the heart."

Better yet, maybe he'd just shoot Gecko. The fool had to go and torch that apartment before they were sure O'Toole was in there. Cenicero like a raging bull when he found out it was only his girlfriend went up in smoke. If they failed this time, there'd be no mercy. Cenicero's orders had been plenty clear—*You fockers want to see another full moon come up over Miami, you better bring O'Toole and every fockin' penny back here pronto!*

Jose gave the fender a final kick then stepped to the edge of the highway. He raised his hand to shield his eyes and read aloud from the green overhead sign. "Florence, twenty miles. "We ain't even outa South Carolina yet.

"So what we gonna say to Cenicero when we call him tomorrow and say we ain't found no O'Toole?" Gecko said.

"Ain't what we're gonna say, you hemorrhoid on a pig's ass. Is what Cenicero gonna do when he find out we ain't even got near Baltimore yet, let alone found this *bolsa de caca* O'Toole. That's when you better start counting your *cojones*."

14. "I Met Her Today"

Herb Polaris hauled himself into the van's leather seat and readjusted his rear-view mirror. A lost cause, this whole trip. No sign of O'Toole. What was a hell of a lot worse, no Konstanze. Two whole hours scouring the neighborhood after he left Floyd's whacko mother without so much as a clue. Where in blazes could the cat have gone?

He reached to scratch his head in puzzlement, then realized his cap was missing. Must have left it back there in the kitchen when he was talking to Lotte O'Toole. He'd have to go back and retrieve it, even though he'd had about all the Gypsies and disappearing picture frames he could take. The real kicker had been Lotte's claim that one time the Gypsies broke in and stole all the plumbing pipes, replaced them with smaller ones. "I could tell all right," the Loony-tunes woman declared. "The faucets haven't flowed the same since."

Every time he'd tried to steer the conversation toward Floyd, Lotte had turned cagey. "I don't dare talk about Floyd," she'd informed him, arms folded tight against her chest. "He's got this important undercover job that if anybody knew about it he'd have to kill them.

He'd coughed to conceal his snort of disbelief. Sure— Floyd O'Toole was a secret agent. And he, Herb Polaris, was Luciano Pavarotti.

She'd hedged, too, when he asked her when was the last time Floyd came by to visit her. Her answer was another hoot— "Must have been about the same week the Gypsies stole the gold earrings my grandmother left me.

No difficulty translating that—Floyd appeared, the earrings disappeared. Odds were a hundred to one that anytime that scag showed up, something valuable went missing. Bottom line, hanging around this low-rent neighborhood was a waste of time. No sign of Floyd and Konstanze had deserted him. Nothing to do but get his cap then head on back to Newark.

He glanced across the street at 2744. The porch light had been turned on and giggling gaggles of women were spilling out of the O'Toole house. Some headed off toward the bus stop, others climbed into cars. The daughter's Elvis fan club that Lotte O'Toole said met in their basement. Some family, these O'Tooles—Floyd a two-bit chiseler, the mother bonkers about Gypsies, and the daughter an Elvis groupie.

More women poured from the house and then the guy with the cameras came out and stowed his gear into the trunk of the Toyota. The woman with him slid behind the wheel and started the motor. Judging from the smoke shooting out of the car's tailpipe, she'd better get that valve job real soon.

When it seemed the last of the Elvis bunch had gone, Herb heaved a sigh and climbed down from the cab. He'd reached the middle of the street when the door to the O'Toole house swung open again and two more women came out onto the stoop. He approached and introduced himself. The older of the two, or at least the plainer one, said, "Yes, Mama mentioned she talked to you." The younger one, a broad with the hair that had been seriously teased gave him the once over before she took off toward the bus stop, hip-swaying down the sidewalk on three-inch heels. Partway down the block she swiveled around to call over her shoulder, "See you at work tomorrow, Vangie,"

Herb sized up Vangie O'Toole as she waved to her friend. Not a bad figure, but none of her friend's va-va-vroom, that was for sure. No fancy dresser, just jeans and a t-shirt with *Elvis-4-Ever* printed on it. Under the porch light her hair looked to be a medium color, somewhere between blond and light brown. He guessed her age at mid to late twenties but then he wasn't much good at figuring women's ages, besides which they were always changing them.

He explained to her that he'd forgotten his cap.

She looked puzzled. "I thought Mama said it was a cat you were looking for. She said it's name is Konstanze."

Here we go, Herb thought. Cats…caps…she'll probably tell me that Elvis has my cap or the Gypsies came and stole it. Speaking slowly the way he would for a six-year-old, he said, "Yes, I did tell you mother that I lost my *cat*, but now it's my *cap* I'm looking for. Konstanze's my cat's name."

She tilted her head and sent him a puzzled look. "Yes, well, it *would* be a little strange if your *cap* was called Konstanze," she said.

For a moment he wondered if she was putting him on. Or maybe she only understood Elvis-speak. "I think I left it in the kitchen," he continued in the same tone. "My cap, that is."

Again that puzzled look, but after a moment's hesitation she opened the door and motioned for him to follow her. Inside the narrow front hall, he could see through the archway to the living room where Lotte O'Toole was planted in one of the overstuffed chairs, a pencil in her hand, a pad of paper on her lap and her attention riveted to Alex Trebec's figure on the TV's flickering screen.

Vangie nodded in her mother's direction. "Mama keeps score while she watches Jeopardy," she said. "By now she's 2,488,350 dollars ahead. Plus whatever she wins tonight."

Herb rolled his eyes. The daughter was just as flaky as the old lady. Best just to humor her a bit then grab his cap and go. "So your mama's gonna be rich as Ross Perot," he said. "What's she going to do with all that dough when she collects her winnings?"

Vangie gave him a puzzled look. "There aren't any winnings," she told him. "It's just a game Mama plays."

With that she turned and marched ahead of him into the kitchen. When she spotted his Aragon Transfer Company cap hanging from the back of a chair, she handed it to him without saying anything more, her expression clearly annoyed. He reached to take it from her. "Say, I didn't mean…. It's just that talking to your mother I got the impression…."

"My mother may seem a little strange, Mr. Polaris, but she isn't stupid."

Herb felt the crimson of his cheeks deepen. "I really didn't mean to imply…."

"It's okay, I'm glad you found your cap."

He turned to go, then stopped and pulled one of his business cards from his pocket. "Look, if you happen to spot Konstanze, would you or your mother call me?"

Vangie took the card and studied it. Her voice a little softer, she said, "Mama mentioned that you were awfully upset about losing your cat."

He scratched his head. "I can't understand it. All the years I've had her, Konstanze's never pulled a stunt like this before."

"Maybe she'll show up. Cats can be that way, you know, they come and go as they like."

He stared down at the cap in his hands. "I was sure hoping she'd turn up before I left. It's gonna be a lonesome trek up 95 tonight without her keeping me company."

"Would you like a cup of coffee before you leave, Mr. Polaris. Mama keeps the Mr. Coffee plugged in until she goes to bed."

Herb accepted her offer with thanks and took the seat that she motioned him to. "Coffee will be great. It'll help keep awake on the long haul back to Newark."

"Is Newark where you have your headquarters?"

She stooped to remove cream from the refrigerator and he noticed again that her figure wasn't at all bad. "Headquarters?"

"Mama said you were some sort of law officer. I just thought...."

"Guess my uniform had her confused. I tried to explain that I own a trucking company, Aragon Transfer. My warehouse is in Newark, New Jersey."

Vangie gave a rueful grin. "You'll have to excuse Mama. Once she gets an idea in her head it's hard to change it."

She began pouring his coffee, and Herb took the opportunity to give her a closer once over. Kind of nice, the way her eyes lit up with little gold sparkles when she smiled. What color were they, anyhow? Somewhere between green and brown was as close as he could come. He liked that she didn't pile on a ton of makeup. That brush of freckles across her cheeks made it easy to see what she must have looked like as a little girl. All in all, not bad looking, but not quite the way he expected an Elvis fan to look. A little touchy about her Mama, though. Best to stick to the subject of cats. "You seem to know a lot about cats," he said. "You ever have one?"

She set his cup down in front of him. "Yes. But that was years ago. Dad brought this cute little kitten home from the route. It turned out that Floyd—that's my brother—Floyd had allergies to animal hair. So I couldn't keep her."

At the mention of Floyd, Herb's sensors flipped into alert. "This brother—does he live here with you?"

"Floyd? He's been gone for years. Ever since Dad died. Would you care for sugar?"

"No, thanks. I suppose your brother does come to visit you and your mom every so often, though?"

Just like her mother, Vangie turned her eyes away when she spoke about Floyd, staring toward the screen door at the rear of the kitchen and the maple tree outside. "I suppose he *intends* to come," she said. "Last time we saw him was December three years ago. On his way to Miami. Driving this big Lincoln Continental. Said he couldn't stay, that he was on an important assignment. We haven't seen him since."

Something in Vangie's tone warned Herb not to push farther. He took a cookie off the plate she offered. "So with your Dad dead and your brother gone, that leaves you all alone to look after your mother?"

Vangie poured herself a cup of coffee and sat down opposite him. "I was hoping you actually were a police officer so that you could convince Mama nobody's broken into the house."

"Because of the Gypsies?"

"Mama gets confused at times," Vangie said, not looking directly at him. "She has this idea in her head that if she's left alone something bad will happen."

He nodded. "Lotte told me about the Gypsy thing."

Vangie seemed relieved that he understood without her having to explain. He watched her take a sip of coffee, obviously debating how much to tell him. Hazel—that was the color of her eyes. Summer eyes.

"My Elvis-4-Ever Fan Club, the group that was meeting here tonight, they're planning a trip to Graceland in August for the tenth anniversary of Elvis's passing. Fans from all over the world will be there. I want so much to go, and I've even paid my deposit for the trip, but I'm scared if I say anything about it to Mama she'll get upset."

Okay, so the girl *was* an Elvis groupie, but she seemed like a decent sort, and a person couldn't really blame her for being protective of her mother. "Couldn't you just hire someone to come in and stay with your mother while you're gone? Like a neighbor lady or someone she trusts?"

"That's what I keep hoping Mama will agree to. Some of the girls in the club say that I'm foolish to miss out on the Graceland trip. They claim that once I was gone she would manage fine by herself. But they don't understand how it is with Mama, how hard her life has been."

He stirred his coffee for a moment. "You ever talked to a doctor or maybe a psychiatrist about her?"

"Once this man I was….a friend of mine….he persuaded me to take Mama to a psychiatrist. The doctor examined her and said that she had something called Capgras Syndrome and that people who suffer from it believe as she does that people or objects in their environment are stolen away and replaced with others."

"Is there any cure?"

"The doctor said if she came to him for therapy three times each week he might be able to improve her condition, but

Mama refused to go back. She said that was the exact time the Gypsies would come and take her things."

Herb grinned and shook his head. "Her warped way of thinking does have a kind of logic behind it."

"That's what makes it so difficult to deal with. Sometimes she almost has me believing the Gypsies are real. Anyhow, after my...friend...moved away, Mama seemed much better."

***

Traffic on 95 was heavy and Herb had plenty of time while he was driving to mull over what Vangie O'Toole had told him. He deduced that the friend she'd mentioned had been a lot more than that. He could also make a damned good guess that Lotte's Gypsies always managed to put in an appearance the moment Vangie tried to carve out a life of her own. A blasted shame, a nice girl like that chained to a psycho mother and stuck with a shitheel of a brother besides. No wonder she'd latched onto her Elvis club for an escape.

The blast of a horn behind alerted Herb that he'd drifted into the wrong lane and he swung the wheel. Why the hell was he worrying about a girl he'd barely met, a girl half his age? He had his own problems to deal with. The last thing he need was to get involved in all the craziness in that O'Toole family.

***

Vangie paused at the foot of the stairs. Sometimes it seemed that the Gypsies and Baltimore Gas and Electric Company were in cahoots. Ever since the picture incident, Mama had insisted on burning every light in the house. Always the same argument—"They could come back, you know. Take everything this time."

At least tonight Mama had an old John Wayne movie on TV to keep her company, her favorite. Mama loved when John Wayne took the reins in his teeth and galloped breakneck toward the villains yelling, "Fill your hand, you sonsofbitches."

Vangie paused on the landing listening to the sound of a truck revving its engine. Mr. Polaris. Herb. He must be leaving. Said he was going to check the neighborhood once more for his cat. Never did mention why he'd come to Dundalk in the first place, just mumbled something about a special delivery.

He'd acted a little strange at first, talked to her as if she were deaf or something, but maybe that was because he was so concerned about his cat. Somewhere between forty and fifty years old at a guess. But handsome. Strong jawline. The sideburns of his coppery-colored hair barely touched with gray. His nose looked like it might have been broken at some time, but that didn't really detract from his looks. A little like the Jessie Wade character Elvis played in the movie, *Charro!* Polite, too—thanked her several times for the coffee and for promising to keep an eye out for his cat.

She climbed the stairs, suddenly aware of the ache in her calves from being on her feet all day. Mr. Polaris was gone now, and she had other things to worry about. She'd given the club treasurer her deposit and in two weeks the rest the money would be due, but that wasn't the main concern, it was persuading

Mama that she'd be safe with Mrs. McWhirter while she was gone.

Vangie groped for the light switch inside her bedroom door. The string of forty-two blue Christmas lights—one for each year of Elvis's life—that surrounded the amphitheater gleamed blue-black off the mannequin's wig and multiplied the image of her own face in the mirrored alcove behind him.

"Why did the Gypsies have to come back?" she asked, not sure whether the question was directed to Elvis or those cloned Vangies in the mirror. "Just when things start to work out fine, why do they always ruin it?"

No answer came.

That was the trouble, there *were* no answers, nobody who could tell her how to deal with Mama, no fairy godmother to wave a magic wand say, "Go on, Vangie, go to Graceland."

Vangie pulled Elvis's apricot-colored jumpsuit from behind the curtain that concealed her clothing and turned the costume so light sparkled off the sequined palm trees on the back. She lifted the mannequin from his platform and disconnected the wire leading from the tape player on her nightstand then stripped off his American Eagle costume. This was the only time he seemed less real, when his plastic chest was exposed and she could see the speaker tucked inside the jagged hole where his heart would have been. Up close, the places she'd patched, the tip of his nose and his left index finger, were a little less perfect than she would have liked. Still and all, it was incredible luck, the mannequin falling off the truck and Dennis saying that since it was damaged she could take it. The wig was another piece of good fortune, it being on sale, the color just right, the fit perfect, exactly covering the crack that stretched from ear to ear across to top of the mannequin's skull.

The fresh jumpsuit in place, she returned Elvis to his niche, settled the aviator frames on his nose, re-connected the speaker wire, and stepped back to admire the effect. Perfect. A slight adjustment of the belt buckle leveled the rhinestone initials *TCB*, Elvis's personal motto, "Taking Care of Business." Afterwards, she slid the jumpsuit's zipper tab down a couple of inches so his gold chains—well they looked like gold—would show.

"Maybe I should have brought the reporter up here and let the photographer take your picture," she told Elvis, "but some of Miss McLeod's questions made me feel little uncomfortable. 'Could you tell me why you are such a devoted Elvis follower, Miss O'Toole? Can you explain the impact Elvis has on your daily life?' How could I explain that off the top of my head?"

She'd probably talked too much as it was, telling Miss McLeod that when the kids at St. Ignatius were going through tough times it felt as if Elvis was right there in the ward. Had he reporter understood that, or how his song, "Take My Hand," sometimes played inside her head at moments she most needed it? Maybe she should have explained how Elvis had been a way of holding onto her Dad after he was gone.

Dad had loved Elvis and Elvis's music, always played Elvis songs on the record player, listened to Elvis songs on the radio. "Look what a poor boy from Tupelo, Mississippi, turned out to be," Dad would say. "Came from nothing and made a name for himself." Dad had promised her they'd go to Graceland some day, see the place where Elvis lived. "Next year, Vangie, next year for sure." They never got there, but after Dad was gone, it seemed like Elvis and his music was something he'd left behind for her, something nobody could take away.

"But talking about that would have been risky," she told Elvis. "Lacey McLeod seems different from those reporters who called the fans Presley worshipers and Elvis junkies, but you can never be sure. Tell the reporter that stuff, and chances were her article would come out sounding screwier than Mama and her Gypsies."

Vangie gathered her robe and headed for the bathroom at the end of the hall. Four more weeks. Once Mama's nerves were settled, she'd pick the right time, say very calmly, "The trip's only for five days, so I'll be home practically before you know I'm gone."

But the nagging worries refused to be hushed. What if she was all the way down there in Memphis and Mrs. McWhirter called to say Mama was prowling endlessly though the house, upstairs and down, terrified of what might be lurking in the darkness? All too easy to picture Mama going totally berserk if no one was here to calm her, to show her that "those horrible things out there" were only shadows.

Back in her room, Vangie sagged onto the end of her bed and stared at Elvis. "I don't mean to complain about the way things are, but sometimes it seems as if I'll be stuck like this my entire life. Much as I love Mama, it isn't fair."

Elvis glowered thoughtfully.

"That Mr. Polaris knows that Mama's fears are more imaginary than real. That picture frame really *doesn't* look any different if you came right down to it."

Elvis seemed to answer: *Even if your Mama's terror is nothing but illusions, even if the Gypsies are only mirror images, dark shadows in the night, fear is fear, not something you can shrug off.*

Sometimes Elvis could be awfully hard to live with. Vangie sat on the edge of the bed a moment longer to sort through her Elvis tapes, but tonight none of her favorites seemed right. She finally settled on one that contained a song she was less familiar with, "Long, Lonely Highway." She flipped off the lights, climbed into bed, and pressed the PLAY button of the tape player on the nightstand. From the darkened niche across the room, came the words of the song, offering consolations in Elvis's sweet soothing voice until her eyelids grew heavy and her breathing slowed.

Mr. Polaris—Herb, he said to call him—he really did care a lot about his cat....

• I Met Her Today •

NOTICE TO ALL CLUB MEMBERS

THE BUS COMPANY HAS INFORMED ME

THAT WE WILL LEAVE THE BALTIMORE BUS STATION

PROMPTLY AT 10:30 ON THURSDAY, AUGUST 13.

PLEASE REMEMBER TO CARRY WITH YOU A SMALL BAG WITH

EVERYTHING

YOU WILL NEED FOR OUR OVERNIGHT STAY IN JONESVILLE

SO THAT THERE IS NO NEED TO UNPACK THE SUITCASES

FROM UNDER THE BUS.

ONLY FOUR MORE WEEKS!!!!!!

BRENDA SUE HIGGS, PRESIDENT

ELVIS-4-EVER FAN CLUB

15. "Too Much Monkey Business"

The dark liquid streaming from the coffeepot wasn't the only thing brewing this morning. Mama was jittering about the kitchen, nervous as a wasp trapped inside a windowpane. Back and forth she flitted, back and forth, opening and closing cupboard doors. "Gone, gone, gone. It was here, I tell you," she repeated, "and now it's gone."

Vangie opened a new box of tea bags and slipped an English muffin into the toaster. How to head off Mama's notion that more things were disappearing? Let that idea take root and inevitably it would sprout like Jack's beanstalk, heaven-high and treacherous to boot. "Don't you remember? You opened that can of Campbells pork and beans for dinner last week."

The rapid flap, flap, of Mama's slippers against the linoleum was the only response. "And the sardines, two whole tins of them. Totally disappeared. It all adds up, just like the picture frame and the way they broke my lawn ornaments.

Vangie, waiting for the kettle to boil, stared through the screen at the maple tree outside the back door. Its leaves hung limp and listless in the heavy morning air. The night he left for good, Floyd had shinnied down the maple's trunk. But then he was a man, much easier for them to slip away. Or maybe Floyd's desertion had nothing to do with him being a man, maybe it was just that he had no guilt about leaving Mama and her behind, never gave it a second thought. A lot different from the way Herb Polaris who was so concerned over losing his cat.

AS if Mama had picked up on that thought, she said, . "That cat fellow, the one that was investigating—if a fellow like him was around, I'd feel a lot safer. He's not a leaver like Floyd."

Vangie stared at her mother. Never before had Lotte compared Floyd unfavorably with anyone. It was always Floyd's return that would save them.

The toaster's annoyed *Sproinggg!* startled Vangie back into the present. She extracted the English muffin, poured water over the teabag dangling in her cup, then carried her breakfast to the table.

But even as she ate, the calendar nagged at her – Wednesday already...July 15th and only twenty-nine days left. She'd saved her trip money and Dennis had agreed she could have the time off, so the only hurdle left was getting up the nerve to tell Mama about the trip.

Earlier, she'd braced her self to tackle that, and she would have, too, if only Mama hadn't started rooting about in the cabinets, checking the refrigerator, claiming food was missing.

Next it would be the Gypsies stealing peanut butter and finishing off the leftover meatloaf.

"The milk, too," Mama announced. "That bottle was a lot more than half full when I set it in here last night. This whole situation is beginning to add up."

The English muffin stuck like sawdust in Vangie's throat. This held all the danger signals of another really bad episode. Keeping her voice deliberately calm, Vangie asked, "Add up to what?"

Lotte raised her head from the vegetable bin. "I'm not saying. But I got my ideas. Just look what happened the other night. No way the wind blew that ball off its pedestal and broke off the mama duck's head."

To keep Mama's mind from barreling any farther down that dangerous track, Vangie exclaimed brightly, "The Golden Girls will be on tonight, Mama. TV Guide says it's the episode where Blanche tries to seduce the postman and Dorothy and Rose end up going to jail."

"Reruns," Mama snapped the refrigerator door shut. "Nothing but reruns the entire summer. Never did understand how come those TV people are able to get three whole months off when your dad was lucky to get two weeks. Always seemed to me there's a lot more work to running a garbage route than there is to goofing off in front of a camera."

With Mama's sidetracked for the moment, Vangie forced a playfulness she didn't feel into her voice. "Just think, Mama, how nice it would be if I got three months vacation from the

Kmart, if Dennis called me right now and said, 'Vangie, don't bother to come in until September...we're going into reruns.' Then I could have time to read some new books, go for walks. Maybe even take a little trip."

Mama ignored the emphasis on 'a little trip,' but at least her attention had been distracted from the mysteriously disappearing food. "Be nice if it was like that," she agreed. "Heaven knows, hard as you work, you deserve a nice long vacation. Sleep late as you like in the mornings. Do anything you felt like doing. Or do nothing at all clear to September if you wanted. Now you take that slutty-looking Rebecca on Cheers—there's a woman looks like she never gets out of bed if she can help it."

Once caught up in speculating about her favorite TV characters, Mama was no longer on the prowl and the tension in Vangie's chest eased a bit. Still, she watched closely as Mama stretched on tiptoe to select a box of cereal from the cupboard above the stove. If Mama chose the Cheerios or Honey Toasted Flakes, that would be a sign her nervousness had passed. Grape Nuts or the All Bran, watch out.

Mama lifted down the box of Shredded Wheat biscuits. No clue there.

***

Darla slipped a coin into the soft drink machine's slot. "Tom Selleck. I'm telling you the guy's a dead ringer."

"Really? I didn't notice," Vangie reached into the Mister DoNut box, selected a pastry whose orange icing exactly matched Darla's nail polish.

"Well he was noticing you plenty."

"Good grief, Darla, the guy just came back to get his cap."

Darla set her soda can on the carton of Maxi-Pads they were using as a table. "So what did the two of you talk about?"

Vangie pulled up a plastic chair that had been returned damaged after the Sizzlin' Summer Sale-Out. "Mostly we talked about his cat disappearing. Her name's Konstanze. He said she was named for a character in an opera. And then I told him about the trip to Graceland and how hard it was to get away because of Mama. That's all."

Darla popped the tab on her Coke. "So did he ask you out or anything?"

Vangie rolled her eyes—Darla was impossible. . "Get real. The guy's from New Jersey, for gosh sakes."

"So? They don't date in New Jersey?"

"Besides, he's...he's older."

"I can tell you right now that if Tom Selleck asked me out, I wouldn't ask to see his birth certificate."

16. "Good Time Charlie's Got the Blues"

Floyd swore when his shirt caught on a nail as he slithered through the basement window. Once outside, he slipped from the safety of the maple tree's shadow and crouched close to the ground. He'd only gone a dozen feet or so when the sight of a police car oozing its way down the alley jolted him like the sting from a cattle prod. Heart pounding, he crouched behind a pile of overflowing garbage cans and sucked in a careful breath. The reek of food rotting in the sultry heat almost made him gag—in his haste, he'd knocked over a bag filled with reeking crab shells.

The patrol car crept closer, red and blue flashes from its rooftop lights bouncing off chain link fences and garbage cans. Moving slowly, its spotlight etched across the back yard fences toward his hiding place. Floyd's ribs rattled with fear—one false move and he could end up as target practice.

After what seemed an eternity, the cop car rolled on past and turned out of sight at the far end of the alley. Floyd stood up shakily and brushed the grit from the knees of his trousers.

Expensive threads when he'd bought them. Now they looked like something out of a Salvation Army barrel.

Slipping from shadow to shadow, he left the alley and hurried down the street. Even though it was three a.m., this was a hairy business, risky as hell. But he had to get out—he was going nuts in that that basement tomb. Especially with the damned cat and her constant whining. Sardines were the only thing that really shut her up, and he'd used up the last of Mama's supply.

At the 24-Hour Sanitary Market, Floyd picked his way down the aisles, gathering supplies from the market's limited offerings. Tuna fish and sardines for the cat. Dinty Moore Corned Beef...cheese...crackers....Chef Boyardee spaghetti— stuff he could eat cold. Cigarettes. He'd have to get them at the register where they kept them locked up. He took a chance every time he lit up in the basement—the old lady upstairs could smell smoke from half a mile. She had a nose that picked up scents like a vacuum cleaner sucking up dust bunnies. Thank God for the lavatory Pop had installed in the basement. At least he had water and place to go to the crapper without having to sneak upstairs. Flushing was the tricky part, always having to wait until Mama went out or had the TV blaring at top volume.

Pickles. Maybe some Oreos. He finished filling his basket.

At the checkout counter Floyd kept a nervous watch on the door and the parking lot beyond. The dark-skinned, dark-haired man behind the register extracted the cigarettes from their locked cage and totaled his purchases. Floyd handed him a hundred. The clerk cast a suspicious eye on the money and then on him. "Don't keep these kind of monies at night," he said, placing a sibilant hiss on the s's.

"It's all I got," Floyd told him.

"No change," the man declared flatly as he shoved the Ben Franklin back across the counter. "Bill's too big. Besides, I don't think he's any good."

"Look. Make you a deal. The stuff I've got here comes no more than twenty bucks or so. How 'bout if we say the hundred covers it? You keep the change."

The man's frown couldn't hide the greedy glitter in his eyes. He held the bill up to the light, then stuffed it in the register and pocketed sixty-three bucks.

His purchases bagged, Floyd turned to leave, but hesitated as headlights swept across the parking lot. Pulse racing, he ducked behind a display rack, ready to run if necessary.

The guy getting out of the car looked okay. Maybe a little too okay for Dundalk at three in the morning. Stores this part of town didn't get many customers dressed in business suits, starched shirts, and striped ties. Floyd crouched lower.

The moment the man shoved open the glass door, Floyd's heart sank. The guy was Willie Durzowitz, the geeky kid who'd been in his class at Dundalk High, the one whose briefcase and pencil-loaded pocket protector had made him the gang's favorite target. Back then Willie had been their patsy for every trick from de-pantsing to "scuba training" in the boys' lavatory toilets. Willie was still carrying the briefcase, only now it was an expensive gold-initialed leather one. Sonuvabitch must have made it big. Everything about him, from the blow-dried haircut to his polished Guccis, shouted money.

Floyd hesitated. Willie had always been too nearsighted to see past the end of his nose. Maybe if he was careful, he could sneak out the door without the jerk recognizing him.

Floyd's attempt to conceal his face and slink past might have succeeded if the grocery bag he was carrying hadn't split, sending cans of Meow Mix and Chef Boyardee rolling across the tiled floor. Too late he made a grab for the jar of pickles. It hit the floor, and glass shattered, the vinegary mess splattering onto Willie Durzowitz's Italian loafers.

Clumsy with fear and frustration, Floyd ducked down to gather his scattered purchases. He had to get the hell out of here before Willie fingered him. But even that thin hope collapsed when Willie exclaimed, "My God, Floyd O'Toole."

Floyd rose reluctantly, clutching the split grocery bag against his filthy shirt, all too aware of the dirt stains on the knees of his trousers, the smell of sweat from his unwashed body, plus the added aroma he'd picked up from the garbage.

Willie recoiled from the odor. Shifting his face slightly away, he said, "Man, what's happened to you?"

"Nothing." Floyd retrieved a can of Spam from under the bread rack. "In a hurry. Gotta go."

But Willie stood blocking the way with no apparent intention of moving, and, judging from the muscles the well-fitted suit didn't quite hide, Willie didn't look like someone who'd be easy to push around any more. Even the glasses were gone—sonuvabitch must have gotten contacts or maybe laser surgery.

Willie pursed his lips as if recalling some bit of trivia that was eluding him. "Say, O'Toole, last I heard, you were in Vegas or Miami or someplace like that."

"Yeah. Well, right now I'm on my way to New York. Got a big deal working there."

"Oh. Right. That's good to hear." Not bothering to hide his knowing smirk, Willie reached into his inside suit pocket and pulled out a card. "You ever need a good lawyer, I'm a partner now at Forthright, Forthright, Wells and Tompkins."

Floyd took the card and pretended to examine it. "Well," he blustered, "when the deal I'm working on takes off, I might just need someone to give me advice on the legal angles. If I do, I'll give you a call."

"You do that. And say, O'Toole, if you need a few bucks...."

"I got money." Floyd snapped, stuffing a can of Meow Mix into his pants pocket.

Willie flicked the last of the pickle juice from his loafer with a crisp handkerchief. "Anyhow, hold on till I grab a pack of cigarettes, and I'll give you a lift. Got my Jag parked right outside."

***

Floyd forked up another mouthful of cold Spaghetti-Os. "I shoulda cold-cocked the patronizing bastard. Treating me like some charity case. Offering me a ride in his lousy Jag."

Konstanze, happily munching a sardine, ran a delicate tongue over her whiskers before meowing agreement.

"Damned punk Durzowitz putting on airs like he's somebody now. Even his lousy card was engraved." Floyd scraped the bottom of the can for the last few Spaghetti-Os. "Thought he was impressing me, talking about how he lives out in ritzy Greenspring Valley now. 'Don't get down here to grimy old Dundalk very often these days. My firm's handling a class action suit for the steelworkers that have been exposed to asbestos. Multi-million dollar case.' Like who gives a crap?"

Floyd stared morosely at the canvas bag on the workbench. "I coulda shown the jerk what real cash looks like." But could he? Somehow nearly two hundred fifty Gs—it has shrunk by a few hundred what with the Indian that gave him a ride and the high-jack prices they charged in the fast food restaurants and other expenses along the way—the cash didn't seem real anymore…might as well be fake Monopoly money for all the good it was doing him. The dough couldn't buy him a plane ticket and it couldn't get him a decent place to stay. Having to keep the bag glued to himself day and night was worse than toting along a bratty four-year-old with a runny nose. Doze off for a minute in the wrong place and the bag and the money would be gone. A person couldn't trust anybody.

He scratched at a blob of yellow paint that was peeling from the workbench. Four days in this basement hole with nobody but the cat to talk to had him spooked. Running into Willie Durzowitz had made it even worse. "Hard to believe that guy was just a scrawny punk back in high school," he told Konstanze. "'Course I felt kinda bad that time the gang took his glasses and put them on the railroad tracks, let the train run over them. Willie's old man beat the shit out of him for losing them, banged him up so bad Willie was out of school for a week. I never felt right about hassling him after that."

Konstanze's twitched her tail. She understood.

Floyd tossed the empty can into a corner. "But hell, I had it tough myself. Took a lot of crap off guys that wanted to rub my nose in it because my old man worked the garbage route. 'Here comes O'Toole, the garbage man. Got his fancy bellbottoms from a garbage can.' 'Yay, O'Toole, whose garbage is your old lady cookin' for dinner tonight?' Stuff like that they'd yell. Even the asshole teachers kind of smirked when they found out what Dad did for a living."

Stupid, talking to a cat, but at four o'clock in the morning who else was there? "With girls it was more embarrassing. Like in the eighth grade, that time with Sally Durant and her bitch-friend, Denise Parkwell."

Even after all these years he could remember how he'd anguished for weeks trying to get up nerve enough to ask Sally Durant for a date. Sally, who wafted through the halls of Dundalk High in a glow of blondness, hungry male eyes recording her every move, Sally whose bubbling laugh and tinkling, little-girl voice sent chills up his spine, not to mention their effect on other parts of his anatomy. "The morning I finally manage to ask her, my hands are sweating so bad I can feel the cover of my notebook getting slimy," he told Konstanze. "I even have it figured out what I'll do when Sally turns me down—make out like I was only been joking when I asked her to go out with me. Nearly wet myself when Sally says she'll think about it, let me know after last class.

"I'm so psyched my feet never touch the ground the rest of that day. Half the time I couldn't tell you what classroom I'm in. Shoot—I'm so excited I got trouble remembering my own name. I'd just seen *Saturday Night* Fever, so I'd gone out and bought the white suit with the black shirt like John Travolta wore in the movie. All I can think about is my date with Sally, where we'd go, what we'd do, what we'd say to each other. I even make up these imaginary conversations. *Oh, Floyd, I never realized you knew so much about baseball.* But then I'd start sweating over what the hell I'd do if it turned out she didn't like baseball."

Konstanze's cocked head invited him to continue the story.

He lit a cigarette and stared into the smoke for a minute. "When the dismissal bell finally rings, I'm in such a rush to find Sally that I take those steps to the basement locker room two at a time. Then, when I'm just about to the row where she has her locker, I hear voices, girls' voices, Sally's voice. No way I'm gonna ask Sally for her answer in front of her friends, so I back out of sight. That's when I hear this Denise Parkwell, say, 'You're actually thinking of going out with Floyd O'Toole?'" He imitated for Konstanze the way Denise's voice had screeched to a higher register on his name and the sneering way she'd minced, "So where's he going to take you, Sally? Down to the dump to shoot rats?"

"I wait for Sally to tell Denise to bug off. But she doesn't. Instead, I hear her say, 'I can't believe you thought I was serious about going out with him. You didn't actually think I would date Floyd O'Toole.'"

"Then some other girl—I didn't recognize her voice—she chimes in, 'Well I should hope you were kidding about dating him. Otherwise, you could end up going to the prom on a garbage truck'."

"I never made that same mistake again," Floyd told Konstanze. "The girls I hung out with may have been low rent types, but at least they weren't phonies like Sally and Denise and the rest of that crowd."

A twitch of Konstanze's ears signaled her agreement.

17. "Stranger in My Own Home Town"

India Marlowe stared at her image in the dressing table mirror as Dina Roberts read aloud from her notepad: "Bootsy deWinter. Husband William Westland deWinter is with Upwood, Tolliver, Whistler, and Church, Baltimore's oldest, most prestigious law firm. Son, Westland deWinter, a freshman at Princeton. Two daughters, Amy and Sarah, both at the Saint Mark's County Day School."

India's French-manicured nails pawed through her jewelry box, shoving aside the rejected pieces. "Amy. Sarah. Saint Marks. Son at Princeton" she parroted, head tilted to examine an earring, an impressive central emerald surrounded by a cluster of diamonds. "What do you think?"

"Ummm. A bit much with the necklace." Dina continued with her list. "Simmy Barnes. Hubby is Torrance 'Torrey' Barnes of Barnes Steel. Torrey a gentleman rider who has won the Maryland Hunt Cup three times."

"Barnes Steel, Maryland Hunt Cup," India repeated absently. "What the hell—green's my color. I'll wear these anyhow."

Dina shrugged. "Your call. Next on the list is Carolyn Cutworth Colwell. Known for obvious reasons as 'CeeCee.' Unmarried. Old family money, banking and commercial real estate. CeeCee very much into horses. Matter of fact, she rather resembles one, especially from the rear. Tends to dress like a stableboy, so watch out for mud on the carpets."

India responded to Dina's grin with an amused shake of her head. The best part of this luncheon would be when the ordeal was over and she and Dina could dish about these women.

But for now, Dina was all business. "Elaine DuVall, first cousin to Senator Duvall. Big in the Garden Club. Famous for her estate's display of daffodils each spring. Don't forget to ask how her bulbs are doing. Crestie Roland – that's Crestie, not Cristie – family goes back to the Calverts, Altar Guild at St. Johns, only you've got to pronounce it the British way—'Sinjins', not 'Saint Johns.'"

"Sinjins," India echoed dutifully. "Daffodils. And it's Crestie, not Cristie."

"Good. Next is Nina Haines Sylvester, wife of the philanthropist Cameron Sylvester, patroness of the Symphony, sponsor of a number of young musicians, some of whom are rumored to make her marriage a bit more...ah...bearable. Be sure to mention how thrilled you were with the first flautist's performance in the Spring concert."

***

Ruthella Wiggins, her starched white apron stretched across ample hips, bustled from the sink carrying a bowl of radishes she'd slitted into precise little roses. "Sure some big changes at Gwynnbrook since that lady came," she remarked. "Old Missy would never have served that California Salad."

Mazie Figgs, not daring to take her eyes off the Newburg sauce she was stirring, nodded. "Girl, you can say that again. She din't waste no time gettin' rid of Missy Stowell's fine old antique furniture, neither. That glass and chrome stuff makes the dining room look like some furniture store. Not to mention them mirrors stuck around ever' place you turn."

"What for you reckon Mister Stowell want to go and marry a has-been movie star, anyhow?"

Mazie snorted. "Ever'body in the Valley knows he ain't exactly what you'd call bright. It was his Mama ran things, made the decisions 'round here. Once she was gone, wasn't nobody to stop him makin' a fool of hisself."

***

The shrill of the telephone interrupted the luncheon table chatter. India excused herself to take the call. "My agent, no doubt," she explained as she removed her napkin from her lap and placed it next to her plate. "The man simply never lets me have a moment's peace."

"Did you notice the diamonds?" Bootsy Tolliver whispered to Nina Sylvester when India had left the dining room.

"Notice? My dear, I thought I was going to be blinded. Hasn't anyone ever told the woman that one doesn't wear that sort of thing before six?"

Crestie Roland surveyed the dining room with dismay. "What she's done to this beautiful old house just makes me ill, absolutely ill. That Philadelphia sideboard she got rid of was over two hundred years old. And can you imagine replacing Mary Stowell's lovely Minton china with this horribly tacky *stuff.*"

Murmurs of agreement floated around the table. "So gaudy. No taste whatsoever."

"And the napkins," Elaine DuVall exclaimed. "Pink. And folded like swans. Do you suppose that's the way they do it out there in Hollywood?"

"She *is* pretty, though," CeeCee Colwill remarked wistfully. "Although I rather expected her to be...bigger...somehow."

"Oh they're all like that out there," Bootsy reported knowledgeably. "Great big heads and these little tiny bodies. Makes them photograph better, I've heard."

"Oh, I do hope it wasn't a mistake making her honorary chairman," Nina Sylvester sighed. "All this discussion of 'publicity.' It would be just too dreadful if she turned our affair into something...well, you know...something *vulgar.*"

India returned just then to announce, "Ladies, I have the most exciting news. You'll never guess who that was on the phone. Madonna's agent. He said Madonna would be delighted to donate one of her bustierre's for the auction."

There was a clatter of china as CeeCee Colwill's cup slipped from her hand.

18. "Stay Away"

Jose Espada guided the Chevy into the lane leading to the take-out window. "So what you gonna have this time, Gecko?" he grunted.

"I don' see why we all the time gotta be eating McDonald's," Gecko groused. "Mes vientres, already they full of gas from nothing but these damned cheeseburgers."

TAKE YOUR ORDER, PLEASE the amplified voice demanded in the metallic tones of a rake scraping the bottom of a rusty barrel.

Espada ignored the demand. "Fifty times I done tol' you, hombre—the boss says O'Toole ain't shown up at his girlfriend's place in New York. Most likely place for him to be hiding out is here, Baltimore. Cenicero say if we wanna stay healthy we gotta stay on this job every minute, find O'Toole, get the money back."

"Already one whole week we been chasing this slippery bastard, driving aroun' in this junk-heap of a car, eating this slop," Gecko whined.

"So whose fault is that, estupido? If you'd stole a decent car we wouldn't been stuck in South Carolina four days getting ripped off by a half-assed grease monkey what calls himself a mechanic."

"So how I'm supposed to know the damned tow truck driver gonna haul us thirty-five miles back in the country? How I'm supposed to know the garage fellow he's gonna keep us there until he finds a junkyard with the part we need? I ain't no fortune teller."

"Always you don't know nothin' 'bout nothin'. Now you want to give up looking for O'Toole. I'm telling you for the last time, *hombre*, you wanna take a chance of screwing up when you're working for Cenicero go right ahead. Me, I'd like to live a little longer."

"Why can't we at least go inside? Sit down for a few minutes. Already today we eat breakfast and lunch in this damned car. I'm sick of talking to this clown sign three times a day."

"So you wanna go sit in some restaurant where a cop might walk in and wonder what two guys that look like us doing in this white honky neighborhood?"

YOUR ORDER, PLEASE screeched the metallic voice.

"Hokay...Hokay! Just keep your *pantalones* on." Espada snarled, then demanded of Gecko: "So say what you want, *caca de caballo*."

"Same damn thing, I guess."

"Hokay," Jose told the sign. "Make it two cheeseburgers, double order of fries, two chocolate shakes."

***

Floyd scrambled feet-first through the basement window, pulling the sack of hamburgers in after him. Reeling from shock, he leaned against the cinder-block wall, his heart pounding out an arrhythmic cha cha cha.

Maybe he was mistaken. Maybe it wasn't Jose Espada behind the wheel of that beat-up Chevy. Or Gecko in the passenger seat.

Yeah. He must be getting stir crazy. Holed up in this dump with a damned cat was enough to make anybody start seeing spooks. No way Cenicero could have figured out he was here in Dundalk.

That was the trouble with packing so much cash, made you feel like every creep who gave you the hairy eyeball was out to get you. Still, why take chances? Next time the old lady left the house, the loot was getting stashed in a safer spot. Then, if he had to make a quick getaway, he could travel light, come back for the dough later.

Jose and Gecko. Couldn't have been them. Could it?

And what was it with Angelina's father? Twice now he'd risked sneaking upstairs to use the phone only to have the old fart refuse to take a collect call. "O'Toole? Don' know no O'Toole. Tell him he got the wrong number." Bet your ass when he showed up in New York with a couple hundred Gs in his pocket deParco would sing a different tune.

His nerves unstrung, Floyd nearly yelped aloud when Konstanze brushed up against his leg. "Damned cat—ought to wring your neck and be done with it. You're the reason I gotta take these chances, risk getting caught. By myself I could get by with taking a little bit of this and that from the kitchen upstairs, but no, Your Majesty's gotta have her milk, her sardines, an' nothin' less than Chicken-of-the-Sea brand tuna."

Miffed at his criticism, Konstanze leaped first to the workbench then to the highest shelf above it. From there, she stared down at him with her most pissed off expression. Little wretch was going to give him away yet, always whining to be let outside, or else sneaking off into the main part of the basement whenever he cracked open the door to get a little ventilation. Last night had been a really close call. Barely time to coax Konstanze back into the coal bin when Vangie came downstairs to mess around with her Elvis stuff.

Floyd dug the paper cone of French fries out of the bag and opened a catsup packet with his teeth. "I gotta get the hell out of here before this place drives me nuts." he muttered. "Tomorrow night that mob of women will be here again. Talk about weird. Half of them are bawling by the time they get through that dumb candle-lighting business. Then that broad talking about how last year at Graceland she got up every morning at five to go sit by old Fatso's grave and pray. Jesus."

Konstanze turned up her royal nose at the French fry Floyd offered her.

"You sure are one particular broad." He reached into the bag and broke off a chunk of meat for her from one of the Big Macs.

Konstanze carefully examined the hunk of hamburger before nibbling a dainty bite.

"At least the Elvis groupies aren't around all the time," Floyd said. "It's Mama's got me climbing the walls. Just my lousy luck this coal bin's right under the spot where she watches TV all day and half the night, the volume turned up full blast so I gotta listen to that shit whether I want to or not. Freak shows, all of them, like on Phil Donahue this morning, the dames who kicked their husbands out of bed so they could sleep with their dogs."

Konstanze, head tilted to one side, seemed skeptical.

"It's the truth," Floyd told her. "But Mama had the right idea. She shouted at one of them to put a flea collar on her husband and feed him Alpo."

Konstanze dismissed the issue with a delicate sneeze.

Floyd squirted more catsup on his fries. Mama's TV shows were bad enough, but it was even weirder when she was on the phone with her lady friends. By now he know all about Mabel McWhirter's hot flashes and how Hilda Martin's daughter got pregnant after her husband had a vasectomy and what brand of laxative it took to keep old Elsie Phane regular.

He paused to offer Konstanze another fry, which she haughtily refused. "Can't blame you," he said. They're greasy as hell."

He stared bleakly at the opposite wall as he took another bite of hamburger. He was sick and tired of this setup, having to time his trips to the John when he could flush without anybody hearing. Another week and he'd be needin' a dose of old Elsie's blasting powder. Just like it was too risky to wash his clothes except when Vangie and Ma were both out. He felt like a damned fool running around in this blouse of Mama's and Vangie's slacks. And now one of his socks had gone missing.

***

The signal from the D.C. radio station began picking up static. Without taking his eyes off the road, Herb Polaris pushed the "Scan" button. That brought up a country music station playing an Elvis oldie, "Suspicious Minds". Herb hummed along with the tune.

He must be getting soft in the head. Konstanze was gone, that's all there was to it. Three days since she'd disappeared. He'd left his number. Vangie or Lotte would have called by now if they'd spotted her.

Damned odd, though, Konstanze picking the exact street where O'Toole's family lived to pull her disappearing act. Especially since O'Toole was the only human besides himself the cat had ever taken a fancy to. Even before Floyd rescued Konstanze from the fire, she'd followed him around the warehouse, snuggled up in his lap during lunch. Probably because of the sardines O'Toole ate. Stank up the joint, but sardines were ambrosia to Konstanze's royal palate.

As for trying to find Floyd O'Toole, screw him. That nickel-and-dime punk wasn't worth risking his own neck, let alone violating the strict rule he'd lived by these years—*Look out for Number One because nobody else will.*

Strange, though. For some reason he couldn't get the O'Tooles out his mind. Lotte O'Toole and her Gypsies. Vangie O'Toole stuck in Dundalk with a crazy mother, a dead-end job, her Elvis groupies.

Herb, forgetting for the moment that Konstanze wasn't there to listen, spoke aloud. "Oh, hell, even Floyd's not someone I can throw to the wolves. The guy wasn't really all that bad. Probably never had anybody to steer him toward a decent education, show him that his schemes and stupid cons weren't the way to make it. Maybe if I'd taken more time, talked to Floyd when I had the chance, things might have turned out different."

Lost in his thoughts, Herb almost failed to see the tiny red convertible cut directly in front of him. His foot went automatically to the brake. He swerved, barely missing the car as it shot across three lanes of traffic and down the off ramp. Crazy dame. From the brief glimpse he'd gotten of the woman behind the wheel, she was a blond with all the right equipment. Reminded him of the story the Overland driver had been spouting: "Here I am, hauling ass up 95, when this rag-top pulls up alongside me on the left, just hangs right there even with my cab. So I looks down and here's this babe, nothin' on below the waist, not a stitch, just this li'l old cut-off T-shirt that din't hardly cover her bazooms. I damn near run my rig right through the ass-end of a Greyhound bus."

You'd think those truck jockeys at the I-95 Truckerama would have learned by now that any time some bozo started his yarn with "I ain't feedin' you no bull," he was. Instead, the whole bunch had sat there with eyes big as the headlights on a Peterbilt, drinking in every last detail even though they'd heard that same damned story, or some variation of it, a thousand times over. Sometimes the woman behind the wheel was altogether bare-assed naked. Other times she had on nothing but a little garter belt and black stockings. In one version it was a couple, both of them naked, with the gal either jerking the guy off or else going down on him.

Women—always the Numero Uno topic with truckers. Not that he was above a little of that. The waitress at the Denver truck stop. Gertie, his ever-willing bookkeeper. The gal who ran a boarding house up near Portland, Maine. But the deal was always strictly on his own terms. A nice time. No kinky stuff. Treat them decent. Pay for what you get. Above all, no strings, no noose around the neck, no involvement. At least that's how it had been ever since....

Well, no use thinking about her. Just leave it that he was unlucky when it came to women.

Right from the beginning, unlucky, his own mother dumping him like an empty six-pack on the cold, stone steps of a church. No note, not so much as a scrap of paper to prove that once for a few hours or days he'd actually belonged to somebody. But it had taken Marissa to bring home the lesson that he was on his own, always would be.

Marissa. The image of her as she had been that day the nuns brought her into the orphanage barged uninvited into Herb's mind. Ten years old. Arms and legs like sticks protruding from an oversized dress. A mop of dark hair pulled down over her face so no one could see the disfigurement, the tears when the cruel teasing began. "Scarface." "Zipper Head." "Little Frankenstein."

Sister Berta, the same Sister Berta who'd given him his name and introduced him to classical music, had assigned him the responsibility for Marissa. "She's so tiny, so fragile, Herbie. I realize—you realize—that an orphanage can be a cruel place. If someone strong doesn't look after her, I'm afraid she won't survive."

"Treacher-Collins Syndrome" was the term Sister Berta used to describe Marissa's condition. "I looked it up at the library," Herb told the non-present Konstanze. "In the medical dictionary it was called Mandibulofacial Dysostosisin, a whole mouthful of words I couldn't pronounce, but I wrote them down anyhow, just in case I ever needed them. The book showed pictures of people with Treacher-Collins that almost made me sick—ears all distorted or missing, eyeballs bulging, some of them with huge mouths and very small jaws.

"Marisa had some of those same things, but when I looked at her I didn't really see them. Sister Berta was right, though, about the orphanage being a cruel place. Six guys bigger than myself I had to beat up to make them stop calling her names. And another, Roe Walker, who beat the crap out of me twice. But the third time I won, ground Roe's face into the dirt of the play-yard when he yelled at Marissa, "Hey, Dogface, where's your chin?"

Herb leaned forward to check his side view mirrors, then settled back again. He'd been fifteen when Marissa arrived, and all set to run away from the orphanage first chance he got. He'd saved every penny he'd made from running errands and washing cars and hustling newspapers and doing whatever it took to earn a little change. At night he lay on his cot, bone tired, but never too tired to count that day's addition to his hoard, let his imagination spin out the future he'd so carefully planned. He'd find a small town in the mid-west where the air wasn't ninety percent carbon monoxide and ten percent garbage smells. He'd get a job, save his money. After a while he'd open a little music store, stock it with classical tapes and records, all the great music of the world. He'd even picked the name. *Parsifal Music Store, Herb Polaris, Proprietor.*

Of course not everyone in that little town would understand or appreciate classical music right off the bat. But gradually he'd introduce them to wonderful passages from his favorites, just the way Sister Berta had done with him, break them in gently, start with the better known arias like Madame Butterfly's "Un bel di", and Verdi's "Celeste Aida." Later, he'd introduce the more obscure ones like the "Royal Hunt and Storm" from Les Troyens.

And maybe, just maybe, one day this beautiful girl would walk into his shop. "Mr. Polaris, I'm looking for a recording of 'Arabella.' Can you help me?"

As he led her toward the shelf where the Strauss operas were located, she would burst into Arabella's beautiful, "When the right one comes, neither of us will doubt it for a moment." Music. His life would be filled with beautiful music.

Then Marissa had arrived. Two more years of orphanage hell he'd endured because he couldn't bring himself to abandon her. "Herbie, I hurt my knee when I fell down." "Herbie, I can't figure out what Sister Adrian means by irregular fractions."

"Herbie." Always "Herbie" when she needed something. Or maybe she knew it was he who needed her, needed the satisfaction that came from helping her grow strong and secure, like Konstanze after she had finally gotten her belly full of milk and found a warm hand to stroke her fur.

By the time Marissa was twelve, he'd graduated from high school, and even Sister Berta agreed it was time for him to leave. But instead of heading for the Midwest, he abandoned his dream, stayed close by. Wasn't long, though, before he realized that his job as a loader in a Newark warehouse was a dead end, that the only way out was to study and pass the test for a commercial driver's license. Which he did. But every Sunday it was back to the orphanage to take Marissa her treat for the week, to let her know that if anything went wrong, if anyone mistreated her, they'd have Herb Polaris to deal with.

Three more years went by. Marissa turned fifteen, and overnight it seemed her body changed from girl to woman, a body that turned men's heads, at least until they got a glimpse of the face that she still tried to conceal by combing her hair forward in an exaggerated Veronica Lake hairdo.

For all that time his own life was wrapped so intensely around Marissa that he could not imagine it ever being any other way. Guys at the warehouse kidded him about his "secret woman" and, in a sense, she was that. His secret. His woman. What others saw as a disfigurement was invisible to him, simply a transparent screen behind which was hidden the real beauty and tenderness that was Marissa. His Marissa.

On the Sunday Marissa celebrated her sixteenth birthday, he was leaving the orphanage when Sister Berta stopped him. "Herbie, I have the most wonderful news."

Right off, he'd felt an uncomfortable gnawing at his insides. If the news Sister Berta was bringing him was so wonderful, why did she turn her head away so that the wimple hid her eyes. "Mother Superior just heard of a doctor in Chicago who has had remarkable success in rebuilding the facial structure of patients with Treacher-Collins Syndrome," Sister Berta told him. "This Doctor Victor Kalama is quite young, I understand, but marvelously skilled. Already patients are coming from all over the world to his clinic." She halted for a moment, then sighed, "How wonderful it would be if our Marissa could take advantage of Dr. Kalama's services."

"But Marissa's face doesn't *need* changing," he protested. "She's beautiful the way she is...."

Sister Berta didn't answer with words. Just looked at him. Stared right through him with eyes that saw too damned much. Funny how a woman who'd spent practically her entire life in a dumpy black robe, lived surrounded by other women exactly like herself, funny how she was able to look inside a man and know exactly what was there. *Is it that she looks all right, Herbie, or is it that you don't want to see her changed, don't want to take the chance of her becoming pretty?*

"Of course," Sister Berta sighed, "the operation won't be possible. It turns out the procedure is tremendously expensive. Mother Superior has checked with Dr. Kalama. He is willing to lower his fees for Marissa, but even then the cost of the operations and the long hospitalizations they require are far beyond the resources of our poor order."

Sister Berta's words followed him back to his one-room flat, hounded his heels as he headed for work next day, engraved themselves on every bill of lading. Deep down he knew even then that somehow, somewhere, he would have to find a way to get Marissa to Dr. Kalama, allow the doctor to create for her a new face. No one in this world deserved that chance more than his Marissa.

Money. He needed money. A lot of it. Considering the slow rate at which the dough he'd been saving toward his music store was accumulating, it would be years before he could earn enough to pay for Marissa's operation. Then an unexpected opportunity arrived. He was approached by Vittorio, Consigliere of the dePaola mob. "A simple thing, Kid. You load up this rental truck, drive it down to Miami. Then, instead of deadheading back, you pick up a little cargo for us. When you return the merchandise, you get an extra ten grand cash for a coupla days driving."

That assignment was completed to the mob's satisfaction. Vittorio gloated. "Looks like we finally got ourselves a nice, reliable moving man."

Vittorio even went so far as to recommend him to several others who had "special cargoes" to transport. Almost without realizing it, he fell into what would become his lifetime career. But at the time Vittorio first approached him, all he'd cared about was getting enough money for Marissa's operations.

Marissa's elation when he and Sister Berta told her about the surgery was almost explosive. If joy and gratitude had been atomic energy, she'd have blown up the whole convent.

"Now don't expect miracles," Sister Berta had warned Marissa when they put her on the plane for Chicago. "Remember, this is a long, tedious process and there are no guarantees." Marissa was so focused on him, so eager to show her gratitude, that she was totally oblivious to Sister Berta's words. Herb felt as if he had been able to do for her what God could not.

The convent had arranged for Marissa to stay in their Chicago residence during the years she'd be undergoing the series of operations. He drove up there to visit her after the first surgical procedure. Maybe he was expecting too much too soon. No way to hide his shock at the scars and swelling. "Herbie," she begged when he was leaving, "don't come back until it's all done. I want you to be able to look at me and see a whole new person."

Reluctantly, he promised. After that, he wrote letters almost daily and sent gifts and counted the days until the final operation. At first, Marissa responded promptly, every letter he sent matched by one of hers. Then, as the months wore on, her replies became less frequent. By the time a year had passed, entire weeks would go by with only a brief, say-nothing note from her. He told himself it was because of the pain she was enduring, the agony she was going through. He begged her to send pictures, but she refused, insisting he was not to see her until she was "whole."

By the following April, Dr. Kalama's name began to figure more prominently in her letters.

> *Today Dr. Kalama took me to the park across the street. We had lunch together by the waterfront. Afterwards, we fed the crumbs to the seagulls off Lake Michigan. They were so cute, almost tame. One who looked a little like Sister Adrian even took a piece of cookie from my hand. Dr. Kalama says I'm doing incredibly well, that I'm his prize patient. Next month he is taking me to a medical conference in California to show the other doctors his success.*

He'd told himself he had no cause to be jealous. The guy was Marissa's doctor, for God's sake. If Kalama was being nice to her, so much the better. But wasn't it strange how many operas had doctors as vile characters? Dr. Malatesta, the schemer who switched the brides in *Don Pasquale*. "Dr. Dulcamara" the snake-oil salesman in Donizetti's *L'Elisir d'amore*. And if there was nothing to this Dr. Kalama business, how come his own heart seemed to be echoing Don Silva's sad aria from *Ernani* – "Infelice e tu credevi." "All unhappy, I believed you."

Dr. Kalama. Always Dr. Kalama. She and Dr. Kalama went to the museum together. Dr. Kalama showed her a painting of a beautiful woman and said that was what she was going to look like when he was finished her surgery. Dr. Kalama was taking dozens of photos of her so that he could determine exactly how the jaw bone would be broken, ground down, re-set. Dr. Kalama – Victor – said he could already guarantee that with the final operation she was going to be absolutely beautiful.

Beautiful. Yes. Doctor Victor Kalama's masterpiece. A creation so beautiful that when it was completed, the good doctor could not bear to part with it. Had claimed it for his own.

Herb suddenly realized his fingers were so tight on the wheel that they had cramped. He'd done it again. Let the memories run on, reached that part that was always too painful to deal with. He punched the radio's 'off' button and began watching for the Dundalk exit. One thing for sure, he'd never had to repeat the bitter lesson he'd learned from Marissa, that caring too much was a game for idiots. Since then, there'd been no more involvements. No woman who claimed him for more than a night or so.

Not that it was such a bad life he'd carved out for himself. In fact, it was a pretty damned good one. By now he owned his own warehouse, had his own small fleet of trucks. Picked his own jobs, some of them legitimate, some of them a little on the twilight side of the law, but those handled in such a way that not even the other drivers who worked for him knew what went on. He'd never got caught, never ended up on the wrong side of the wrong people. And never cheated anybody. He was proud of that.

Proud, too, that he could do little things to help out Sister Berta and the nuns at St. Anselms, especially now that they were in serious financial straits, barely hanging on since the orphanage had been closed down. The load of fruit he'd picked up in Florida would add a little punch to the sisters' diet. Of course they'd end up distributing most of it around the neighborhood, same as when he gave them money. "Use this to turn up the heat this winter," he'd tell them. "No sense in you freezing just to save a few bucks."

Sister Berta would simply smile and give him that "We'll see what the Lord intends," line, then go right ahead and use the dough to buy shoes for some school kids or to pay doctor bills for some eight-months pregnant woman who couldn't afford medical care. Crazy. Too damn stubborn to use the money for their own needs even though half those women in the convent would end up with colds and flu or worse next winter.

An overhead sign reminded Herb that in a few more miles he'd have to make a choice, head on back to Newark or take the Dundalk exit.

Newark. Definitely Newark.

Konstanze had deserted him for good. Like everyone else, she was loyal only so long as it suited her. There wasn't a chance in hell, either, of finding O'Toole before Cenicero's hoods caught up with him. Nothing to indicate that O'Toole had come anywhere near 2744 Shirley Avenue. A waste of time to go back there. Better to wash his hands of the whole business.

Herb momentarily shifted his glance from the road ahead to the empty seat beside him. Ah, what the hell? He was dead-heading back from D.C. anyhow, might just as well have one more shot at finding his Lady. Life without her had about as much flavor as instant mashed potatoes.

***

Herb had scarcely tapped on the screen door before Lotte O'Toole appeared. "It's you. Come on in." She opened the door for him. "I was just getting ready to put on a fresh pot of coffee."

Herb was taken back. Somebody ought to warn the old girl that even Jack the Ripper could put on a uniform. "I was wondering, Ma'am, if by any chance my cat might have shown up."

"Oh, there's cats all right. Cat smells, cat hairs, cats drinking my milk, eating my tuna fish."

"Cats stole your tuna fish?"

"Not the cats. The Gypsies. They keep cats, you know." She ushered him into the kitchen. "It's not something I usually brag about, but I do have the gift of second sight. That's how come I spotted the milk bottle right off. Course when I told Vangie that, she just shook her head and sighed. Well, she can sigh all she wants, but I've seen the signs. They're here."

Not sure how to respond, Herb seated himself uneasily on the plastic seat of the chrome-framed chair toward which Lotte O'Toole waved him. If anything, the old girl seemed even fruitier than last time. Did all that gibberish mean she'd actually seen Konstanze,? "I'm looking for just one   particular cat Mrs. O'Toole. Like I told you before, she's a Persian, dark grey with brown paws and blue eyes. I was hoping you might have seen her."

"I don't recall mentioning to you that my name's O'Toole. But then I suppose you FBI fellows got all kinds of records on everybody. Well, I can tell you right now, I'm no Communist. Lived right here in America my entire life. My Aunt Hulda was German, though. But I don't think you ought to count that against me."

"Honestly, Mrs. O'Toole, I'm not investigating anyone. I'm just looking for my cat...."

"Funny thing about cats. Now you take my son, Floyd. Allergies. Cats make him sneeze something awful. But would you believe cats just *love* Floyd? If there's a cat within fifty miles, the creature will come rubbing up against that boy, simply won't let him be."

Herb leaped at that opening before her mind tracked off in some other direction. "I believe you mentioned your son when I was here before. Any chance he's been around lately?"

"They sure teach you FBI fellows how to ask questions, don't they? How many criminals you shot, Mr. Polaris?"

19. "And the Grass Won't Pay No Mind"

Floyd stared unbelievingly at the coffee can that had clattered to the floor. Could it be what he thought? He pried open the lid and sniffed. Oh, Mama, just the stuff he needed. Like manna from heaven dropped right at his feet.

Maybe the damned cat was worth the trouble she caused after all. She'd been climbing around on the top shelf again, poking her nose into the spaces where the joists and the outer basement walls met. Must have knocked the can loose, some of his stash he'd long since forgotten. Even a packet of cigarette papers inside. Thanks to good old Konstanze, the party just got going.

***

In late afternoon the heat was still wretched. Vangie shed her work clothes then stepped into the shower and stood for a long grateful moment under the cool spray. Refreshed, she gave a quick dab with the towel, and slipped into shorts and a tank top. An enticing odor came wafting up the stairwell—Old Bay seasoning. Mama was in the kitchen fixing their favorite summertime dinner—crab cakes, coleslaw, sliced Eastern Shore tomatoes and lima beans.

Feeling cooler and definitely hungry, Vangie pulled her hair into a ponytail, then hurried downstairs. At the bottom of the stairs she stopped short at the sound of voices coming from the kitchen, one of them masculine. She peered through the doorway. Herb Polaris was sitting at the table with Mama, the two of them chatting away.

Herb jumped up from his seat as she entered. "Your Mama has invited me to stay for dinner and everything smells so good I couldn't say no. Hope you don't mind."

"Mind? No. Of course not," was the best she could stammer. She wished now that she'd put on something a little nicer, maybe done something with her hair. Darla was right. Herb did look like Tom Selleck, especially the way his eyes crinkled when he smiled.

"Mr. Polaris has come back about his cat," Mama said, then added without pause, "Vangie, you can set the dining room table. We'll use the Sunday dishes."

Stunned that Mama had invited a man she hardly knew to have dinner with them, Vangie retreated to the dining room and began laying three places. She took the dishes from the china cabinet Dad had found on his route and placed them on the table—another route find—as she mulled over her mother's bizarre turnabout. Ordinarily Mama suspected any stranger of either being a Gypsy or else connected to Gypsies in some way.

Then there was the question of what Herb Polaris was doing back in Dundalk. His cat, Mama had said, but neither she nor Mama had called him to report any sighting of Konstanze. To detour all this way, he must really care about that cat. Of course Darla would put a different spin on that, claim it was her, Vangie, that drew Herb back here. That was ridiculous, of course.

During dinner, Mama kept up a running account of the adventures of her favorite soap opera characters. Several times Herb attempted to include her, Vangie, in the conversation. He described the plot of novel he'd picked up at a truck stop, but for some perverse reason, she didn't let him know she'd already read it.

So far as she could tell, Herb was enjoying his food. He kept complimenting Mama on her cooking. "Why is it the crab cakes I ordered at a restaurant down in South Carolina last week didn't taste anything like this?"

Mama gave a disdainful snort as she spooned another helping of lima beans onto Herb's plate. "You order a crab cake anyplace but Maryland, they serve you some doughy mess that's more filler than crab. Here in Maryland we know all you need is good back fin crab meat, a little mayonnaise, Ritz cracker crumbs and just the right amount of Old Bay seasoning."

Herb grinned. "I'll remember that. Unless I'm in Maryland, I'll stick with the meat loaf."

"Better than that, any time you want crab cakes, you just come on by here and I'll fix them for you. My husband always said mine beat any he ever ate."

That invitation was surprising enough, but Vangie nearly choked when her mother paused while and said, "Why don't you just stay the night, Mr. Polaris? You could use Floyd's old room."

Vangie could tell Herb was also taken aback, but after a moment's pause he said, "Certainly would be a relief not to make that long haul back to Newark tonight."

Under pretense of needing Mama's help, Vangie pulled her into the kitchen. "Mama," she whispered, "what's going on?"

"There's clean sheets on Floyd's bed but I'll need to put out some towels," Mama said.

"Mama, I can't believe you asked him to spend the night. We hardly know Mr. Polaris."

"What more is there to know? Any man who goes to all that trouble over a runaway cat must have a good heart in him."

"But...."

"Besides," Mama went on ignoring her protests, "with a man in uniform in the house, nobody will bother my stuff."

Seeing it was useless, Vangie gave up. When they returned to the dining room, Mama announced, "After dinner you're welcome to watch Wheel of Fortune with me if you like, Mr. Polaris. The fool that won fifteen thousand last night got lucky when he guessed Lake Titicaca. That low-cut dress Vanna White had on gave him the exact clue he needed."

Vangie cringed, but Mama's outrageous remark didn't seem to faze Herb. "Thanks anyhow, Lotte," he said. "I'll just help Vangie with the dishes if you don't mind."

Left alone in the kitchen with Herb Polaris, Vangie felt awkward and tongue-tied. He reached behind her to take a dishtowel from the rack and she felt the tension of his nearness. She gave a nervous start when he asked, "So, Vangie—your mother said you work at the Kmart. Tell me about your job."

"Not much to tell, really. I'm the assistant manager."

She would have left it at that, but he kept pushing her for more details. While she washed and he dried, she told him about the new program she'd designed for keeping track of the Kmart's returns on damaged merchandise and how she'd organized the payroll deductions so that they didn't have to be refigured each week."

Herb seemed impressed. "Programs like that could be a big asset in my business," he said.

Vangie began to feel more comfortable talking to him. He laughed aloud when she told him about some of the many mishaps Brandi and Shari always seemed to be having at their registers. She also told him how good Flo was at dealing with difficult customers, and how Opal on her cashier's salary was raising her alcoholic daughter's four children.

"So what do you do outside of work," he asked after a while. "I mean for fun?"

She watched as he carefully dried the platter the crab cakes had been served on. Herb had large hands, with strong, well-shaped fingers. Dad's hands had been like that. "I don't have too much free time," she said. "One night a week and on Saturdays I have classes. I'm studying accounting."

Herb whistled. "I give you a lot of credit," he said. "That's got to take real commitment."

Vangie pointed with the sponge to one of the open cabinets. "That platter goes on the top shelf next to the gravy boat. Mama gets upset if everything isn't put back in the same place."

She watched as he reached to put the dish carefully in place. Darla would have approved on Herb's broad shoulders and his slim tapered body. There was a bit of gray sprinkled through his reddish hair, but hardly enough to notice.

"So what's your plan once you have your degree?" he asked, closing the cabinet door.

She paused, thinking, with a rinsed plate in her hand. "What I'd really like is a job where I could use what I've learned about accounting but still work with people...and where I'd be doing something more worthwhile than writing out rebates and exchanges."

"From the way you've stuck with it, I'm sure you'll get there. Lotte told me you also spend a lot of time with the sick kids at the hospital."

Vangie felt her face color—Mama had certainly given Herb Polaris a lot of information about her. "The cups go in the cupboard to the right of the sink," she said. "Actually, spending time with those kids is the best part of my week."

She described what it was like on the ward, told him about Tandora's slow recovery, Betsy the Brat's tantrums, Danny's struggle with his prosthesis. "Some days, though, I hate being there. The worst is when a kid we thought was free and clear gets re-admitted. The look in the parent's eyes...." She gave an involuntary shudder, then hurried to add, "But then sometimes one of the kids pulls through against all odds...."

By the time the last of the dishes were dried and stowed, Vangie felt surprisingly comfortable talking to Herb, almost as if they had gone to high school together, or met at some family get-together, distant cousins twelve times removed.

Herb folded the damp dishtowel and hung it on the rack. Vangie noticed that he seemed to be pondering something. "So tell me about this Elvis club of yours," he said.

The way he said "this Elvis club" put Vangie on the defensive, and her answer came out stiffer than she'd anticipated. "I realize Elvis's music isn't grand opera and he's not Pavarotti, but he's had an important influence in many people's lives, not only as a singer but as a human being."

"Hey, I didn't mean...Elvis was a great performer...it's just that I've always been more into opera...."

Vangie saw that he was struggling and she relented. "My Dad got me started on Elvis," she explained. "He said he knew the first time he heard him sing that Elvis was going to turn the music world upside down. So I was listening to Elvis's songs from the time I was little. Later, after Dad died, I happened to meet Brenda Sue Higgs. At the time, her Elvis fan club was looking for a meeting place so I offered our basement. It gives the club has a nice place to meet and plenty of space to store all our memorabilia."

"Can I have a look?"

***

Vangie tried to decipher Herb's expression as he wandered about the basement room examining the club's collection of tapes, books, pictures, and souvenirs. She was never certain how outsiders would react. Elvis seemed to either fascinate people, puzzle them, or turn them off. Herb definitely wasn't turned off, although he seemed oddly distracted. "You smell anything, like something burning?" he asked.

Vangie paused to sniff the air as she slipped the cassette with Elvis's Hawaiian concert into the tape deck. "I can't tell. Sometimes when Mama forgets to clean the lint filter in the dryer we get a sort of burned odor."

"I suppose. Or could be it's the seasoning your Mama used on the crab cakes, that Old Bay. That's probably it."

Afterwards, Herb stopped to sniff several more times, as if something in the air disturbed him, but he didn't mention the odor again. They listened to Elvis's rendition of "Early Morning Rain," and Herb mused, "I'm an opera buff myself, but after hearing you describe what Elvis's music means to you I figure it must be a lot like the tight feeling I get in my gut when I hear Licia Albanese sing Madame Butterfly."

Vangie sensed that was a compliment to Elvis.

***

Floyd stared numbly at the cat. The little she-devil must have put some kind of spell on him.

Weird, the way she'd climbed up in his lap the minute he lit up. Got this blissed-out look on her face when he blew a little smoke her way and pretty soon she was flyin' high. Now she was totally zonked.

It had to be the grass that was giving him hallucinations. Stronger stuff than he realized, really had him tripping.

The whole thing had to be just a reefer dream. Imagine thinking he'd heard Herb Polaris talking to Vangie—that was a hoot. Fat chance those two would ever meet. Some trip. Now Elvis was out there, singing his guts out. He ought to get up and take a look, but that was too much trouble. Far out.

Konstanze was a lot like old Elvis, the cat knew how to party. Maybe when he and Angelina took off for Mexico they'd take Konstanza with them. *May-he-co. Yo, Pedro. Another of those rum punches.*

20. "An Evening Prayer"

Vangie flicked off the light switch at the top of the basement stairs, aware that Herb was following close behind. Good thing she'd remembered to shave her legs. As she closed the basement door, he offered, "What say I take you and your mom out for some ice cream? Dessert's on me."

Lotte said she hated to miss Alex, but chocolate chip sounded tempting. The three of them climbed into the truck's cab, Herb at the wheel, Vangie in the middle, Lotte next to the window. Vangie pointed out to Herb some of the neighborhood landmarks as they rode along, the church, a little park, the kindergarten she and Floyd had attended. "Right over there on those monkey bars is where I fell and knocked out a front tooth," she told him.

"Vangie was lucky it wasn't a permanent tooth," Lotte said. "But she couldn't pronounce her S's for a whole year until the new tooth came in."

"Betcha couldn't say 'Sister Susie sitting on a thistle'," Herb teased.

Vangie laughed. "No. And I couldn't blow bubble gum either."

Herb grinned at her. "Hey, that's a nice laugh. I'll have to think of some good jokes so I can hear it more often."

Herb Polaris wanted to hear her laugh more often. Did that mean he was planning to be around for a while? Nice, that warm feeling when he downshifted and their thighs happened to touch. Had he noticed that, too?

Oh, stop it, Vangie told the voice in her head. *He's just doing this to show his appreciation for dinner. Not like this is a date or anything.*

A weird date it would be, with Mama sitting right there. That was the real enigma. Herb was just the type of serious guy that Mama's sixth sense always picked up on. Like Larry Bendall. Soon as Larry entered the picture Mama had started seeing Gypsies all over the place. Day and night she'd prowled through the house, worrying over every little noise, every object out of place, tying strands of thread across the doorways so she'd know immediately if Gypsies had been there. Then, after she and Larry announced they were engaged, came the phone calls at work. "Miss O'Toole, we got a call there's been another emergency at your house." Home she'd fly, to find the police searching for the intruders Mama insisted she'd seen, only no trace of them could ever be found. Finally, it had gotten so bad the police refused to come when Mama called them. That was worse in a way. Day after day she'd come home to find Mama cringing in a closet, terrified, crying that the Gypsies were after her for sure.

At first, Larry kept calling, "When are we going to be able to go out and have some fun, Vangie?" After a while, his calls stopped. She didn't need his letter to know that their engagement was off. Months later she'd run into Larry's mother in the grocery store. "Oh, yes. Larry's married now," Mrs. Bendall had gloated. "That nice Finster girl. A baby on the way already." Mrs. Bendall's satisfied smile had made Vangie want to crawl into the frozen vegetable case and die.

But Larry Bendall was history. So far, Mama didn't seem to see Herb as a threat. Not that his taking them out for ice cream meant anything serious…just a friendly gesture on his part.

Back at the house afterwards, Herb excused himself to take another look around the neighborhood for his cat. He came back nearly an hour later looking tired and discouraged. "Nothing," he said. "I've got to pull out early in the morning, so I'll say goodnight now. Thanks again, Mrs. O'Toole for your delicious dinner and for your hospitality. Vangie, it was nice seeing you again." With that, he headed up the stairs.

Vangie waited a while before going upstairs to her room so Herb would have time to use the bathroom. When she did go up, it felt strange, knowing Herb was just steps away in Floyd's old room. "I know he'll be gone by morning," Vangie whispered to the mannequin as she turned back her covers, "but it was really nice having someone to talk to."

For some reason Elvis seemed to resent that remark.

"Besides you, I mean," Vangie quickly added.

Elvis still seemed a little distant, his expression a bit miffed. *So now you're becoming an opera buff? You really dig that 'Dona e Mobile' tape he was playing in the truck?*

Liking one kind of music doesn't mean I can't appreciate other kinds, does it?

Isn't he a little old for you?

I'll be twenty-eight come January.

Sure, and this trucker guy will be —what? – forty-five? Forty-six?

I think Mama really likes him.

She also thinks Floyd is the salt of the earth.

To end the imaginary conversation, she lifted Elvis from his niche, stripped off his costume, and slid his stiff limbs into the tiger costume—his favorite. She checked to make sure the speaker cord was concealed, then set the mannequin into the niche and stepped back to view the effect. The tiger reflections were spectacular…a whole jungle of prowling beasts. Perfect.

Would it be a dumb idea, the thing Pearl had suggested? "I swear, Vangie, I've tried it and it works," Pearl had insisted. "Before you go to sleep you light a candle for each year since Elvis died. I burnt those candles the night before I was to go back to the doctor and sure enough, he said that the tumor wasn't cancer. Eudora said she used the candles to wish for her boss to give her a raise. The very next week she got an extra five in her pay envelope."

Vangie went to her dresser and took out the nine votary candles she'd bought a couple of weeks before. Who knew?

Maybe it would take a little magic to get Mama to agree that it was all right for her to go to Graceland. It certainly wouldn't hurt anything, and might even help the odds a bit. She placed the candles in their glass containers around Elvis's niche and lit each one.

Snuggled in under the covers, Vangie raised her head to take a last peek at her handiwork. The candles along with the blue Christmas lights and the reflections of the tiger on Elvis's back made a pretty display. What should she wish for? The trip to Graceland, of course. For Mama to forget about the Gypsies. For Herb to find his cat. Maybe even for Herb to come back again to Dundalk.

***

A warm, soft cloud wafted Floyd high, high, high, then swept him south until he could see palm trees and white sand. Cool! This must be Mexico. Him and Angelina stretched out in beach chairs, her in a hot-looking bikini that didn't leave much to the imagination. "Tell me this ain't the life, Babe." He lifted a tall frosty glass from the tray the beach boy placed on the table between them.

Angelina grinned and gave a lazy stretch, only it wasn't Angelina at all, it was Konstanze. "Your girl friend's gone," Konstanze told him, "but you'll always have me."

"You can't stay here," he told her, "Herb Polaris and Jose are both looking for you. Better get movin'."

It wasn't Konstanze who got up from the beach chair, it was Mama. "Time to get dressed, Floyd." She shoved an ugly green jumpsuit at him.

"Hey! This ain't mine."

"See, it says 'Floyd' right here." Mama turned the jumpsuit so he could read his name over the pocket.

He tried to push the garment away, but his arm was weaker than a baby's. "Mama, you're crazy. I ain't putting this thing on."

"Juan! Diego! Come here," Mama yelled.

Two beach boys came running. "He won't put it on," Mama told them.

"I'm tellin' ya this dumb outfit ain't mine. Ask Angelina, she'll tell you. I got myself a classy wardrobe now."

But Angelina was nowhere in sight.

"Make him get dressed. He's late for work," Mama told the beach boys.

The two beach boys grinned happily as they held him down, forced his legs into the trousers, buttoned the front of the greenish uniform then stood him on his feet.

"Oh, my, don't you look nice." Mama pulled a huge badge from her purse and pinned it to the front of his shirt. *Floyd O'Toole, Sanitation Engineer* it read. "Just the way your father looked every morning when he left for his route."

"I'm not Dad. And I don't want to go on the route."

His protest was interrupted by a harsh, grinding sound. A huge garbage truck came rumbling down the beach toward him.

Closer and closer. He tried to run, but his legs felt like overcooked spaghetti and he knew with sickening certainty that the garbage truck was going to get him...going to get him...going to get him....

***

Sometime before dawn, Vangie heard the engine of Herb's tractor-trailer rev up. She took a quick peek at the alarm clock then snuggled back to steal a few more minutes of drowsiness. Last night had been fun. Mama rarely ever laughed the way she did when Herb told that story about his driver getting lost in a snow-storm out in Montana, having to live for five days on his load of beef jerky and Twinkies. "So bloated by the time the highway patrol found him they practically had to pry him out of the cab."

Mama was in a good mood, so today might be the right time to tell her about Graceland. Herb said the best way to do it would be to come straight out, say "I'm going, Mama," and tell her that Mrs. McWhirter had agreed to come stay.

Vangie swung her legs out of bed. No reason to keep thinking about Herb. He was gone. Even his cat seemed to have disappeared for good. But who could tell? "Maybe crab cakes seasoned with Old Bay will bring him back," Vangie told Elvis.

Elvis didn't respond, but then peanut butter, bacon and banana sandwiches would have been more his style.

The morning sun cast harsh leaf patterns against the bathroom window shade, a sure sign that the heat wave hadn't broken. After she showered, Vangie considered herself in the mirror on the back of the bathroom door. Her legs actually *were* pretty nice. Herb had definitely noticed. Maybe she should buy a new outfit for the trip to Memphis. That shade of teal green...how would that look with her complexion? Risky relying on sales clerks for advice. "It's really *you*," they'd say, even if the color made her look as if she'd been stranded for three months in a cave.

Back in her room, Vangie began dressing for work. The lingering smell of wax reminded her how ridiculous it had been, lighting candles around the Elvis mannequin before going to bed last night. If only a statue *could* make wishes come true. She glanced ruefully at the remains of her little ceremony, the globs of wax and blackened wick stubs left in the bottoms of the glass containers.

Elvis was looking good, though. The mirrored tiles that lined his niche reflected endless multiples of the tiger pattern on the back of his jumpsuit. She adjusted his belt so the raised letters "TCB" on the buckle were exactly centered. She started to switch off the Christmas lights, but their reflection in the mirrors was so pretty she decided to leave them on. "I'm telling Mama this morning, so keep your fingers crossed for me," she told Elvis, then grinned at her own foolishness. Talking to a mannequin. Next she'd be calling those 900-line psychics on TV. *Ah, yeeess...you have recently met a man, noooo?*

Mama was already at the breakfast table when Vangie came down, the pages of the *Baltimore Star* spread in front of her.

"Mr. Polaris likes his coffee good and strong in the morning. Said my pancakes were the lightest he's ever eaten."

Vangie blinked. "You got up and fixed him breakfast?"

"No trouble. He's a hearty breakfast eater, like your Dad used to be."

Mama rustled through the newspaper pages for several minutes, then announced, "Weatherman says temperature's gonna hit a hundred again today. Can't remember when July ever stayed hot like this."

Vangie set the teakettle on the burner. "A scorcher for sure. All our suppliers have run out of window fans. And we've had to re-order three times on beach towels and umbrellas."

Tell her, Vangie...tell her now, that inner voice prodded.

She was going to do it, she just had to lead up to it, feel Mama out a bit first. She took a deep breath as if she were about to leap off a high dive. Only with Mama there was no way of knowing whether the water below was six feet deep or six inches. "It seemed like every other person who came through the check-outs yesterday was going someplace," she said. "We practically sold out of those new travel bags we that are on special."

Mama didn't look up from her newspaper. "Says here they're looking for all kinds of tie-ups on the Bay Bridge this weekend. Makes you wonder what folks get out of tearing all over the countryside, swarming about from place to place when they could stay nice and cool and comfortable right in their own homes."

Vangie's trouble sensor went on alert. "Most people enjoy getting away, doing something different once in a while."

"You ask me, they could save themselves a lot of trouble just by turning on the TV. Take yesterday – Phil Donohue was talking to these ladies that had turned themselves into men. Now if that's not different, you tell me."

"I don't mean that kind of different, Mama. What I meant was seeing other parts of the country, getting to know about other places."

"They had the exact opposite on last week," Mama said, "men that get a thrill out of dressing up in women's panties and garter belts. One of them was a bulldozer operator, huge galoot of a fellow. You'd think he'd be downright uncomfortable, driving one of those big machines all day wearing a bra and panty hose."

The cautious approach wasn't working. Vangie sucked in a deep breath. "Mama, about this trip to Graceland next month, I'll have all sorts of interesting things to tell you when I come back, who I saw, where we went. And while I'm gone, you and Mrs. McWhirter can have yourselves a nice visit, go downtown shopping, maybe invite Mrs. Hamerhoff and some of the other ladies over to play Canasta." Running out of breath, Vangie finished lamely, "Or you two could go see a movie."

Mama didn't emerge from behind her paper. "The TV's got all the movies on it a person needs," she said. "Last night after Mr. Polaris went to bed I watched that John Wayne one again, the one where he takes the reins in his teeth and gallops his horse right into the bad guys, shoots them down. Now I don't see how a person could want much more excitement than that."

Vangie's Cheerios were as soggy as her brain. She needed to find another angle to convince Mama. But before she could say anything more, Mama exclaimed, "Would you look at this. piece in here about India Marlowe. Says she's taking riding lessons so she can go foxhunting with her husband's crowd. Seems to me a person's got to be plain foolish to go racing around over the countryside after an animal that they can't even eat once they catch it."

Vangie seized the slim opening. "You know, Mama, India Marlowe was one of the few people in Hollywood who was nice to Elvis when he was making movies. Those other stars turned up their noses at him, but Miss Marlowe asked him to parties and told everyone he had the makings of a fine actor. And speaking of Elvis—"

"Always wondered why foxhunters have to wear those red coats."

"When I'm down there in Graceland with the girls I'll call home every night. That way I'll know that you're all right."

"Says here the President's going to sign this bill that'll let all these foreigners into the country."

"Mama, did you even hear what I said about going to Graceland with the girls?"

"Foreigners," Mama muttered, then lowered the paper to stare directly at her. "Of course I heard you. You said when you're at Graceland you'll call home every night. I'm not deaf, you know."

Vangie nearly collapsed with relief. What a dolt she'd been to worry so. Mama was perfectly fine with the idea of her going to Graceland, hadn't raised a fuss at all.

21. "So High"

Floyd tried to sit up, then fell back with an agonized groan. His head felt the size of a cheese wheel and twice as thick. The entire house could have collapsed around him while he was passed out last night, and he'd never have known the difference.

He lifted Konstanze and set her on her feet, but she flopped down dishrag flat, like she didn't have a bone in her body. Totally spaced out. Pupils dilated. The cat was still high from his smoke.

Floyd rubbed at his eyes with both fists. Crazy damned dreams all night long, that nightmare about the garbage truck. Another one with Herb, Melva, Elvis, all jumbled together, impossible to remember.

Had the cat really gotten loose in the basement when he went to take a whiz? Seemed like he'd heard her knocking stuff over in there, but that was probably a dream, too.

He was still too groggy to think straight. Or maybe this whole thing was just one long hallucination, a nightmare that he'd wake up from any time now.

Floyd curled up on the workbench, his head on the sack of money. Within moments both he and Konstanze had slipped back into some other world.

***

Vangie gaped in astonishment. Lisa Marie doll heads were scattered across the basement floor like the remains of some mass guillotining. Several were chipped, two completely broken. Last night when she and Herb were down here, they'd been neatly lined up on the shelf waiting to have their bodies attached. Now something, or someone, had knocked them down.

She stooped to pick up one of the heads that had survived the fall. Beside it on the rug lay a cluster of fur that looked as if it had come off an animal, possibly a cat. For days now, Mama had been insisting that there were cats around. Could there be something to her suspicions after all?

But that was silly. Those doll's heads falling, just a stupid accident. As for the fur, Eudora and Darla both had cats. They'd probably carried the fur in on their shoes or clothes.

She started to replace the first doll head then halted, her hand in midair. Was that a sneeze? Mama, perhaps? No, the sound hadn't come from upstairs, more like from the lavatory or the laundry room.

There it came again. Muffled, as if someone had tried to cover it, and this time definitely from the powder room.

She tiptoed to the closed door at the far end of the room and leaned her ear against door panel. No sound from within. Mama's imaginings must be getting to her. Sure, Gypsies were hiding out in the basement powder room. And Elvis was driving a truck in Tennessee. She seized the knob and jerked open the door.

"M-My God, V-Vangie." Floyd, perched on the commode, made a grab for the trousers bunched at his feet.

Vangie staggered backward. Craziness must be genetic. She really had lost her mind. Floyd…Elvis…the Gypsies – they were all living here in the basement.

***

Vangie struggled to make sense of Floyd's bizarre story. "You say these people—this gang—they're after you because you're an undercover narcotics agent? That you broke up their big drug deal?"

Floyd tugged at a lock of his scraggly hair, the way he'd always had of doing when he was trying to cover up something. "Yeah, well, I can't explain all the details, Vange. Top secret. But I can tell you they're dangerous. That bunch will stop at nothing to knock off a narc. That's how come I've got to cool it for a week or so."

"But the police? If you're an undercover agent, wouldn't they protect you? I think we ought to call them right now, tell them what you just told me."

"Hey, no. It's a lot more complicated than that. You see, guys that work on top-secret stuff like I do, we aren't allowed to blow our cover, even when it puts us in danger. Like the CIA."

"So what do you plan to do?"

"Well, I gotta lay low for another week or so until the heat's off. After that, I'll get out of here, report back to headquarters. All I need is for you to hide me out for a few days, bring me some food. Yeah, and get me some clothes. I had to take it on the lam so fast I ain't got nothing but what's on my back."

***

Vangie prepared for bed, still struggling to sort out what was real and what was lies. The downward curl of Elvis's lips seemed to express skepticism. *Floyd always lies, especially when he's in trouble, which is most of the time.*

That was true. Even when Floyd was a little kid he lied his way out of every scrape. "It wasn't my fault. Those bigger guys made me do it."… "The stupid teacher never gave me a fair chance." That was Floyd.

Whoppers, phony excuses, broken promises, she'd heard them all. Like that time in sixth grade when he got caught shoplifting and swore someone else must have slipped the cigarette lighter into his pocket. The times he hooked school, stole from parking meters, got caught smoking pot—never his fault. Worst of all, he'd would take money from Mama's purse and then pretending he'd seen Gypsies lurking around the neighborhood.

"What if a gang of drug dealers really is after him?" she asked Elvis. "I can't just turn my back on him. After all, he *is* my brother."

Doesn't this story sound as phony as every other lie Floyd has told you over the years?

Lies. Floyd's story about being an undercover agent was about as durable as a scoop of ice-cream in 90-degree heat. If she helped him, she could be putting Mama and herself in danger.

Vangie stared across the room at the mannequin, but the dark glasses concealing Elvis's eyes stared back at her, blank and clueless. Elvis was no help.

22. "This Is My Story"

Mike Dowling grabbed for the dashboard as Lacey McLeod swung the Toyota onto the two-lane road that bisected Greenspring Valley. "If you wouldn't mind slowing down to sixty or so, McLeod, I'd like to check this light meter again," he groused.

"Okay, okay. You can take your foot off the phantom brake now," Lacey retorted. "By the way, Dowling, those were nice shots you did for my article on 'Fashions for the Fourth.' Good skin tones."

"Thanks, Lace. That's high praise coming from a 'Noo Yawk' reporter lady."

"*Ex*-New York reporter lady, if you don't mind."

"I still don't know how you could give that up. Me, if I ever managed to get a photo of mine in *Time* or *Newsweek*, I'd be heading for the Big Apple so fast all you'd see would be my smokin' rear end."

"Well, that's because you're not a single mother with a four-year-old to consider. After Jake and I split, it was just too tough raising a kid solo in the city. My last nanny quit in the middle of the day, left Tissie alone in the apartment. That curdled it for me. Here in Baltimore, decent day care may cost an arm and a leg, but at least it exists."

"But don't you miss the excitement, being right in the center of things?"

"True. When I took this job with the *Star* I didn't expect to get stuck covering fashion shows and church bazaars."

Mike shot her a grin. "I can account for the fashion assignments, McLeod. Considering the slapped-together appearance of most of our female reporters, it's obvious why Avery hands that stuff to you. Even in an outfit from J.C. Penney you'd manage to look straight out of the pages of *Vogue*."

"Can't help it, Dowling, it's genetic. My mom was an editor with *Women's Wear Daily* for over twenty years. Fashion's in my genes."

"And in your jeans." Mike turned to gesture toward to an elaborate Italianate mansion perched on a nearby hilltop overlooking acres of lush green. "Jeez, they must manicure these lawns with nail clippers. You ever wonder how it would feel, Lacey, to live like this?"

"Considering that I'm driving a car with 120,000 miles on its odometer and in serious need of a valve job, plus that I just spent two frantic hours trying to find a baby-sitter for a kid who's too croupy and miserable for the day-care center, it's a little hard to imagine."

• This Is My Story •

Lacey floored the accelerator to pass a slow-moving horse van and Mike held his breath until the Toyota was safely back in the right lane, then asked, "Tissie's sick?"

"Ears again. I felt like a dog leaving the poor kid with my landlady, but what else could I do? After practically getting down on bended knees begging Avery Wilder to let me cover something meatier than the annual St. James Ladies' Bazaar, I couldn't afford to turn down this assignment."

Mike nodded. "By the way," he said, "that was a great story you did on that Elvis Fan Club. Took talent to write about women who dote on the Maharajah of Memphis without making them sound like kooks. I hear that the Great One actually gave one of his infrequent grunts of approval."

Lacey flashed him a grin. "Yeah...Avery actually used the 'S' word to describe that piece – 'satisfactory.' Said I didn't take cheap shots at Elvis fans the way most reporters do. Thank God I got an attack of conscience and did an in-depth on Vangie O'Toole instead of playing on the bizzarro aspects of the story."

"Why did you decide to focus the article on her? "

Lacey downshifted for a sharp curve. "She changed the mental image I'd had of an Elvis fan. I could see she has a strong sense of connection to him and realized I needed to get more of that into the story."

Mike picked up Lacey's notepad from the seat between them. "Let's have a look at the agenda for your interview with la Marlowe. Want my input? Ask her if she's bored out of her skull living in a mausoleum with an old geezer who smells like a stable."

"You're rotten. Although if what Hannah duLaine told me over lunch yesterday is true, you're closer to the mark than you might think."

"So dish already. What nasty little secrets did our society maven spill over the vichyssoise?"

"Well, according to Hannah, the ex-movie queen seems to have set so many aristocratic teeth on edge with her 'Hollywood ways' that marriage number five may be headed for the rocks already."

Mike sighted through his camera's viewfinder on a fenced pasture where several brood mares were grazing, their stiff-legged colts cavorting close by. "I guess hobnobbing with this stuffy Greenspring Valley crowd isn't exactly like a day at the bull-fights or dancing the night away in some Greek bistro," he said. "Maybe you should quiz her about that."

"Fat chance. According to this memo from Marlowe's secretary, my interview is to be focused *exclusively* upon Marlowe's honorary chairmanship of St. Ignatius's fund-raiser. We'll discuss the kick-off reception at which Miss M will preside as hostess, the fund drive, et cetera. "

Mike's expression was cynical. "Bet your press pass the lady will leave the fund-raising job to others."

"Then there's the grand finale, the banquet and charity auction to be held at the Civic Center on August 8th."

Mike gave his head a cynical twist. "And of course the only reason the Valley set will turn out for all this fancy folderol is because they care so intensely about the *deah* little kiddies at St. Ignatius, not simply because they're all dying for an up-close glimpse of Marlowe."

Lacey acknowledged that with a shrug. "I understand you got your orders, too, regarding exactly what photos will be permitted."

Mike nodded. "Strictly limited to shots of the house and grounds. Pre-approved stills of La Marlowe will be provided. And you can bet *they'll* be at least 20 years old and shot through linoleum. Hey, isn't that the entrance to Gwynnbrook just ahead?"

Lacey brought the Toyota to a shuddering halt, the front bumper barely clearing one of the pillars that marked the entrance to Gwynnbrook's oak-colonnaded driveway. A guard approached from the gatehouse and asked for their credentials. As they waited for him to swing open the massive gates, Lacey muttered under her breath, "Tara redux."

***

India Marlowe greeted them as they entered the drawing room. The image the movie star presented was so far removed from the Lacey's mental picture of her that ten minutes into the interview she was still groping to get a handle on the "new" India Marlowe. Since when had Marlowe abandoned her wild Rodeo Drive wardrobe for simple linen shifts graced only by a sedate string of pearls? Where was the unrepressed, sex-obsessed "other woman" who bared all with abandon in Technicolor? Who had spirited away the India Marlowe who once mouthed obscenities in Sensuround and who had substituted in her place this aloof, gracious society queen who drawled her A's in perfect pseudo-British fashion? "Ah've just taken the *greatest* interest in those *dahling* little children at St. Ignatius. As Ah told Daniel, Ah feel it is mah civic duty to lend mah support to this worthiest of causes."

When Marlowe excused herself for a moment to consult with her secretary who was hovering discretely to one side, Lacey exchanged a quick glance with Mike who simply shook his head bemusedly. If this was an act, the woman was good, damned good. Easy to understand how she'd copped those two nominations for best supporting actress. Only an occasional deliberate exposure of the famous Marlowe legs—a sight duly appreciated by Mike—revealed the woman who had played tramps and villainesses so convincingly.

But as the interview continued, Lacey's frustration began to build. The carefully programmed responses Marlowe was ladling out wouldn't make for a very exciting article—she could have gotten juicier tidbits from the press packet.

As if aware that Lacey was itching for something a bit meatier, the woman who had been introduced as Marlowe's secretary interjected smoothly, "Miss Marlowe was quite impressed by your piece in the *Star* about the Elvis fan who spends her free time working with those children in the cancer ward."

• *This Is My Story* •

The famous India Marlowe had actually read her article?
Annoyed with herself for feeling flattered, Lacey stammered her appreciation.

"Indeed yes," the star drawled, taking her cue from her secretary. "In fact, we decided it would be great publicity—for the fundraiser, that is—if Ah were to meet this woman...ah..." she paused and glanced toward the secretary.

"Vangie O'Toole," the secretary supplied.

"Yes, present Miss O'Toole with an award. Dina has already contacted the Mayor. He agrees completely."

Lacey consulted her notes. "We're scheduling the feature on you for August first so it appears the week before the auction. If the award is presented before then, I could include it as a human interest angle."

"Lovely," India Marlowe cooed, then added, "This is just a little aside, but you might be interested to know that when Elvis arrived in Hollywood for his first movies we were at the same studio. I was just a starlet then, of course. Anyhow, the studio's publicity department arranged a date for us. Turned out to be quite an evening.."

India Marlowe paused as if reflecting, then went on, "Do you know, that was the first time I'd ever ridden on a motorcycle. And Elvis was quite amazing. An intriguing combination. Such a sexy hunk, but a little boy underneath it all."

Although this information set her reporter's glands to salivating, Lacey managed to keep her voice noncommittal as she asked, "A little boy, you say? In what respect?"

India Marlowe shrugged knowingly. "Missionary. Total missionary. Sweet as they come and equipment to die for, but a baby between the sheets. I remember...."

Dina Roberts stepped forward to interject smoothly, "Perhaps it would be helpful to Miss McLeod to set a date for the award ceremony in case she wishes to include those details in her article."

"Oh. Of course." India Marlowe instantly stepped back into her role of Lady Bountiful of Gwynnbrook Manor. "A mahvelous idea."

***

Dina Roberts escorted Lacey and Mike back out into the foyer then handed Lacey a packet consisting of several neatly printed pages. "A few suggestions for your article. Some background on Gwynnbrook, information about the kickoff reception that will be held here next Saturday, figures of receipts from last year's auction, Miss Marlowe's bio, and some clippings about her past charitable efforts."

"Thanks. This will be very helpful."

Dina extracted a page from the packet. "You'll see that lending Miss Marlowe's name to the event has already generated a lot of interest in the affair. Here's a list of some of the prizes we've already received for the auction—a Cadillac El Dorado from one of the dealers in town, a trip to Egypt from a travel agency, a designer gown from delaRenta."

"Thanks," Lacey repeated. "I appreciate all this."

The secretary smiled ingratiatingly as she returned the list to Lacey. "Oh, and it might be best if you didn't include Miss Marlowe's remarks about Elvis. That was off the record."

Dina Roberts spotted the disappointment Lacey couldn't quite conceal at having to abandon what had been the spiciest part of the interview and quickly added, "We haven't said anything publicly yet, but there's an exciting new role coming up for Miss Marlowe. Usually we'd reserve an item like that for the national press, but we're considering breaking the story locally. Could be a real coup for the reporter we give it to."

***

When Vangie arrived home from work, Lotte greeted her at the door waving a long, creamy envelope. "For you. Looks real important. Some kind of official seal on the front."

"You open it for me, Mama, please."

While her mother's attention was focused on opening the envelope, , Vangie discreetly shoved the bag she was carrying into the hall closet. The last thing she needed was for Mama to see the clothes she'd bought for Floyd.

Lotte read to herself the words printed on the stiff, creamy stock, then announced excitedly, "It says the mayor and Miss India Marlowe are going to present you with an award. Something to do with your volunteering at St. Ignatius." Mama's face reflected her awe as she handed the letter to Vangie.

Vangie scanned down the page. "City Hall, 11 A.M. this Friday," she mused. "I suppose I could ask Dennis to switch my days off."

"Aren't you thrilled to be getting an award and meeting a big star like her?"

For Mama's sake, Vangie tried to appear more excited, but with Floyd in the basement and fearing how that could affect her chances of going to Graceland, meeting India Marlowe in person had to take second place in her thoughts.

"India Marlowe." Mama rubbed her fingertips across the raised emblem on the letterhead – *City of Baltimore, Office of the Mayor.* "And to think I bought last week's *Enquirer* just to read the story about her having cancer. Leastways, that's what the headline said: *India Marlowe Stricken by Cancer.* When you read the story inside, you found out she didn't have cancer at all. Just said she was 'stricken by grief' when she found out some producer she'd worked with has it."

Leaving Mama to gloat over the invitation, Vangie started upstairs to change from her working clothes. Mama called after her, "What do you think I ought to wear?"

"Wear, Mama?"

"For the award thing. You think that purple I wore to Mr. McWhirter's funeral will do?"

***

Vangie handed Floyd the bag of clothes. "Like I promised, I won't tell anybody about your being here, but you've got to leave before the 12th of next month. I'm taking a trip then, and I wouldn't feel right about going if you were still in the house."

Floyd switched the shirt he was wearing for the new one Vangie had brought. "No sweat, Babe. The minute I get things set up in New York, I'm out of here. All I need is for you to keep this on the q-t for another day or so."

Vangie turned her back as Floyd slipped out of his rumpled trousers. "You really ought to tell Mama, though," she said. "She thinks the house is full of Gypsies, that they've been taking food from the kitchen."

"No way. We can't say squat about this to Mama. If she ever let on to anybody about me being here, it would be taps. Besides, now that you know I'm here, you can slip me some food."

The sound of a zipper closing allowed Vangie to turn around. "I still think it would be safer just to call the police, let them protect you from that gang until you can get back to your headquarters."

"Look, Sis, you don't understand. It's a dog-eat-dog business. Last year one of our agents turned himself in to the locals and that was the last anybody saw him alive." Floyd drew a finger across his throat for emphasis. "Living here in Dundalk like you do, you got no idea the kinda stuff goes on out there in the real world."

23. "Steppin' Out of Line"

Before leaving the phone booth, Jose Espada hooked an inquiring finger into the coin return slot. It came up empty. Gecko called to him from the open car window, "So what's Cenicero say?"

"Stupid sonvabitch." Jose hissed. "You want the whole goddam neighborhood to know?" He jerked open the driver's side door and slid beneath the wheel. "Maybe you like we should ride around with a sign on this junk heap car, 'These here two guys gonna rub out the double-crosser O'Toole?'"

"*Jesus, Maria y Josef.* I only ask what the boss wants we should do now."

"Cenicero says it's middle of July already. He says he's sick to death of excuses. He says tomorrow we gotta get inside that house, find out for sure if the double-crossing bastard's hiding in there."

"Cenicero got some ideas how we supposed to do this?"

"He say whenever the old lady she goes out, we go in. Simple as that." Jose turned the key. With a hoarse whine, the motor ground over, then quit.

"Sonvabitch." Gecko hissed through his teeth. "When this job she's over, I'm gonna run this piece o' shit car in the river."

Jose turned the key again. The engine reluctantly started. "We don' catch this O'Toole soon," he predicted, his voice thick with gloom, "I got a feeling me and you gonna be in the trunk when she goes in the river."

24. "Tiger Man"

For two whole days after her marijuana jag, the cat had done nothing but lie around purring and staring booby-eyed at the coffee can. Now that her buzz had worn off she was touchier than a rattlesnake and hungry as a boa constrictor. Scarcely finished the last lick of tuna, she was already whining for more.

"Cool it, cat, I gotta think." Floyd rubbed his aching head. "Gets weirder and weirder. First you show up. Then I spot that beat-up old car with Gecko and Espada or else their clones inside. To put the cheese on it, Herb Polaris turns up here the other night."

Konstanze's ears shot straight up at the sound of Herb's name.

"Yeah, it was Herb all right. Lucky thing you were too spaced out to realize he was around, otherwise you'd have given us both away."

The pitch of Konstanze's complaints subsided somewhat as Floyd's fingers traveled the length of her spine.

"So what was Herb was doing here in Dundalk? Not like him to be in cahoots with either the gang or the cops. I couldn't ask Vangie—the less she knows the better."

A motor-like purr expressed the cat's total indifference to anything except the hand that was stroking the delicious spot behind her ears.

"Anyhow," Floyd said, "there's no hidey-holes in this coalbin. I gotta stash this dough someplace else where nobody can get their hands on it, not Cenicero, not Herb, not even my crazy Mama's Gypsies."

When Floyd's hand withdrew, Konstanze's purr shifted to the loud, demanding *MMVVRRROOOWWW* that was her hunger signal.

"Cool it," he told her. "You've cleaned me out of sardines and I can't take a chance going out with Cenicero's goons hanging around. Soon as Mama leaves and it's safe for us to sneak upstairs, I'll fix you something."

Floyd listened carefully for sounds from above. Finally the front door slammed and the TV was silent. That much luck at least—he'd been scared that the storm rumbling off in the distance would keep Mama from going to the beauty parlor with Mabel McWhirter. He hoisted the canvas bag with the money.

With the cat at his heels, Floyd crept cautiously to the head of the basement stairs and listened again. Not a peep, so it was all clear. "What with hairdos and gabbing over lunch, they'll be out a coupla hours at least," he told Konstanze.

The minute he eased open the door to the kitchen, Konstanze slid past him and, with a single leap, rocketed to the top of the refrigerator. From her high perch she glared down at him, screaming an insistent *MMVVVRROOOWWW*.

Floyd set the canvas sack on the table and began rooting through the cabinets. More luck—Mama had bought Star-Kist this time, not that store brand Konstanze hated.

He opened the can before piling lunchmeat and cheese on a sandwich for himself. Hunger overcame caution. He ate the sandwich in huge bites, washing it down with gulps straight from the milk bottle. After they'd finished eating, he hid the empty tuna can under the garbage in the pail and added water to bring the milk to its former level in the bottle. That done, he hoisted the sack of money. "One good thing," he told Konstanze, "with all the junk the old lady's got laying around this dump, it'll be a cinch to find a safe place to stash this dough."

Konstanze was too busy licking her whiskers to comment.

But finding a place to stow fifty thick packets of bills turned out not to be so easy. Every drawer and cabinet was stuffed full, every niche and closet either too obvious or too small. The grandfather clock that was missing its works would have been perfect, but even a dumb cluck like Gecko would be smart enough to look there. The big, ugly vase that stood waist-high in the front hall, the one Mama called her "Greek urn," looked like a better possibility, ought to be room enough to hide an elephant underneath the plastic lilacs and Madonna lilies.

"Nah..." he told Konstanze, "too risky. That vase is the first thing Cenicero's hoods will spot if they come in the front way. Upstairs in one of the bedrooms is better."

His old room. Mama's room. Floyd's frustration grew as he scouted both of them. "No luck here," he told Konstanze. "Closets, the back of dresser drawers, and under mattresses are all places they'll look for stash. The bathroom won't work either, only a linen closet and the toilet tank in there. Neither will work."

Konstanze trailed close behind as Floyd shoved open the door to Vangie's room, but barely managed to avoid being stepped on when Floyd jumped backward and slammed the door. "Cripes—there's a guy in there." he said. "A big sucker. Staring straight at me."

He drew a shaky breath, then eased the door open a crack to peer cautiously inside. He let out a gust of relief. "That ain't a man, it's nothin' but a store-window dummy."

He opened the door wide and flipped the light switch. The string of Christmas lights surrounding Elvis's niche flicked on. "Holy Crackers," Floyd gasped. Mirrored images of the huge, sequined tiger that adorned the back of the mannequin's jumpsuit glittered from every angle, red rhinestone eyes as menacing as those of a real jungle cat.

Konstanze went sniffing about the room while Floyd searched for potential hiding places. "Man, Ol' Vangie sure is hooked on Elvis. Even got his face on her bedspread."

Floyd touched the "Play" button of the tape-recorder on Vangie's nightstand and music blasted from the Elvis mannequin.

The cat let out an offended screech and shot between Floyd's legs, cleared the width of the room in one leap, and landed on top of Vangie's dresser.

"Cool it" Floyd told Konstanze. "So what if it ain't that opera stuff you like so much?" He stepped closer to the mirrored niche, listening. "The music's coming from inside the dummy's body. Wonder how Vangie rigged that up?"

A tug on the jumpsuit's zipper gave the answer. "Jeez, there's a hole in his chest."

Floyd stepped back to think, a tedious process that involved twisting his mouth to one side, hunching his shoulder and rubbing the back of his head. "You know, this Elvis dummy might be the perfect place. I could stuff these wads of bills inside the legs and Vangie would never notice, not even if she took the speaker out."

Getting the money into Elvis proved a lot trickier than Floyd had figured. After removing the speaker, only a few packets would fit through the small opening at a time. What was worse, the mannequin's legs didn't connect with its body. He'd have to shove the entire two hundred fifty grand into Elvis's gut. Konstanze deserted the dresser to come perch atop Elvis's wig. "Hope the old boy don't mind that he's gettin' stuffed with something other than cheeseburgers and corn dogs," Floyd told her.

He was down to the last few packets when Konstanze let out a warning *MMMMVVVRROOOWWW*. Floyd sat back on his heels and listened. Down below a car door slammed. He crept to the window, pulled back a corner of the curtain and craned to get a better view. A car had just pulled into the alley next to the garbage cans, the same green Chevy he'd spotted before. Two guys were getting out. "Oh, shit—it's Espado and Gecko." Floyd dropped the corner of the curtain and ducked out of sight. "I gotta get out of here, pronto."

He hastily rammed the last few wads of bills into Elvis, stuffed the empty canvas sack into the cavity on top of the money, then shoved the speaker back into its hole. With fumbling fingers he zipped Elvis's jumpsuit, then turned and sprinted for the bathroom at the end of the hall.

The bathroom window, had been his old escape route when he was a kid sneaking out to smoke pot with his friends or rip off car stereos. Not it was his only hope. Luckily, the maple tree's branches hid the window from the alley. He shoved the curtain aside and tried to ease open the lower sash. It was stuck. He struggled to rock it loose, cold sweat creeping down his back. After what seemed an eternity, the window inched open. He slithered through the narrow frame and out onto the porch roof.

Crouched low against the shingles, Floyd waited, his heart beating so loud he was afraid the pair down below would hear it. Nails screeched and then came the sound of wood splintering. The sonovabitches were jimmying the kitchen window. Mustn't panic.

Heart pounding, he waited until Espada and Gecko were inside the house, then with a quick shinny he was down the maple tree's thick trunk. He hit the ground in a crouch. At that moment the storm broke, and the rain began pelting down. Floyd took off full speed down the alley, the same as when he'd escaped from the house on Casaverde, only this time there was no waiting rental car, no sack of money in his arms, nothing but a frantic need to put distance between himself and two guys who would kill him dead without batting an eye.

***

Jose Espado swiveled his huge head, staring from one side of the living room to the other. He expelled a snort of disgust. "This damned *casa*, she's so full of junk the *dinero* and O'Toole both could be anywhere." He stepped over a smashed lamp base and the pile of sofa cushions, their stuffing bulging where they had been slit, then shoved Gecko ahead of him toward the stairs. "Come on, we done wasted enough time down here..."

"I don' like the way this damn cat keep following us aroun'," Gecko whined as they climbed to the second floor. "*Mi abuela* – my gran'mother – she say when a *gato* is looking at you like that she's putting on you the, how you say, the *ojo malo,* the curse of the tiger."

Between Gecko's complaints and the menacing crashes from the storm overhead, Jose was about to snap. "I'm sick and damned tired of you whining all the time about voodoo, the "evil eye," your damn *abuela*. We don't find O'Toole and this money pronto, we're gonna have more than some crazy tiger curse to worry about."

They reached the landing and Jose kicked open the door to the front bedroom. He and Gecko pawed through Lotte's wardrobe, tossing garments to the floor in a disordered heap as streak after streak of lightning splintered the darkened sky beyond the window. From one corner of the closet Jose extracted a rumpled green uniform. "What this doing here with woman's dresses?" he mused aloud. "Maybe is a man around after all."

Still puzzling over the uniform, he sent Gecko to check out the room across the hall. A moment later, he heard his partner yelp, "*Jesus, Maria y Josef!*"

Jose bolted from the room and found Gecko staggering back into the hallway, trembling and crossing himself. Gecko turned as if to make a run for the stairs, but Jose grabbed him by the shirt and hauled him back.

"*Santa Maria!*" Gecko moaned. "What I'm telling you about bad luck. No way I'm goin' in there," He pointed shaking fingers toward the closed door.

For the hundredth time, Jose cursed the fact that he was saddled with a superstitious idiot. "And I'm telling you, *hombre*, the only bad luck we got to worry about is when we tell the boss we ain't found O'Toole and the money."

Shoving his partner ahead of him, Jose kicked open the door Gecko had indicated, then halted, stunned by the spectacle of hundreds of mirrored tiger images staring at him from the blue-lighted niche. "*Que es...?*"

Gecko pulled fearfully away, whimpering, "Is a holy shrine. Ain't no way I gonna mess aroun' with no saint." He crossed himself again.

Jose, his bravado rapidly shriveling, edged slightly backward toward the door. "Maybe. But it sure ain't no saint *I* ever seen before."

The uncertainty in his voice intensified Gecko's fears. "So how much you know about American saints, hah? You think somebody burn all these candles jus' for fun? I'm telling you, *hombre,* I don' mess with no saints."

Jose hesitated and Konstanze, who was crouched unseen into the niche behind the mannequin, chose that moment to spring onto Elvis's shoulder, fangs bared, every hair on end. From her gaping jaws came an unearthly screech, the defiant scream of a jungle cat.

Gecko leaped backward. "The curse of the *tiger,*" he cried, crashing into Jose in his haste to escape. At that same moment, a lightning bolt crashed to earth, splitting the maple tree outside the bathroom window. The house shook and reverberated with a sound like doomsday itself.

Jose's machismo deserted him. In his headlong descent of the stairs, he was only dimly aware of the siren whose persistent shrilling tapered into a thin wail as a police car pulled to the curb in front of 2744 Shirley Avenue.

NOTICE TO ALL CLUB MEMBERS

RE: GRACELAND TRIP

THERE HAVE BEEN COMPLAINTS THAT

THE 30 ELVIS-4-EVER PINS

EACH MEMBER RECEIVED ARE NOT ENOUGH.

OUR TREASURY CANNOT AFFORD TO ORDER MORE,

SO BE CAREFUL TO EXCHANGE WITH

FANS FROM CLUBS WHOSE PINS YOU REALLY WANT,

ESPECIALLY FOREIGN COUNTRIES

SUCH AS JAPAN AND SOUTH AFRICA.

ONLY THREE MORE WEEKS!!!!

BRENDA SUE HIGGS, PRESIDENT

ELVIS-4-EVER FAN CLUB

25. "Where Did They Go, Lord?"

The storm had passed, trailing behind diminishing growls of thunder, by the time Vangie and Opal left the Kmart. "That was a some crack of lightning," Opal remarked. "Thought for a while there we'd lose the electricity."

"You ever thought about how storms always seem to act out little dramas?" Vangie said.

Opal checked her purse for change. "How you mean, little dramas?"

"Well, first you feel all this tension building, as if something important is about to happen. Next the wind begins to howl, lightning splits the sky, and then come the booming crescendos of thunder."

Opal shot her a quizzical glance. "Booming crescendos? Who you been talking to, girl?"

Vangie grinned and shifted her bag to the opposite shoulder. "I guess that does sound like the way Herb Polaris talks about opera. Herb says people think opera is highbrow and hard to understand, but usually the stories aren't any more complicated than a romance novel or a Western movie."

Opal cocked her head at Vangie, eyebrows raised. "You mean to tell me all that screechin' and hollerin' is just like another episode of 'As the World Turns'?"

Vangie nodded. "Or 'High Noon.' Mostly there's a beautiful heroine, a villain who puts the heroine in danger, and a handsome hero who comes to rescue her."

"Funny," Opal mused as they climbed aboard the bus, "Can't picture Gary Cooper warbling' in Eye-talian."

As usual, riders were crammed into the 5:15 so tightly that for one person to move, three others had to crunch out of the way. It was only some five or six stops later that Opal and Vangie were finally able to claim seats. Vangie sank into hers with a sigh of relief. "Today's been a killer," she said, "what with all last week's sales reports due."

Opal snorted. "Yeah, and Dennis two weeks behind in his record keeping...as usual. So tell me more about this Herb dude you been seeing."

"Not really *seeing*. He only came back because he's really upset about losing his cat."

"I hear you, girl. So how come ever since you met this dude you been going around humming opera tunes. It's got so I can even recognize that one about some Donna A Mobil Lay."

Vangie grinned ruefully—that was the only one she knew.

Opal stood as the bus approached her stop. "So what was this Herb guy doing in Dundalk in the first place?"

Vangie shrugged. "That's what I haven't quite figured out yet."

Opal left, her 200-plus pounds causing the bus to list momentarily before it lurched forward. Vangie's thoughts turned once more to her conversation with Herb about opera. He had made it all sound so simple—good guys, bad guys, happy endings, tragic endings. If only real life was that uncomplicated. If only it wasn't so hard to tell the good guys from the bad ones, the heroes from the villains. Sometimes when it was all over, a person still wasn't sure whether it had been a comedy or a tragedy.

Take Elvis for instance. Now there was a life story that would make a grand opera. At one time he was king of the world, could do anything he wanted. If he felt like seeing a movie at midnight, they'd open the theater for him. If he wanted to fly to Las Vegas, he called his pilot and told him to gas up the jet. If he wanted a cheeseburger and shake at three in the morning someone was there to fix it for him.

Then it all turned sour. Elvis could still have his steak and mashed potatoes anytime he wanted, but every time he looked in the mirror he saw a bloated body. Women practically killed to get at him, but he could never be sure if it was really him they wanted or some crazy notion of him they'd built in their own minds. Even with Colonel Parker, a man he'd trusted like a father, Elvis had to be asking himself why the Colonel kept setting him up with ridiculous movie roles instead of letting him develop into the actor he might have been. What must have hurt the worst was when the guys he'd thought were his friends turned on him, wrote books that made him look selfish and ridiculous. Some of it was lies, but the parts that were true must have hurt. In the end there had been nothing left for Elvis. Except his talent. And even that must have seemed like a tiger that was threatening to eat him up, driving him through the jungle when all he really wanted to do was go home to Graceland, lie down there and rest, enjoy the peace he couldn't find anywhere else. Graceland. Elvis's Eden, his Shangri-La.

Vangie stared through the bus window at the rain-slicked sidewalks, but in her mind she was seeing a white-columned mansion perched on a gentle rise, its windows glistening in the sunset.

She hunched her shoulders tight. Maybe it was silly, this feeling that Graceland held something special for her...something she had to go there to find. But silly or not, the feeling would not go away.

August fourteenth. Less than four weeks. Mama was still okay, hadn't mentioned a word against the trip. The other problem—Floyd—would be gone by this weekend, off to New York. At least, that was what he'd said when she brought him the new clothes and the hair dye he'd asked for. "No sweat. Friday night for sure I'm out of here."

It wasn't altogether clear exactly who Floyd would be meeting in New York or how his going there fit in with his plan for catching the drug dealers in Miami. With Floyd you never knew. His stories were like a cheap pair of shoes, nice and shiny, but with a tendency to fall apart after a couple of wearings. Anyhow, he was leaving soon, and Mama was okay, and in less than four weeks she, herself, would be headed for Graceland.

Then, as the bus neared the corner of Shirley Avenue, Vangie's hopes went as flat as a week-old Mylar balloon. Through the bus's rain-streaked windshield she saw Mama lurching down the sidewalk, arms flapping from her shoulders, pausing every couple of steps to whirl about as if some invisible elastic cord were jerking her backward. Heart pounding, Vangie waited as the bus driver took his deliberate time releasing the door.

***

There was no way to make sense of what had happened to their home. The Gypsies had never, ever done anything like this before: messed, pried, scattered, broken, tossed things helter-skelter. The living room, especially, was a disaster zone with broken furniture, smashed pictures, shattered knickknacks, spilled drawers. Vangie picked up a slashed cushion and squeezed its needlepointed roses against her body, trying to hold back the anger fermenting inside her. "Why would they do this? They've never ruined our stuff before."

"They've ransacked the entire house," Mama rasped. "Every room the same way. And they left their cat behind. It's a sign they'll be back. This time they're coming to get me for sure."

Vangie stared perplexed at the cat who sat on the front windowsill delicately licking her paws. "Her tag says 'Konstanze.' Remember? That's the name of Herb Polaris's cat."

But how could that be? It had been more than a week since Herb's cat disappeared. And what had happened to Floyd? A quick search of the basement had turned up no trace of him. Almost dizzy with puzzlement, Vangie reached to pick up the cat. The reassurance of warm, soft fur beneath her fingers convinced her she wasn't in the middle of a nightmare. "The police...what did they say?"

Mama tossed her head. "Oh, them. Mrs. Aldine said that from the time she heard the glass breaking in the back door and called 911 till the police got here was a good twenty minutes. By then the Gypsies were long gone. Cops dusted all over for fingerprints, but you can imagine how much good that will do. Anybody but a fool would know Gypsies are too smart to leave evidence behind."

***

Vangie's call to the police station brought Officer Cooley of the Baltimore County police, who turned out to be a guy she had known in high school. "Gee, they sure left a mess," Cooley observed when she led him into the living room.

Vangie remembered that in school Cooley had been noted for two things, one, his endless bragging, and two, his tendency to state the obvious—"Guess I got a D on the test 'cause I missed seventeen out of the twenty questions." She remembered how at a high school reunion, one of their classmates had remarked, "Shame Cooley picked law enforcement for a career. He'd have made a great sports announcer: 'Gee, letting the other team get possession of the ball on our own two yard line cost us a touchdown'."

Apparently Cooley had not forgotten her, either. "Hey, you're Vangie O'Toole, the gal that used to run up the curve on the math tests. Never thought you'd still be hanging around here in Dundalk. By the way, did you ever see that girl sat behind you in Bio? Betty something-or-other? You know, the one with the big baz...the redhead that never handed in her homework and still got straight 'A's? Always thought she had the hots for me."

She assured Corporal Cooley that she hadn't kept up with Betty Edelen, known to a few sophomore boys, most of the upper class ones, and several select faculty males as Ready Betty.

Ignoring the mess, Cooley settled himself into Mama's armchair, then launched into an endless saga of his exploits as a law enforcement officer. "So I'm off-duty, ya know, just walking across this parking lot when I see these two guys breaking into somebody's car. I come up behind them and shove my hand down inside my belt like this." Cooley stood to demonstrate. 'I'm packing so hit the pavement,' I tell them. You never seen two guys kiss concrete so fast. Lucky thing they had no way of knowing I got nothing down there but my underwear."

He leered, as if certain the reference to his underwear was too thrilling for words, but Vangie could only picture his shorts as being sort of grimy and with the waistband elastic stretched by his more-than-ample paunch. Regardless, Cooley's boundless ego seemed to convince him that she was impressed. He immediately embarked on yet another story, this time out-

Superman-ing Clark Kent as he foiled an entire gang of bank-robbers, again with no other weapon than his dirty shorts.

Vangie gritted her teeth at the impossibility of steering Cooley away from a drawn-out recital of his derring-do as an officer. He had embarked on yet another episode when Mama appeared in the doorway. With a single meaningful glare, Mama brought Cooley straight up out of her chair. "Since it appears you've wiped out crime in the county, Officer Cooley, how's it possible that this morning's paper has seven robberies, three muggings, a rape, and two murders? And why is that after 10 years on the force, you're still wearing only one stripe on your sleeve?"

His face burning, Cooley pulled out a dog-eared notebook, cocked his head to one side and squinted. "You ladies got any idea who might of done this break-in? Noticed any strangers around the neighborhood lately?"

"Strangers," Mama snapped. "'Course it was strangers. Gypsies, that's who."

Vangie sighed. This was going to be a long investigation.

***

Herb Polaris swore under his breath. A teenager in an open Jeep whizzed past, doing at least eighty, blond girl snuggled up next to him, radio blaring. Kids. Thought being young gave them some special immunity from accidents. Seemed like lately the highways were full of fools—fools and damned fools. To be honest, he'd have to put himself in the latter category. If he had the sense he'd been born with he'd be halfway up 95 to Newark right now instead of heading for Dundalk again.

Floyd O'Toole wasn't going to show up at the house on Shirley Avenue, and Konstanze was gone, gone for good. Why couldn't he just accept that?

Herb took his eyes off the road long enough to switch tapes. Wagner? Nah, enough *Gottdamerung* with the storm and this traffic. Maybe the Vivaldi. Konstanze had loved "The Four Seasons."

Konstanze—he still couldn't shake that spooky feeling, he'd got when Vangie took him down to the basement to show him all her Elvis stuff. Almost as if Konstanze had been close by, watching him.

And that smell. Just the vaguest whiff, but it had been dogging him ever since. The same smell that used to cling to O'Toole's clothes when he came back to work after lunch break. The sweet, sickish odor marijuana left behind.

But if Floyd was holed up anywhere around that house, he was sure laying low. Vangie, then? Herb shook his head. With that open expression, Vangie wasn't the sort who could conceal a lie with any success.

Helluva difference between brother and sister in that family. Floyd dumping his responsibilities like an empty six-pack, Vangie so damned conscientious that she had no life of her own. Easy to see when she talked about going to Graceland how much that meant to her. Maybe he should tell her that he'd actually driven past Graceland once himself. But no use puncturing her pipe dream. If she got there, she'd see what she wanted to see. To him, hauling a load of Vidalia onions through Memphis at four in the morning, it was just a fancy white house setting on a knoll, iron gates in front. Graffiti slathered all over the stone wall that surrounded the place. *Good luck in heaven, Elvis. I can't forget you, Elvis. I'm just a prisoner of rock and roll.*

Not that Lotte O'Toole was ever going to let Vangie get as far away as Graceland. Looking at Vangie's situation made a person almost grateful to have no family at all. The orphanage may have been no easy upbringing, but at least it had knocked one lesson into his head: getting mixed up in another person's life was a flytrap that sucked you in, then ate you for lunch.

Why was he spending so much time thinking about Vangie O'Toole, anyhow? Stupid. Just like the impulse that led him to buy that prism in the truck-stop. A piece of silly junk. Hunk of glass with Elvis's face etched on it. But seeing it sparkle there, innocent as a rainbow in the midst of bill caps with slogans like "What I Like Best Rhymes with Truckin'" and mud flaps with naked babes on them, well, that little glass ornament reminded him of Vangie.

He wouldn't actually give it to her, though. Presents were just another knot in the noose. *Blest be the ties that bind*—what a crock that was. Since Marissa he'd avoided those traps, stayed free, gone about his business, never let anyone get too close. That was the big pay-off of trucking. You sat up in the cab, looked down on the world, saw it all, but weren't a part of it, nobody to intrude, your space your own, total control over how fast to go, how far, when to turn, which direction to head. You could listen to the radio or not, play whatever music you wanted, adjust the heat and the AC to suit yourself.

Music was another open highway, flowed like macadam under your fantasies. Dive into a mountain brook, duel with a knight, fly higher than the astronauts. It was all there on the tapes.

All in all, considering where he'd started from, the things he'd had to do to get where he was, this was a damned good life. Nobody to answer to, nobody to say, "Do this, don't do that," to ask where he was going, when he was coming back. A great life.

So why the hell was he heading toward Dundalk? Exxon station up ahead. Room enough to swing the rig around, roll on back to Newark. All he needed to do was ease up on gas pedal, hit the brake.

Ah, what the hell? He'd give it one last shot. Strictly for Konstanze's sake. This time, if she didn't show up, he'd call it quits, put her and the entire O'Toole family out of his mind once and for all.

***

Herb stared about him, dazed by the extent of the destruction. Somebody had really done a number on the place. Before, what with Lotte's collection of furniture and ornaments from the garbage route along with Vangie's Elvis stuff, the O'Toole's living room had been a little weird but kind of homey and interesting. Now, thanks to some asshole, it was all garbage again.

Herb watched Vangie replace a table lamp that had been knocked to the floor, center it on a crocheted doily and flip on the switch. Lamplight did great things for her hair, picked up golden highlights and gave it a nice soft sheen. Pretty. And the way her skin glowed, like it was lit from inside by candlelight. But then Vangie was pretty down deep where it counted. Quality. The genuine article.

Vangie caught him staring at her. "I can't tell you how much I appreciate your staying to help get things straightened out," she said.

Herb felt his face turn as red as Mama O'Toole's velvet-covered settee. What the hell was wrong with him anyhow? Here he was, mooning like a school-boy over a woman nearly twenty years younger than him...well, *fifteen* years, at least. If Vangie thought of him at all, it was probably as some kind of father figure.

One thing for sure, it wouldn't do to let her catch on how flustered she made him feel. He'd stick around just long enough to get this joint straightened up a bit and then it was *Adios Dundalk* for him and Konstanze.

Konstanze—there was the biggest mystery of all. At this very moment Her Royal Majesty was perched in the windowsill of the O'Toole's living room, licking her paws. The furry little broad had made herself right at home, acted like she'd lived here from the day she was a kitten.

Herb shook his head in puzzlement, then picked up an amethyst vase and a cracked bust of Nefertiti. He started to put them back on the mantelshelf, but paused when Vangie shook her head. "No. The vase has to go on the right," she directed. "Between the bisque doll and the souvenir cup from Atlantic City. Mama gets nervous if things aren't the same,"

Herb sighed and shifted Nefertiti a quarter-inch to the left, turning her so the crack wouldn't show. This latest episode was a puzzler for sure. "You know," Herb admitted, " till now, I suspected this Gypsy thing was all in Lotte's imagination. But after this…" He swept his arm across the devastated living room.

"It wasn't the Gypsies this time."

Herb stared at Vangie, surprised by the conviction in her voice. "Then who…?"

Vangie set a vase of artificial peonies on the end table before answering. "There's something I've got to tell you, but I couldn't say anything in front of Mama. You remember I told you I have a brother? Floyd? Well, a couple of days ago, I found Floyd hiding in our basement."

Bingo! So Floyd *had* been here, right under their noses all the time. "So where is he now?"

"Gone. When I got home today, the house was like this. No sign of Floyd. Just Konstanze sitting on top of my Elvis mannequin."

"You didn't tell your mother Floyd was here?"

"He made me promise not to. Said he was a secret agent on a special assignment, that some crooks were after him so it wasn't safe to tell Mama."

Had Vangie actually bought that line—O'Toole a secret agent? No. Judging from the skepticism in her voice, Floyd hadn't fooled her. But did Vangie have any idea of what she was getting into if Cenicero's hit men ever found out who she'd been sheltering? "What about the cops that came to investigate the break-in? Do they know Floyd was hiding out here?"

Again Vangie hesitated. "Floyd claimed the police couldn't be trusted either, that some of them were in with the gang." The glance she gave him pleaded for understanding, clearly torn between common sense and the line Floyd had fed her. "I realize that sounds absurd, but I didn't know what to do. Floyd promised he was only going to stay for a few days and then he'd be gone."

Herb tried not to let Vangie see how this latest revelation shook him. Should he tell her that Floyd was his real reason for coming to Dundalk in the first place? If he did that, he'd have to tell her about the Miami business. Knowing too much could be dangerous for her. Now that Floyd had disappeared again, it was probably best to keep quiet about all that. "So who does your mother think did this?"

Vangie exuded a huge sigh. "Gypsies. She's convinced now that they've been in the house all along."

Lady Konstanze pranced across the room to perch herself on an armchair. Herb reached over to scratch behind her ears. "Don't you think a dose of reality might be the best thing for Lotte? I mean, Gypsies, for God's sake."

Vangie touched the photograph of her father she had just replaced on the mantel. "I can't explain it exactly, but Mama *needs* to believe in the Gypsies. It's like her way of shutting out real dangers inside her head."

Those words confirmed what Herb had suspected all along. Vangie realized her mother's hallucinations were just that, but she was too soft-hearted to call Lotte's bluff. What a depressing set-up way for a girl—woman—like her. And not much hope that the future held anything different.

Still, it wasn't his concern. Soon as the house was back in order he and Konstanze were splitting. Floyd was gone, and whether or not Cenicero caught up with him, sooner or later the creep would do himself in. Nothing anyone could do about that.

Konstanze climbed to the back of the chair. Vangie fished the prism Herb had given her from the pocket of her skirt and swung the glass ornament gently in front of the cat. Konstanze seemed to relish the game. Each time the prism slowed its swing, she batted it with her paw to set it in motion again. Vangie laughed and laid her cheek against the cat's fur. Herb was struck by how comfortable the two of them looked, playing together. Made him wish....

Enough. He'd soon be as bonkers as Lotte O'Toole. Time to hit the road. Hang around here much longer and that sticky old web called commitment would be wrapping itself around him. He was forty-eight, damned near forty-nine. Much too old to get involved with someone Vangie's age.

He bent to retrieve a lava lamp from the debris, then carefully placed it on the table by the sofa. The minute the job was done he and Konstanze were gone, this time for good.

26. "Money Honey"

Vangie drew back the bedspread and folded it. Maybe the Gypsies weren't looking to carry Mama away at all. Maybe she, Vangie, was the one they hated. Why else had they ruined her chance of going to Graceland? Mama was still downstairs crying over the broken plaster bust of Socrates, the one Dad brought home off the route the very day before he was killed.

Or maybe it was Floyd who wrecked their house before he left. He'd done a lot of stupid things, but never anything so mean and vicious.

Elvis wasn't giving any answers, just watching her from across the room, his expression as cold and inhuman as any other store window dummy. A stupid mannequin. No more capable of feeling than of getting down from its niche and walking. No wonder whoever broke in didn't bother to destroy him. They could see he was a fake.

Vangie slithered out of her skirt, and heard a clink as something fell from her pocket. She bent to pick it up. The prism

Herb had given her. Another fake. Not a magic rainbow-maker, nothing but a piece of glass, something he'd brought for her the way you'd bring a kid a candy bar. She'd been stupid to hope Herb would stay a little longer. Why should he? He had his Konstanze back. By now both of them were halfway to Philadelphia.

Vangie lowered herself to the side of the bed and sat staring at nothing. Funny, Mama seemed to like it that Herb called her 'Lotte.' Probably the first time since Dad died that a man had called her by that given name.

Herb really did look a lot like Alex Trebek, the way the crinkles around his eyes became deeper when he was thinking. He pretended to be tough, but the relief on his face when they told him they'd found Konstanze was like a kid at Christmas. Shy, too. Turned absolutely the color of a terra cotta flowerpot when he handed her the prism. For just a minute it was possible to see exactly how he must have looked when he was a little boy.

Vangie picked up the prism, stood, and started to place it on her bureau, then changed her mind and suspended it from the bottom of her window shade. She flipped off the light and crawled between the sheets. No use dwelling on Herb Polaris. He was history. Floyd, too. Everybody gone. Just her and Mama left. Any hopes of visiting Graceland vanished as completely as the prism's rainbows after the light faded.

She reached across to the nightstand and flipped on the tape recorder. But once again Elvis's voice came out as a harsh croak, the lyrics garbled, the melody as unpleasant as a vacuum cleaner's whine. She switched on the light, hit the "off" button and popped out the cassette. It looked okay. She slid it back into the slot and tried again. For a moment or two, the tape ran smoothly. But then the same thing happened—instead of music, the speaker squawked out gibberish.

She turned off the recorder. Another loose connection. In the morning she'd have a look.

***

Iridescent sparkles from the prism danced across the stacks piled on her bed, the thick green wads of money she'd pulled out of the mannequin. The sight of all that cash left her too dazed to think straight –it felt as if Elvis had given birth to packets of hundred dollar bills.

She must be losing her mind. Soon she, too, would be the one seeing Gypsies everywhere. She couldn't be more stunned if she'd opened her accounting textbook and found that plus meant minus and debits had become credits. "Where did it come from?" Vangie asked out loud. Her eyes, reflected in the mirrors, had the same glassy stare as Elvis's.

A quick riff through one of the banded wads had shown that it contained fifty hundreds. Five thousand dollars. Fifty packets in all. Two hundred fifty thousand total if each held the same amount. Only one appeared to have been broken.

Vangie checked of the packets again. Ben Franklin's picture was on each bill—she'd checked enough bills at the Kmart to know these were genuine. Maybe she *wasn't* dreaming. The money *seemed* real. If that was the case, what to do with it?

For certain she mustn't say anything to Mama. This would be just one more thing to upset her. For now, she'd have to hide it until she could think more rationally and decide what to do with it.

She crammed the wads of bills back into Elvis's torso, praying that by the time she got home from work they'd disappear.

27. "Is It So Strange?"

Lacey McLeod was preparing to step onto the elevator when Mike Dowling signaled for her to wait. "Ran across something this morning that might interest you," he said.

Lacey propped the elevator door open with her shoulder. "Can't stop, Mike, the babysitter leaves promptly at five."

"Only take a minute. You know that O'Toole woman down in Dundalk, the Elvis fan?"

"Vangie O'Toole? Sure. On Friday I'm covering the award she's getting from Hizzoner and India Marlowe." Lacey stepped out of the elevator and allowed the door to slide shut.

"Well, funny thing, I was over at police headquarters shooting some pix of that cop who brought in the gang that was stealing ostriches from the zoo."

"Ostriches?"

"Yeah. Seems there's a big market for them, people setting up ostrich ranches. Sounds nutty to me, but the eggs are selling for thousands of dollars. Anyhow, while I was there, I overheard a couple of the cops talking about a Floyd O'Toole. Seems there's an APB out on the guy and – get this – they mentioned that he might be hiding out in Dundalk. Vangie O'Toole, the Elvis fan? Dundalk? Coincidence? I think not."

Lacey's haste to get home warred with the intriguing possibilities of Mike's news. "Did you get any further information?"

"I was busy setting up the shot and it was just a couple of cops talking in the hall outside."

A loud *Ding* signaled the elevator's return. Lacey waved her appreciation as she stepped aboard. "Thanks for the tip. If it turns out Vangie O'Toole is related, I'll try to pick up something from her."

All the way home, Lacey mulled over Mike's lead. Probably nothing to it, must be half a dozen O'Toole families in Dundalk. But a check of the Baltimore phone book later that evening showed no other Dundalk exchange listings under that name. Odd. Well, it wasn't her beat—a hot story like that would be hard news, not the kind of assignment Avery would give her a shot at.

After Tissie was in bed for the night, Lacey tried to settle down with a book, but Mike's bit of information still stuck in her mind, as irritating as gravel in a sandal. Okay, so it *wasn't* her assignment, but here was a potential "in" to what might be a headline story. Besides, there was Tim McCoskey. Even though they were no longer dating, they were still friends. Tim might share with her whatever dope headquarters had on Floyd O'Toole.

***

"Here's what came over the wire on Floyd O'Toole," Tim told her over breakfast, the only time they could meet when he was on night shift. "Seems O'Toole was the gofer for a gang of Costa Rican drug dealers operating out of Miami. Guy named Cenicero is the head honcho, real nasty character, known for French-frying his enemies. Cops down there broke up a big buy, arrested several of the gang, but O'Toole absconded with the cash and possibly the dope as well. Feds have reason to believe he might have headed for Baltimore. They've asked our help in locating him. How come you're interested?"

"I'm doing a story on somebody with the same family name. I just decided to check it out."

"Wouldn't get involved in this if I were you.. If this O'Toole's double-crossed a drug dealer, you can bet there's a contract out on him. If the Feds do find him, it'll probably be as a corpse."

"Oh, I wasn't intending to *do* anything about this. Just curious about what was going on."

"Sure, sure. And that newshound gleam in your eye is just because you're so excited about those scrambled eggs you've hardly touched."

"Well, a person can't help wondering..."

"Well, while you're wondering, I finally got back on day shift next week. Any chance we could get together Friday night?"

"Could be. If I can get a baby-sitter."

"So shall we consider it a definite date?"

"Single mothers of four-year-olds can't *make* definite dates until they have clearance from at least two pediatricians and the babysitter," she told him, grinning ruefully.

"A definite 'maybe' then?"

"Let's hope."

"Gosh, Lace, don't commit yourself too strongly...a guy could get ideas."

She grinned again. "Adios, McCoskey. I'll call you."

***

In the foyer of the city council auditorium, Vangie, Lotte and Mrs. McWhirter stood off to one side, a little apart from of the crowd of reporters and onlookers waiting for India Marlowe to appear. Lacey McLeod joined them. She noticed that both Mrs. O'Toole and Mrs. McWhirter were obviously enjoying the occasion, while Vangie seemed subdued and distracted.

"You must be very proud of your daughter," Lacey remarked to Lotte.

"Of course I'm proud of Vangie," Lotte said. "Who wouldn't be? By the way, you ever done a piece on Gypsies? Now I could tell you..."

To Lacey's relief, Vangie came to her rescue. "Thanks for the nice article you did on our fan club, Miss McLeod," she said. "Brenda Sue is having it laminated."

"Glad you liked it. So how do you feel about getting this award?"

Vangie hesitated for a long moment as if struggling to gather her thoughts. "Mostly I'm confused as to why I'm getting it. All the club members helped raise the money. I'm not the only one who volunteers at the hospital, several of the others also spend a lot of time working there."

"Must be a thrill, though, having this chance to meet India Marlowe in person."

Vangie nodded. "It will be nice to meet her, especially since Miss Marlowe was one of the few people in Hollywood who were really decent to Elvis when he was making movies. She claimed that he could have been another James Dean if only he'd been given good roles to play."

Lacey nodded. "That's true. Who knows how far Elvis might have gone if he hadn't gotten stuck in silly films like 'Fun in Acapulco?'"

Vangie's face lit. "His early movies proved he had plenty of natural talent—'King Creole,' and 'Jailhouse Rock,' for instance."

"Jailhouse. That's where those people belong, you ask me." Lotte O'Toole pronounced darkly.

"You'll have to excuse Mama," Vangie explained. "We had a break-in at our house a couple of days ago. She's still upset about it."

Lacey felt her reporter's antenna begin to tingle. "Do the police know who did it?"

Vangie shook her head. "They came and took fingerprints, asked a lot of questions."

"Questions," Mrs. O'Toole snapped. "They've got plenty of those. Where are the answers, that's what *I* want to know." With that she went flouncing across the room to examine the portraits of former mayors that decorated the walls. Mrs. McWhirter gave Vangie and Lacey a commiserating smile then trailed after Lotte.

Lacey bit her lower lip as she considered this latest revelation. A break-in at the O'Toole's house? A police report that Floyd O'Toole was headed for Dundalk? Reticence be damned—she was a reporter. She flipped open her notepad. "Vangie, I need more information for the article I'll be writing about the award ceremony. Your family, for instance—to you have any brothers or sisters?"

The startled look on Vangie's face made it clear that the question hit a nerve. Vangie hesitated and just then India Marlowe swept in, surrounded by her entourage and the buzz of excitement drowned any chance for further questioning. Together with Vangie and Lotte, Lacey joined the mob shoving through the double doors into the auditorium.

Once everyone had crowded inside, the Mayor stepped forward to offer a speech about the real Samaritans being the ones who gave of themselves day after day without thought of reward. He then presented Vangie with a gold key stamped with a crest and the words *City of Baltimore*. After making sure the TV cameras were focused in her direction, India Marlowe stepped forward to hand Vangie an engraved certificate and an autographed photo of herself. "Ah'm terribly, terribly thrilled to present this award to a special little person who carries on the tradition of caring for the less fortunate as practiced by mah de-ah, de-ah friend, the late Elvis Presley," she announced. "All of us who care about those de-ah little sick children truly appreciate your efforts on their behalf, Miss O'Toole."

The presentation finished, the movie star wasted no more time. Pasting on a wide, glittering smile, she swept from the room, reporters and photographers scrambling in her wake.

Lacey hesitated. If she stuck to her assignment, she should become part of that school of remoras trailing after Marlowe. But what the hell, she had more interesting fish to catch. She headed off Vangie and her mother as they were preparing to leave.

At Lacey's approach, Vangie grasped her mother's arm and turned abruptly toward the entrance. "Since the break in, Mrs. McWhirter's been kind enough to stay with Mama during the day. They're taking the bus back to Dundalk and I'm going on to the hospital," she said, in what was clearly intended as an end to any further interview.

Lacey hesitated only for a moment. "Wonderful," she gushed. "I'm going in the direction of the hospital myself. How about if you and I have lunch. Afterwards I'll drive you over there."

Vangie slowed only slightly in her rush toward the door. "Oh, no. We couldn't ask you to..."

"No trouble whatsoever. I'm parked right out front."

"Thanks for the offer, but I've got to see that Mama and Mrs. McWhirter get the right bus. The next one for Dundalk might not come for a while. I'm sure you have other things…."

"No problem," Lacey assured her. "I'll just wait with you until they're on the bus and then we'll take my car."

"It's probably out of your way…."

"Not at all." Lacey seized Lotte O'Toole's free arm.

While the four of them waited at the bus stop, Lotte O'Toole scrutinized the photograph India Marlowe had presented to Vangie. "Air brushed," she announced with authority. "Got rid of the wrinkles around the eyes."

***

Remembering the wary look her earlier question had provoked, during their drive Lacey chatted about neutral subjects such as the award ceremony and the charity auction that would raise money for hospital unit. At the restaurant, after giving her lunch order, she excused herself saying she had to call home. "The day-care center is closed this week for vacation," she explained to Vangie. "The only person available to sit for Tissie was an older woman who lives down the hall from us."

When she returned to the table, Vangie asked, "Everything okay?"

Lacey grinned as she slid into the seat opposite. "The apartment will probably be a wreck when I get home. Mrs. Dreyfuss feels her only mission is to keep Tissie happy and occupied, so they make wonderful messes that I'm left to clean up."

"You don't seem to be too upset about that."

"I'm not. Better a baby-sitter who pays attention to the kid than one whose priority is a neat house."

Vangie returned her smudged menu to the wire holder next to the salt and paper shakers. "I remember the messes my brother Floyd and I used to make when we were kids...." she began, then halted abruptly.

Lacey paused, seeking to thread the fine line between prying and casual interest. "I didn't know you had a brother. Does he live with you and your mother?"

Vangie turned to stare toward the window, her closed expression making it clear that was a subject she'd rather not pursue. "Floyd's been gone for ages. He left years ago, right after Dad died."

Lacey casually unwrapped her silverware from its swaddling napkin. "But I suppose you hear from him sometimes?"

"Sometimes." Vangie didn't elaborate.

Realizing she'd have to approach the subject of Floyd from a different angle, Lacey said, "I'll bet all your Elvis club members will be impressed that you got to meet India Marlowe."

Vangie gave her a knowing glance. "Mama said Miss Marlowe was the one reaping the award—the publicity, you know."

Lacey laughed. "Your Mama's no fool. Did you get a load of that necklace Marlowe was wearing? Bet you could buy a house with what those stones cost."

"I suppose when you're a big star you have to dress and act the part, even when you're not on stage."

"I always find it funny at the Academy Awards to see the sort of men who always play rough and ready roles showing up in tuxes."

With the change of topic, the two of them were soon chatting away. By the time their sandwiches arrived, Vangie had revealed how desperately she wanted to go to Graceland, and Lacey found herself telling Vangie about the break-up of her marriage. "Six months after his law firm took in a new junior partner, I found out 'junior' was a woman. Unfortunately, my husband latched onto her gender a lot faster."

"That must have been a really tough time for you," Vangie said.

Lacey nodded acknowledgement. "At least it made me stop and think what I really wanted out of my life. I finally faced the fact that trading a decent family life for the prestige that came from being the wife of a successful corporate lawyer wasn't on my to-do list. That's when Tissie and I made the move to Baltimore."

"Does your ex-husband come visit Tissie?"

"At first he did. Now he just sends presents and excuses. By now the poor kid thinks the UPS man is her dad." Lacey bit into a potato chip with unnecessary force. "But tell me about you. Do you date anyone special?"

Vangie shrugged. "No one special or un-special. Although I did meet a man recently, somebody really nice. Not likely anything will come of it, though...."

"Why not?"

"Well, for one thing, he lives in New Jersey. And even if he did...get interested...there's always the problem of Mama."

"Sounds a lot like me with Tissie. I was sort of dating this policeman, Tim McCoskey. But between his work shifts and my having to find a baby-sitter, we eventually gave up on the whole thing."

Later, as they were preparing to leave, Vangie hesitated, then said, "There's something important I need to discuss, and I don't know who to talk to about it. It's about Floyd...my brother."

Lacey's heart gave a little lurch.

***

At home that evening, Lacey sat puzzling over the startling story Vangie had given her, the fact that Floyd had been hiding out in their basement without either Vangie or Lotte knowing he was there. And now he'd disappeared, presumably at the same time their house was ransacked. "I don't know whether to think Floyd did all that damage, or to worry that whoever did it was after him," Vangie had told her.

Lacey bit the end of her pen, trying to get a grip on the events Vangie had revealed. It was plain Vangie didn't believe Floyd's story about his being a federal agent, but there was also a niggling feeling that Vangie hadn't spilled quite the whole story.

Lacey continued to puzzle over that, but none of the many scenarios she considered pinpointed the story's missing element.

At her daughter's demand for a bedtime story, Lacey closed her notebook. The important thing was that she now had the inside track on an important story, one that that could put her byline on the front pages instead of hidden away in the "About Town" section. If this lead on Floyd O'Toole panned out, it was so hot that even Avery couldn't refuse her this assignment. But could she justify using information Vangie had given her as a friend? In just the short time she'd known Vangie, she'd come to like her, admire her, even.

Even after the bedtime story was read and Tissie safely tucked away, Lacey's conscience troubled her. Still, all was fair in love, war, and journalism. Would Hank Willis or Don Parvech down in the city room hesitate to make use of material like that she'd just pumped out of Vangie? Would Dan Rather shelve a breaking story just because he and some senator he was stalking had become friends?

Okay, so Vangie O'Toole was no sleazy politician. She was a woman working full-time, busting her buns trying to get a college degree, and, at the same time taking care of a mother whose mental state was a chronic worry. On top of all that, Vangie still found time and energy to work with sick and dying kids.

But wasn't she protecting a criminal? Not that one could blame Vangie for holding back information that could get her brother killed. According to Tim McCoskey, Floyd O'Toole's chances of staying alive after ripping off the meanest dealer in Miami were equivalent to his chances of being elected president. "Odds are a hundred to one the mob will knock him off before the Feds get anywhere near the poor stupid devil," Tim had told her. "Wouldn't surprise me a bit if we got a call that there was a body floating in the harbor or stinking up the trunk of some abandoned car."

If Floyd were still in the house with Vangie and her mother, turning him in to the police would have been a viable option, one that might have saved his life. But with him running from both the police and the gang, a newspaper story on him could easily put both him and his family in danger.

Lacey rose and turned out the light. Her conscience had won out, at least for the moment. She'd hold off a bit on the Floyd story, see what developed. Meanwhile, she'd get in touch with Tim again and find out if he had anything new.

28. "Don't Leave Me Now"

From the upper deck, Floyd stared down at the dirty gray line of foam marking the ferry's progress across the Hudson. What a crock. Angelina had turned out to be nothing but a two-bit, good-for-nothing gold-digger. No money, no honey, she'd informed him.

Her dogfaced father was just as rotten. "I ain't taking no chance of seeing my restaurant go up in smoke," the old fart had yelled as he kicked him out of the house. "And no way my daughter's gonna end up anchored in concrete because some half-ass punk was stupid enough to cross Cenicero."

They could all stick it. He didn't need Angelina...plenty of other broads around. Yeah. Once he had his paws back on that 250 Gs, he'd be able walk into any bar and....

But for now he was flat broke. Stashing all his cash in Vangie's dummy may have been a stupid-assed move, but with Cenicero's men breaking into the house he'd had no choice. Now, thanks to Angelina's bastard of a father, he had no place to lay low until it was safe to go back to Dundalk and pick up his dough.

He reached into his pocket and jangled the coins. Only eighteen bucks and change left, hardly even coffee money here in New York.

A shudder ran through the ferry's hull as the engines reversed for landing. Floyd turned to watch as the ship bumped its way into the slip. New Jersey. One last chance. One possible person who might help save his ass.

***

Herb hung up his damp jacket and plugged in the coffee pot. A relief to be back in the Newark terminal after a long, miserable haul. Nothing but rain, rain, rain, all the way through Illinois and Ohio, rain pouring down in sheets, the windshield wipers barely able to keep up.

Saturday night, eight o'clock. The office and warehouse both dead. Nobody around. Might as well go through the mail Gertie had left for him, then head home to his empty apartment.

Konstanze was curled up in the "Out" box. Herb absent-mindedly ran his fingers along the cat's spine as he sorted through the pile, trashing the solicitations for credit cards and the envelopes that assured him he'd already won a million. "You know what you did, you wretched female?" he told Konstanze. "You put me through total and absolute hell, not to mention wasted time and lost jobs. And now you show about as much remorse as a truck-stop hooker."

Konstanze's "Mmmvvrrooow" was as self-satisfied as ever.

Herb shook a finger at her. "I'm wise to you, though, Cat. My gut tells me you had a paw in what went on at the O'Toole's house. But how the hell did you manage to get in there in the first place, and how'd you manage to lay low all that time?"

"Mmmmvvrrooow," she responded, casting him a knowing glance over her shoulder

A loud gurgle signaled that the coffee maker had finished brewing. Herb got up, poured himself a cup, and returned to his swivel chair. Leaning back for a moment, he propped his feet on the desk while he sipped the hot brew and puzzled once more over the mystery of Konstanze's disappearing act. "One thing for sure, you didn't go hungry," he told her. "If you ran off with the Gypsies like Lotte claims, they fed you pretty damned well."

Konstanze gave him her pissed-off look. Same as most broads, she hated to have her weight mentioned. So what?—she had more than a little aggravation coming after all she'd put him through.

If only Konstanze could talk. Who the hell had ransacked the O'Toole's house like that? That was another puzzle that had been buzzing around in his brain all the way to Chicago and back. Most likely scenario was Cenicero's hit men looking for Floyd and the money he lifted from them. Local hoods would have grabbed the TV and some other stuff, but Vangie said nothing was missing. That made some sort of sense, would explain the place being torn apart. Although God himself would never convince Lotte O'Toole that it wasn't the Gypsies who'd invaded the house.

"Whoever did it sure left a mess," he mused aloud. "Wouldn't have been fair to leave Vangie to clean that up by herself."

Konstanze raised her head to fix him with a particularly cynical stare.

"Well, you gotta admit it's a crying shame. Whoever trashed the place ruined whatever chance Vangie had of going to Graceland. All the time we were putting it back together she was trying to hide her disappointment, but any fool could see how important that trip was to her, how bad she'd wanted to go."

Ah, what the hell. Not his problem.

Herb plunked both feet on the floor. Time to get busy, concentrate on these manifests. Konstanze was back. From now on it was the regular routine. Forget about Dundalk, about Floyd, about Lotte and her Gypsies, Vangie and her Elvis groupies. Soon as he finished here he'd give Gertie a call, maybe stop by her place for a late-nighter. A few bucks extra in Gertie's next pay envelope. No more involvement than that. Much better that way.

Herb was going over the manifest on his Chicago run—a tidy eight thou profit for Aragon Movers—when the sound of something striking the window that faced on the alley jerked him into instant awareness. In swift consecutive movements, he ducked down, flipped off the desk light, and slipped his Colt .45 from the top drawer. Wasn't like his customers to give him any grief, but in this business you never knew.

Again the window rattled, a sound like pebbles hitting the glass. Herb crouched down and eased his way across the room, making sure to stay out of sight of whoever was lurking outside. He rose slowly, flattened himself against the wall and risked a quick glimpse around the edge of the window frame. The security lights outside the building picked up a figure crouched behind the dumpster in the alley. A man. Something about the furtive hunch of the shoulders seemed familiar, but the glass was too rain-spattered to make out any more than that.

Herb waited. After another minute or so, the man rose cautiously and flung another handful of pebbles toward the window. This time Herb was able to get a better look. Even though he hadn't laid eyes on him for nearly five years, there was no mistaking the skinny frame of Floyd O'Toole.

Herb tapped on the glass with the barrel of his gun and motioned to Floyd to come around to the warehouse's alley entrance. He unbolted the door and cautiously eased it open. Floyd started to enter, then, spotting the pistol, turned as if to run. Herb collared him with his free hand and dragged him inside.

The rain had plastered Floyd's dyed hair against his scalp. His clothing was soaked through and his shoes squished as he followed Herb back to the office where he stood shivering like a half-drowned mongrel.

"If you aren't one sorry damned sight," Herb exclaimed in disgust.

Floyd whimpered. "I got a little problem, Boss. Cenicero's guys are on my tail. On top of that, the lousy cops got an APB out on me." He sniffed and looked down at his muddy shoes. "I'm broke and I ain't got no place to go."

"You're telling me you got a problem." Herb shoved Floyd ahead of him into his office. "Everybody on the whole damned Eastern seaboard has heard about the dumb stunt you pulled, ripping off that drug money."

"I know, Man, but this setback is only temporary. I had to stash the dough, but soon as I can get back to pick it up I'll be settin' pretty. All I need is a place to hole up till the heat's off."

"So where is it you've hid all this dough?"

The sly look that crossed Floyd's face was as easy to decipher as a porn magazine. "Hid it in Miami, Boss. In a girlfriend's pad down there. Just have to wait till things cool off a little and I'll slip back down and get it. Help me out for now and I'll split with you. Fifty-fifty."

Herb grimaced in disgust. Same old Floyd. Never told the truth when a lie would do. Dumb as a stone, too. Hadn't caught on yet to the simple fact that there wasn't a place in the whole damned country he could run to where Cenicero wouldn't hunt him down. If the cops didn't get to him first. Matter of fact, there was an old score of his own to settle with Mr. Floyd O'Toole, that hijack job on an Aragon truck carrying a load of hot furs. But that could wait. For now, he had to decide what to do with the creep. Herb motioned Floyd toward the office bathroom. "There's a change of clothes in there. Get out of those wet things."

While Floyd was in the bathroom, Herb put the gun away and sat down to think. If he did the smart thing, he'd turn O'Toole over to either the mob or the cops and let them deal with him. The guy was scum...out-and-out undiluted scum.

But there were other considerations. Two of them. First, Floyd had saved Konstanze from that fire. Second, Vangie. Much as he'd hate to turn a rat like Floyd loose from the trap he'd built for himself, Floyd was Vangie's brother.

Herb thought for a few more minutes. Then allowed a grin to slowly shape his face as he reached for the phone.

29. "Edge of Reality"

At breakfast on Monday morning, Mama crowed, "Just let Mabel McWhirter start bragging about her Sammy now." She spread the "Lifestyle" section of the Star so Vangie could see Lacey McLeod's article.

Elvis Fan Awarded for Volunteer
Work with Young Cancer Patients
by Lacey McLeod, Star Staff

Mama bent closer to read it. "Evangeline 'Vangie' O'Toole." She looked up, "See, that's you she's talking about." She shifted her bifocals, relocated her place in the column and continued reading:

Vangie O'Toole never met Elvis Presley, never even saw him in a live performance. But inspired by Elvis's many unsung acts of charity, the Elvis fan has spent hundreds of hours comforting and helping the children in the pediatric oncology ward of St. Ignatius Hospital.

Camille Raish, a nurse at St. Ignatius, had this to say of O'Toole's volunteer work: "When Vangie O'Toole

*walks into the ward with her arms full of teddy bears and
Lisa Marie dolls, it's as if she brings Elvis right along
with her. You can tell by the look on the kids' faces that
she really connects. They all want to know 'When's Miss
Vangie coming'?*

***

As soon as Vangie punched in for work it started. Flo, in
the back of the store ticketing a belated shipment of wading
pools, called out, "Hey, Vange, you're a celebrity now." Dennis
came out of his office to give her a big thumbs up. Darla wanted
to know if any guys had called since seeing her picture in the
paper.

One of the cashiers was late, so Vangie took over her
register. The first customer, an older man, stared at her for a
moment then blurted, "Din't I see your pixture in the Star? Never
did see nothin' in that Presley fellow myself. Guess you gals just
can't resist the way he jiggled his butt around, huh?"

Vangie bagged his purchases, stifling the urge to pile his
six-pack of soft drinks on top of his marshmallows.

Most of the customers, however rained congratulations
on her. Several even asked her to sign copies of the article. The
nicest compliment came from an elderly lady who said, "I
wouldn't walk across the street to meet that India Marlowe, but
I'm proud to be able to say I met a young lady who looks out for
other people."

After Vangie arrived home at five-thirty, any remaining
glow from the attention she'd received at work quickly faded.
Officer Cooley was back. With him were two men in dark suits.

They flipped their badges at her simultaneously, their synchronization as perfect as a pair of wind-up toys. "Our lab has identified prints found in this house as belonging to one Floyd O'Toole, Ma'am," one of them told her.

"Would he be a relative, Ma'am?" the other asked, as if it were his turn to speak.

Vangie could only stammer, "Floyd O'Toole?"

"Yes, Ma'am. Your brother Floyd. Complete set of prints." Now Cooley was "ma'am-ing' her, too.

"Floyd's my brother..." Vangie admitted. "But he's...he doesn't live here."

"Latent prints, Ma'am. Thumb only, but AFIS was able to get a positive match," Dark Suit Number One told her.

"AFIS?" Vangie turned to him in bewilderment.

"Automated Fingerprint Identification System," Number Two supplied.

"Gave us positive IDs on prints of two other known felons as well," Number One added.

"Members of a known drug ring," Number Two interjected. "Costa Ricans."

"Ha," Mama gloated. "Just goes to show how much you fellows know. If you can't tell the difference between Costa Ricans and Gypsies, you got no business calling yourselves law officers. Besides, Mr. Polaris is already on the case."

The look of bewilderment on Cooley's face deepened. "We don't got any Polarises on the force."

Mama's attempt to explain about Herb temporarily side-tracked the men from further questions about Floyd. Vangie, meanwhile, was breathing a silent prayer of thanks that she hadn't let on to Mama that Floyd had been hiding out in the basement.

Still, after they'd gone, Vangie felt guilty and more confused than ever. Should she have told them about Floyd? And what about the money? She'd stashed it back inside Elvis, but it was sitting on her conscience like a truckload of cement. She hadn't even revealed that part to Lacey McLeod. As for Mama, knowing about the money would only upset her more than she was already was. Since the break-in, she'd been prowling about all night, carrying Floyd's old baseball bat.

An unwanted thought kept creeping into Vangie's mind—if only she had someone like Herb Polaris to help her decide. Mama was right about one thing—the house would feel a lot safer with him around...uniform or not.

30. "He'll Have to Go"

Herb Polaris joined Placido Domingo in the rousing refrain of *Toreadore!* Konstanze covered her ears with her paws. He reached to tickle her ribs. "Damned music critic."

Herb laughed aloud as he downshifted for the Dundalk exit. It was going to be great, revealing that money to Vangie, loot that was hers to keep, cash that no one would ever be able to trace or claim. Before taking care of Floyd O'Toole, he'd managed to wring out of the miserable creep the full story, including where Floyd had hidden his illegal stash.

The $250,000 that was sitting in Vangie's mannequin could make a huge difference in her life. Now, if she wanted, she could quit her job at the Kmart, go to college fulltime, hire a bodyguard for Lotte while she went to Graceland. Hell, with all that moola she could *rent* Graceland.

Not that when people got their hands on money they necessarily used it to get what they wanted for themselves. He was proof enough of that. God knows. With what he could get if he sold the warehouse and the trucks and the business, he could easily have the music store he'd always dreamed of owning. Top-notch selection of all the great classics…symphony, baroque, opera. He'd hire a staff that genuinely appreciated music and really knew their stuff. *Try this version by the London Symphony, Ma'am.. I think you'll enjoy the way Pavarotti handles the vibrato in this one, Sir.*

So why didn't he do it? Maybe because he'd never had the right motivation. Maybe it was time to give it some serious consideration.

Weird, though, to think of Vangie with all that dough. Actually, not all that pleasant a thought—money changed people. Marissa had changed, and look where that had left him. Or look at the people who won big bucks in the lottery. Too often, five years later they were broke and in debt. Did he really want Vangie to be any different from the way she was?

Why was he getting so worked up about this anyhow? All he was going to do was tell Vangie about the money, make sure she held onto it for herself, then get the hell out of there. What she did afterwards was her business.

***

Vangie met him at the door. Herb was bursting to tell her about Floyd stashing the loot inside her Elvis mannequin, but, before he could say a word, she nodded toward Lotte and motioned him to be quiet. Later, when Lotte went into the kitchen to start dinner, he started to speak, but Vangie put her finger to her lips and signaled for him to follow her upstairs.

The Elvis mannequin in his little grotto was as Floyd had described him. Vangie unzipped the front of the costume and began pulling out packet after packet of hundred dollar bills. "Two hundred forty-nine thousand, three hundred and sixty dollars," she said. "One of the packets was broken."

Herb whistled at the sight of the actual cash. "So you found all this inside the Elvis mannequin?"

Vangie nodded, staring stared thoughtfully at the stacks of bills. "Floyd could have hidden it there, but I don't think he had any money. I even had to buy clothes and food for him. Then the police said they found fingerprints from members of a drug gang, but why would they break into our house and leave money behind?"

Herb hesitated, having second thoughts about revealing where the money came from. Would Vangie feel better or worse if she knew the truth about Floyd and his gang? "Any way you look at it, I figure the money's yours," he assured her. "You can do a lot with two hundred fifty thousand."

"Yes." Vangie stared out the window. "That money *could* do a lot."

Herb looked away out the window. Here it came. Already Vangie was beginning to realize that now she had the means to change her life, change herself even. New clothes, a car, a house in a nicer neighborhood. Soon she'd *be* a different person. No more need for him, a forty-nine-year-old trucker—well, forty-eight and a half—with a shady background.

What the hell was he thinking about anyhow? Just because he'd admired the way Vangie stuck by her Mother, just because he enjoyed being around her, why assume she had the same feelings for him? His only reason for coming back to Dundalk had been to tell her about the money. Nothing more.

Caught up in those thoughts, he was surprised when Vangie asked if he'd mind staying for dinner, said she needed his advice on how she should handle "the problem of the money." Funny. Not many people who'd just had two hundred fifty grand dumped in their laps would refer to it as a "problem." But he'd stick around a bit, help her take it to the bank or bury it in the back yard or whatever she decided to do with the damned stuff. Besides, Lotte O'Toole was clearly delighted that he was back. "It always feels safer when there's a uniformed man in the house," she'd told him before tottering happily off to the kitchen.

Vangie seemed unusually quiet during the meal. Lotte, on the other hand, insisted on giving him a blow-by-blow description of that afternoon's Geraldo program and a synopsis of the latest "Designing Women" episode.

He expected that when dinner was finished, Vangie would tell him what she planned to do with the money, but she seemed distracted and quiet. Soon after, Herb made an excuse to leave. He'd done what he came to do and it was back to Newark, back to business as usual.

Once they were on the Interstate, he mused aloud to Konstanze, "Odd how Vangie never even mentioned the money again. Probably thinking about how many Mercedes she can buy with over two hundred grand. Anyhow, the loot's her problem, it's out of my hands. From now on Vangie and her lousy money are on their own."

***

With nearly two hundred fifty thousand dollars sitting inside Elvis, it was impossible to concentrate on "Partially Owned Subsidiaries" and "Intercompany Sales of Intangible Assets." Maybe that's what the Elvis money was, an intangible asset, something not meant to be touched. On the other hand, what Herb had said made a lot of sense. "You ask me, Vangie, you oughta use that money, quit your job at the Kmart, go to college full-time like you were telling me you wanted to."

It was tempting. No more blue-light specials. No more covering up for Dennis. No more breaking in cashiers who spent more time telling each other about last night's date than waiting on customers. The best part would be going to regular classes, not having to memorize stuff like "consolidated retained earnings" and "deferred income liability" late at night with eyes so bleary they could scarcely see the numbers on the page. She could sit for the CPA exam, get licensed, be qualified for a meaningful job.

Nearly a quarter of a million dollars. So much money. Even a small part of it would be enough to buy a used car, get that dishwasher for Mama. Look at the way Elvis had splurged. If she followed his example, she might hire a limousine so she and Darla could ride home from the Kmart in style…buy Mama a new Cadillac…rent an amusement park and invite all the Elvis-4-

Ever Fan Club members. But then there'd be the IRS. Flashing a lot of cash around would be an open invitation to an audit. *Yes, Agent Jones, I found it all in Elvis!*

Sure, Miss O'Toole…and I'm Frankie Avalon.

But who was she kidding? She'd never feel right about spending that Elvis money. It wasn't hers. Half jokingly she said aloud to the mannequin, "Come on, Elvis, give me the answers. What am I supposed to do with all that cash?"

Vangie suddenly felt a prickling sensation run down her spine as if Elvis was trying to give her the answers she needed. She shivered.

The money was put there for a purpose.

An involuntary shudder ran through her body. A purpose, the voice was telling her. But what purpose?

Look in your accounting book. What does it say?

This was ten times weirder than any of Mama's "episodes." Still the voice was so compelling that she reached instinctively for her accounting text. The book was open to the chapter on Real Estate. The words "best and highest use" seemed to jump off the page at her.

***

At breakfast, Vangie mulled over the words for the hundredth time. "Best and highest use." What did it mean? What would be a "best and highest use" for two hundred fifty thousand dollars? That would be easier to answer if she knew for sure where the money came from. Something to do with Floyd which meant something illegal, but what and where and how?

The phone rang just as she was preparing to leave for work. Mama answered. "For you," she said. "That reporter woman."

Lacey McLeod's voice was charged with excitement. Something had come up, she said, something too important to discuss on the phone. Could they meet and talk? Mystified, Vangie agreed to meet her at noon.

***

Lacey McLeod squirmed impatiently in the booth at Benny's Lunch, her eyes focused on the door. No Vangie as yet. It was still early, but the rush she'd gotten from Tim's McCoskey's latest news had her on edge. "This Floyd O'Toole was hooked up with a big drug gang down in Miami. Seems he ripped off the cash from one of their drug deals, then high-tailed it out of town. Now his prints show up in that house in Dundalk. And—get this—the cops also lifted prints from two other members of the gang."

Lacey squirmed in anticipation. Here it was, the inside scoop on Floyd O'Toole practically in the palm of her hot little hand. Positive I.D. of the fingerprints in the O'Toole house, Tim said. No matter what it took, this story wasn't getting away. A front-page byline. Maybe even a raise. The way day care costs for Tissie had gone up this year, God knows she could use the money.

Getting Vangie to cooperate would be the key. It had been obvious that Vangie still felt a sense of loyalty to her brother. But surely when she was confronted with the evidence she'd spill what she knew concerning Floyd's whereabouts. With drug dealers hot on his trail, Floyd was a dead pigeon unless he gave himself up.

Actually, it turned out to be easier than Lacey had anticipated. Before she could even broach the subject of Floyd, Vangie hesitated a moment. "I need to ask your advice." Her tone made it obvious something serious was coming.

Lacey decided to play it light until she found out what was on Vangie's mind. "You want to know if you can wear a print top with a striped skirt?"

Vangie shook her head. "I...I found something," she said. "Something I don't know what to do with."

"Does this 'something' you found have anything to do with your brother Floyd?"

Vangie showed no surprise at Lacey's question. "Yes. Floyd."

Vangie sat frozen in thought for a very long time and some instinct told Lacey to restrain her curiosity. Her patience paid off. When Vangie spoke at last, her words were electrifying. "Two hundred fifty thousand dollars. It was inside my Elvis mannequin."

In a flash, Lacey saw the headlines—"Drug Loot Found in Elvis Mannequin. Star Reporter Breaks Mystery of 250 Gs in Elvis." Oh, this was the big one, all right. It was all she could do to restrain herself from jumping up and rushing to a phone.

But a hunch told Lacey there was even more on Vangie's mind. *Never assume you've heard the whole story. Sometimes the most truth is revealed after you think you've got it all—* Rule Number Eight in the "Interviewing Techniques" textbook. Again Lacey waited patiently while Vangie withdrew into deep silence. Then, as if she'd finally reached a decision, Vangie straightened, stared thoughtfully across the table at Lacey and announced, "I need your help."

"My help? For what?"

"The money. I've been trying to decide what I should do with it. Last night.... Well, let's just say that Elvis helped me decide. 'Best and highest use.' I didn't realize right off what that meant, but now I understand."

"You've decided on the 'best and highest use' for the money?"

Vangie nodded. "If it came from a gang of drug dealers, I realize I can't give it back to them. And Floyd's gone, so I can't give it to him. It doesn't belong to the police, either. But there is one place where that money could do a lot of good…the kids at St. Ignatius. I want you to help me figure out a way to get it to them without anyone knowing where it came from."

Lacey was almost too stunned to stammer. "You…you're going to *give away* all that money."

Vangie nodded. "It's the only way. But nobody must ever know where it came from. You'd have to promise that."

Lacey could only sit staring at Vangie, as her hopes for a front-page spread imploded. No story about Floyd. No screaming banner headlines. No raise. It wasn't fair…it just wasn't fair.

But in her heart she already knew she couldn't, and wouldn't, refuse Vangie's plea.

So how *could* a person donate two hundred fifty thousand bucks without anyone catching on to where it came from? The two of them sat for a long time pondering, trying one idea after another. No matter what scheme they considered—and there were many—neither Lacey nor Vangie was able to come up with a solution.

31. "Here Comes Santa Claus"

Vangie stepped from the elevator. Heather McNair's parents were standing at the counter fronting the nurse's station, their faces creased with concern. They were showing the duty nurse a sheet of paper, a computer printout. The nurse on duty this Thursday was not Miss Mathews but the tall, cool-looking blond who never really seemed to connect with the patients. "You'll have to take that up with Accounting," she said, scarcely glancing up from her charts. "All the billing's handled down there."

The McNairs turned away from the desk, Mrs. McNair looking as if she'd cry at any moment, her husband's mouth set in a grim line. "All I want to know is how they come up with nine hundred dollars that our insurance doesn't cover and what the hell is this Item 20? They make the damned bills so complicated nobody can read them."

Mr. McNair's complaint was one Vangie had heard often from patients and their families. He was right about the hospital's billing being difficult to read. "Would you like me to check with the Accounting office...see if I can get an explanation?" she asked.

"Would you?" Mr. McNair handed over the printout. "It's these items here we don't understand."

A quick scan of the figures showed a discrepancy between the total, the amount covered by insurance, and the amount charged to the patient. "If it's okay with you," Vangie said, "I'll take this down to Accounting right now and see what I can find out.".

Nothing was ever as simple as it ought to be. At the accounting office Vangie found herself shunted around to five different people before she finally ended up at the desk of a Mrs. Helmsley who examined her volunteer badge closely before motioning her to a chair. She showed the woman the printout. "The figures in column one don't seem to agree with the totals," she pointed out.

Mrs. Helmsley frowned and pulled her calculator across the desktop. "Hematology, eleven fifty. Lab, nine ninety-five," she mumbled aloud. She frowned again and re-checked the figures. "You're right. Somebody's made a mistake. This doesn't add up."

"I thought so. Actually it looks as if the code for pathology got entered twice."

"You're right. How did you pick up on that so quickly?"

Vangie found herself explaining to Mrs. Helmsley that she loved working with numbers and had taken some accounting classes.

When they were finished, Mrs. Helmsley sat back in her desk chair and surveyed Vangie for a moment. "So what's your ultimate career goal, Miss O'Toole?" she asked.

Funny, that was practically the same question Herb had asked her. The way Mrs. Helmsley put it—"career goal"—made her feel a little more confident in replying, "I guess what I'd really like is to feel I'm using what I've learned in my accounting classes for something more than just waiting on customers at the Kmart, something where I could help people at times when they need it."

Mrs. Helmsley tapped the desktop with the end of her pen. "We've discussed the idea of creating a position to handle patient relations, but the budget's extremely tight just now. If you'll leave your name and phone number with me, I'll call you in case something comes up."

They chatted for a few more minutes, with Mrs. Helmsley asking a lot of questions about Vangie's studies and her volunteer work at the hospital.

When Vangie returned to the ward, Heather's parents stepped out into the hall where Vangie explained to them that they'd be getting a corrected bill. Both thanked her for her help. "Did you notice Heather now has the Lisa Marie doll tucked under her covers?" Mrs. McNair whispered with a smile as they tiptoed back into the room.

But there was no need for quiet. This day even Heather was sitting up to watch the departure of one of the ward's patients. As soon as Tandora spotted Vangie she waved a thin arm excitedly. "*Mi Tia* she is come!" she cried, her face glowing with excitement. Vangie ran to hug the child then greeted the thin, haggard-looking young woman who stared shyly with dark eyes that were exact replicas of Tandora's own.

"Tandora say you her *amiga*...friend," the woman stammered. "She say cannot leave *hospital* until say *adios* for Miss Vangie."

"Tandora's a very special little girl," Vangie told the aunt. "Please take good care of her."

"*Si*. My church have arranged for place for us to live, some people to help us. I will taking very good care."

From the way the woman touched Tandora's hair as they wheeled the child down the hall, Vangie could see that that was a promise the aunt intended to keep. Moments later, the small wheelchair disappeared inside the elevator, and Vangie felt a huge emptiness inside. She reminded herself that the children came, the children left. She could only help them while they were here. Still, the sight of Tandora's empty crib aroused an odd mixture of emotions, jubilation that this one small warrior had survived mingled with a sense of loss for a child who—God willing—she'd never see again.

***

While Tissie was upstairs getting into her pajamas, Lacey McLeod sat with a cup of coffee, debating the big question. How could Vangie give the money to the hospital? No way she could just dump two hundred fifty thousand dollars at the Visitors Information desk. If she got in touch with the hospital's board, there would be all sorts of questions. The ever-present IRS was another factor. If that much dough turned up, Uncle Sam would want to know where it came from.

India Marlowe's fund-raiser for the hospital—did that present any possibilities? The dinner and auction were scheduled for a week from Saturday. But what about the problem of total secrecy? Just then, Tissie called out, "Mommie, my clown's zipper is stuck—I can't get my PJs out."

Lacey went upstairs to her daughter's room and worked free the zipper on the back of the clown doll that held Tissie's pajamas. Then, with the zipper halfway down the clown's back, the answer struck—the perfect way for Vangie to donate the money anonymously.

32. "It Feels So Right"

Herb's heart gave an unexpected quiver when he picked up his office phone late Wednesday afternoon and heard Vangie's voice. "Herb," she asked, "if a person wanted to deliver something to a certain place, but didn't want anyone to know about it, how would they manage it?"

Herb thought for a moment. "Depends. Do you mean deliver something to a private residence or to a warehouse or what?"

"Suppose, for instance, something had to be delivered to the Civic Center in downtown Baltimore, but without anyone knowing where it came from."

"Piece of cake," he told her. "Places like that got security guards, cleaning people. No problem finding someone who'll help slip something in. Why? You got something you want delivered?"

"Maybe. But I would need your help."

When she explained Lacey's plan to him he was stunned. "You're giving the dough away? All of it?"

"It's what he would want, Herb."

He didn't have to ask her who the 'he' was—Elvis.

***

Getting a life-sized Elvis mannequin into the Baltimore Civic Center in the middle of a charity auction wasn't turning out to be quite the 'piece of cake' Herb had assured Vangie it would be. First off, there was both an Afro-American festival and a Shriner's parade jamming the Inner Harbor area. Every downtown street was clogged with pedestrians and traffic. Twice, a cop waved him on when he tried to make the turn into the alley that led to the Civic Center's loading area.

When Herb finally managed to park the van, Lacey McLeod was waiting, but the maintenance man she'd located earlier had disappeared. The security guard sitting on a stool inside the loading exit made it clear he had no intention of abandoning his comic book. "Nobody din't say nothing to me 'bout no more donations coming in. 'Sides, they already started with the auctioning."

Herb peeled five tens from his wallet.

The comic book fell to the man's lap. "Well...guess one more piece ain't gonna make no difference. Lez see what you got."

Herb opened the back of the truck and showed him Elvis.

"You mean you think one of them bluebloods in there—" the man jerked his thumb toward the huge hall, "you mean one of them is gonna buy this thing?"

"Sure," Lacey told him. "Just think how nice Elvis will look in someone's foyer."

"Man, them rich people sure got some weird taste. Say, why you hanging that sheet over it?"

"It's kind of a surprise," Lacey improvised. "What they call the *piece de resistance* of the whole auction."

Herb wheeled the now-concealed Elvis down the truck's ramp. "All you gotta do," he told the guard, "is leave Elvis on this dolly. Then, when the auctioneer gets down to the last couple of items, you wheel him in. If anybody should ask you what gives, just explain that it's a last-minute prize somebody just dropped off."

"An' that's all I gotta do?"

"That's all." Herb removed five more tens from his wallet but did not offer to hand them to the guard. "You got fifty now. Do the job and the rest is yours. A hundred bucks for a couple of minutes work."

"Ain't no bomb or nothing inside that thing, is there?"

"Hey, man, come on—you think I'd be fooling around with this thing if it was loaded to blow up?"

"Okay, but I ain't taking no chances. I gotta feel that hundred in my pocket before this dummy gets in the door."

***

At the head table, India Marlowe squirmed in her seat, the famous green eyes dark with rage. "Not one thing has gone right this whole bloody evening," she hissed when Daniel Dulaney Stowell rejoined her after his fourth trip to the bar. "And after all my hard work to make this event a success."

Daniel swayed into his chair. "Ummm. Must admit that waiter was a bit clumsy."

"A bit clumsy? The stupid fool absolutely ruined my gown. When I stood to be introduced it looked as if I'd wet myself. And this food—an utter disaster. The vichyssoise so salty no one could eat it. The Beef Wellington dry as sawdust and equally flavorful. Then that business with the dessert."

Daniel chuckled boozily. "Ah, yes. Certainly was spectacular, that waiter spilling brandy down the front of his uniform, then running out of the kitchen in flames when they lit his Baked Alaska."

"I see nothing whatsoever amusing about that."

"But you have to admit it added a bit of...flare...to the event." Daniel chuckled at his own pun and India's glare darkened.

Just then the auctioneer's chant interrupted. "Do I hear one thousand for this gorgeous full-length mink? One thousand? One thousand? Nine hundred? Will anyone open the bidding at five hundred....?

"Oh, God," India groaned. "Even the auction is a total flop. Nobody's willing to make an offer on any of the furs with those ridiculous animal rights people lurking about. Just like they refused to bid on the vacation trip to Egypt simply because a couple of British tourists got themselves murdered last week."

What was really driving India's anger was her utter embarrassment—Daniel had been forced to bid in the gorgeous gown she'd worn in her last movie. Three hundred measly dollars was all it brought. No wonder these damned bluebloods still had their old money. They'd been sitting on it for the last two centuries.

Daniel wasn't helping the situation any, either. So far he'd spent the half the evening in the bar and the other half talking with that horse-faced Caroline Carruthers about "withers" and "hackamores," whatever the hell they might be. CeeCee. Judging from the way she kept falling over her own feet, those initials ought to stand for "Clumsy Crone."

India's chain of morbid thoughts was broken when Daniel suddenly exclaimed, "I say, what's going on up there?"

She glanced toward the raised platform at the front of the room. A man in a security guard's uniform was wheeling in a sheet-covered object, a statue, judging by the shape of it. He whispered something to the auctioneer.

The auctioneer picked up his microphone. "Ladies and gentlemen, your attention, please," he croaked. "We have what seems to be a surprise donation."

India craned to get a better look as the security guard removed the sheet. Her mouth gaped open then she leaped to her feet. "What kind of a lousy joke is some sonofabitch trying to pull? Get that thing the bloody hell out of here!"

Laughter erupted from all corners of the room, gleeful waves of mocking laughter that only added to India's seething fury as she stormed toward the stage.

***

Mike Dowling lifted the camera strapped around his neck and pretended to focus on Lacey as he strolled toward her desk. "Miss Celebrity," he said. "I guess we'll be seeing our star reporter on Good Morning, America."

Lacey couldn't hide her elation. Even if her byline was below the fold, it had finally made the *Star's* front page, the header in 6-Point Bold--*Mysterious Donation Stuns Baltimore Charity Function.*

"I damn near croak every time I think about the expressions on the faces of that society crowd when Elvis was unveiled." Mike gloated.

"How about when the auctioneer read the note Vangie taped in Elvis's hand?" Lacey said. "The money you will find inside this mannequin is donated to St. Ignatius Hospital's Fund Drive in the name of Elvis Aaron Presley who truly cared about those in need and often gave anonymously to those he wanted to help."

"And the look on everyone's face when they started dragging those packets of bills out of Elvis's gut."

Lacey rolled her eyes heavenward. "It's almost too perfect. Nearly two hundred fifty thousand bucks from a drug deal that soured, and now it's all going to help those kids."

Mike grinned agreement. "I still think the biggest surprise of all was when that horsey Carruthers woman jumped up and offered five hundred for the Elvis mannequin. Didn't that Greenspring Valley crowd get into it then. Can you believe they bid that mannequin up to fifteen thousand?"

Lacey shook her head. "Elvis himself must be looking down with delight at that turn of events. Especially after the guy who bought the mannequin turned around and donated it to the children's ward."

"Hey," Mike said, "Did you get a load of the look on Daniel Dulaney's face after la Marlowe went ape and made a total fool of herself?"

"Yeah. Looks like Marriage Number Five will end even quicker than the previous four."

Lacey read through her piece once more, this time checking for the flaws and omissions that always seemed to pop up once an article was in print. To her relief, she could find none. The only down side was that she'd thrown away a chance for an even bigger story, one that would have had much more lasting impact on her career. But to expose Vangie and her mother to charges of harboring a criminal would have been, in itself, criminal. They were decent people. The mother a little dotty perhaps, but then who wasn't when you came right down to it?

"You know, "Mike observed, "that Herb Polaris seems like a really decent guy."

Lacey nodded agreement. "No wonder Vangie's so gone on him. You should have seen the way she glowed when she was helping him load the mannequin. I could tell she wanted to go with us to the Civic Center, but she respected Herb's argument that that would be too dangerous. Too much chance that someone might spot her and make the connection between Floyd and the money."

After Mike left, Lacey sat staring for a long time toward the elevators where he had disappeared, but it was Tim McCloskey who occupied her thoughts.

Actually, Tim McCloskey and Herb Polaris were a lot alike. Same easy grin, same lack of pretension, both of them guys who knew who they were, what they were, guys who didn't need to hide behind phony fronts. Maybe it was time she responded a little more positively when Tim asked her out. Heck, maybe she'd even ask him out...or at least invite him along when she and Tissie went to out to the Farm Museum this Saturday.

Anyhow, that was the end of the Floyd O'Toole story, a '30.' This evening she'd stop by Vangie's house, interview the club members who were going to Graceland, and that would wind up her involvement with the Elvis-4-Ever club. In the meantime, before she lost her nerve....

Lacey reached for her cell phone and punched in Tim's number.

33. "I Slipped, I Stumbled, I Fell"

Gecko cringed in the passenger seat as Jose, glowering like a bull with banderillos in his neck, returned from telephoning. "One last chance we got, *hombre*," Jose snarled. "We don' find that money this time, we kiss our asses *adios*."

"I don' wan' to go back in that place. Is *un sitio malo*. *Muy* bad. *Mi Abuela* she say...."

Jose jammed the accelerator to the floor, flinging Gecko back against his seat. "I don't give a shit what your *abuela* say. Tonight we gonna go back to that house, find that money, nail O'Toole."

Gecko grabbed for the armrest. "So what about the girl, the old woman? How we supposed to get them to leave?"

"Cinecero say no more Mister Nice Guys. Soon as it's dark tonight, nine o'clock, we break in, do whatever necessary." He patted the gun in his pocket for emphasis. "I figure this time we go in through that basement window in the back. That way, we take the old lady and the girl by surprise."

"Hokay. But *mi abuela*..."

***

Herb, chewing thoughtfully on the end of a pencil, squinted out his office window. Not a good sign, Lacey McLeod's story getting picked up by the wire services, smeared all across the country. They'd even done a piece about it on "Good Morning, America." That could be dangerous if Cenicero spotted the story and connected it with Floyd. Still, , even if Cenicero got wind of what had happened to his dough, what could he do? He sure wasn't going to haul ass up to Baltimore and strong arm the hospital into giving it back. Of course, he could_take it out of Floyd's hide if he ever caught up with him. But that wasn't likely, either, at least not in the near future.

Herb rolled the pencil reflectively between his fingers. Floyd. At least that problem had been neatly taken care of. Before shipping the punk out on that guano freighter bound for South America, he'd warned him that if so much as he set foot on U.S. soil any time during the next three years he, personally, would see to it Cenicero got a shot at him. No, Floyd was safely out of the mob's reach.

An even more remote possibility, but a much more serious one, was that Cenicero would figure out the connection between that money and the Elvis fan club. If that happened, Vangie might become Cenicero's target.

Herb dropped the pencil on the desk and, with the same motion, scooped up Konstanze from the "Out" basket. "Why am I kidding myself?" he demanded of the cat. "I'd be some kind of creep if I abandoned a woman who's given away all that dough to help sick kids." He retrieved his hat and jacket, gathered up the keys to the small van, and headed for the fenced lot behind the office.

***

Being around the kids usually took Vangie's mind off other worries, but this afternoon it didn't seem to help. Every time she looked over at the Elvis mannequin she was reminded that in a few days the rest of the club members would be leaving for Graceland. Once again she'd be left behind.

She wheeled seven-year-old Donnie out to the playroom. Silly to be disappointed over missing out on a trip when little kids like him were the ones with real troubles, like would he ever be well enough to leave this place, like would the next remission be the last one? Questions that made "Will I ever get to Graceland?" sound downright selfish.

She settled Donnie with the Lego blocks and went back to get the new boy, Rick. Those two ought to get along fine, both of them red-hot GI Joe addicts. As she wheeled Rick past the nursing station, Miss Mathews called out, "Telephone for you, Vangie. Somebody from the accounting office, a Mrs. Helmsley."

It took a moment's thought before Vangie could place the name, then it came to her—the woman in the accounting office, the one who'd taken care of the error in the McNair's billing. "Tell her I'll call back in a few minutes," she said.

Vangie parked Rick's chair alongside Donnie's and dug the plastic soldiers figures out of the toy box, then hurried back to the desk to call the Accounting Office. Why would Mrs. Helmsley would be calling her? Possibly something to do with the McNair's bill.

But it wasn't the McNair's bill Mrs. Helmsley wanted to discuss. "I've been telling our Administrator about you, Miss O'Toole," she said. "For some time now we've been considering the feasibility of hiring someone as an ombudsman, a go-between who would help the patients and their families better understand hospital billing procedures, assist them with insurance forms and such. Would you be interested?"

Would she be interested? Could Elvis Presley sing? Did the Kmart have blue-light specials? Mrs. Helmsley's question bowled her over so she could hardly stammer, "But I'm not sure I'm qualified. I'm only in the junior year of my accounting program."

"That's no problem. A basic knowledge of accounting procedures will be helpful, but the ability to interact with people will be even more so. I understand from talking to the staff on the Pediatric ward that you are excellent in that regard. Also, since hospital accounting procedures are somewhat unique, I think you'll find this position will give you excellent on-the-job training. But we can talk about all that later. Why don't you stop by my office this afternoon and we can discuss what duties the job would comprise, what your salary would be."

As she hung up the phone, Vangie felt giddy with excitement. Could this be Elvis's way of letting her know she'd done the right thing by giving up that money? What would the hospital staff do if she turned cartwheels all the way down the hall? Who cared—Vangie O'Toole was going to be an ombudsman.

NOTICE TO ALL CLUB MEMBERS

SYLVIA WILL BE HANDING OUT YOUR

TICKETS AS YOU BOARD THE BUS

INCLUDING TICKETS FOR SPECIAL EVENTS.

BOARDING TIME IS 10:30 SHARP AND

ANYONE NOT AT THE STATION AT THAT TIME

WILL BE LEFT BEHIND.

BRENDA SUE HIGGS, PRESIDENT

ELVIS-4-EVER FAN CLUB

34. "Fools Rush In"

Vangie's earlier exuberance dissolved when the women from the fan club discussed final plans for the trip. Earlier she'd given Dennis notice that she was leaving the Kmart but agreed to stay on until the end of August. She might as well be working— for her, Graceland was nothing more than an impossible dream. Ever since the break-in Mama was more convinced than ever that she was in mortal danger of being kidnapped by Gypsies. "Look what happened the minute I left the house. Next time it's me they'll be taking."

Vangie struggled to keep a smile glued to her face as she admired the display Cara had designed for her Memphis motel window. She assured Vera that the candles she'd made to place on Elvis's grave, one in the shape of a motorcycle, the other a guitar, would be unique. She even admired Aarona's new Priscilla-style hairdo. But it became harder to keep smiling when Lacey McLeod showed up to interview the women who were going on the trip.

Tomorrow, while they were on the bus, rolling toward Memphis, she'd be in the Kmart, dealing with Rubbermaid garbage cans, polyester blouses, and bags of kitty litter. After that, home. Mama, another evening of "Jeopardy" and old John Wayne movies. Even her Elvis mannequin was gone now. Tonight the mirrors that lined his niche would reflect nothing but her own face.

Herb was gone now, too. Back to Newark.

***

It was eight fifteen when Herb knocked on the front screen door of the O'Toole house. Lotte O'Toole greeted him with the news that the Elvis-4-Ever Fan Club members were gathered in the basement. "They're down there settling up last minute things for the trip some of the girls are taking."

Herb noticed that Lotte cleverly avoided mentioning that Vangie would not be going with the others. As if aware of the omission, Vangie's mother immediately launched into a description of a talk show about a couple who were raising their adopted son along with a baby chimp.

Herb was still trying to extricate himself when Vangie came upstairs to get some lemonade and cookies. Was it seeing him or spotting Konstanze that made her face light up like that? Herb couldn't tell for certain. One thing he was sure of—even her welcoming smile couldn't quite cover up the sadness in her eyes. And no wonder. Enough to make anyone miserable, having to listen to the other women plan their trip to Graceland knowing she wouldn't be going. "Do you mind if I take Konstanze down to the basement?" Vangie asked. I'd like to show her to everybody."

"How about if I help you carry down the refreshments?" he said and picked up the tray.

As she followed Herb down the stairs to the basement, Vangie couldn't help thinking the day had turned out to be a roller-coaster of ups and downs. Finding Herb there the kitchen with Konstanze in his arms, a feeling had shot through her, one she couldn't describe except that it made her feel the way she always felt when she heard Elvis sing "If I can Dream." Cheeks flaming, she was unable to hide her delight. Even better, Herb seemed as pleased to see her as she was to see him. He was quick to offer to carry the pitcher of lemonade and tray of cookies.

She and Herb were halfway down the stairs, Konstanze at their heels, when the front doorbell sounded. Vangie paused until she heard Mama call, "I'll get it," then continued on down. Herb's unexpected appearance generated a medley of excited exclamations and knowing glances from the club members. While the women clustered around Herb, Vangie began distributing the refreshments. She had begun pouring lemonade into the paper cups when a commotion broke out up above—loud voices and the thump of heavy shoes across the floor. A moment later Officer Cooley and the two federal officers came bounding down the stairs, guns drawn. Lotte followed close behind, pounding her tiny fists against the rigid shoulders of one of the Dark Suits.

"Freeze!" Cooley commanded as he reached the foot of the stairs. "Don't anyone move.

"You people get out of here," Mama shrieked, continuing to attack the agent with her fists. "This is my house and I say you got no business busting in like this."

"Ma'am, we're federal officers," the man protested, using his forearm to ward off her blows.

"Ma'am, if you interfere we will be forced to place you under arrest," the other echoed.

"Everybody freeze," Cooley shouted again, obviously enjoying his part in the drama.

Meanwhile, like figures in a tableau, Vangie, Herb, Lacey and the club members all stopped motionless, too stunned to do anything but gape as the three men charged into the basement clubroom. "Okay, we got a warrant here for the arrest of one Floyd O'Toole," Cooley announced. "Positive ID on the fingerprints we took from the commode." "I'd advise all of you to stand back and not to interfere with officers of the law."

"Floyd's not here," Vangie gasped.

Ignoring her protest, one of the federal men strode over and flung open the door to the powder room, much to the embarrassment of the seated Eudora Harkins. Crimson with embarrassment, the man slammed the door closed and jerked open the one leading to the laundry room. With his cohort covering him, the man checked out the interior of the washing machine, the laundry tub and the dryer. "Clean," he muttered as he backed out of the room.

The agent swung around and motioned with his pistol to a door on the far wall. "What's in there?" he demanded of

Vangie, who, along with Herb, was trying to restrain her mother from attacking again.

"That's the furnace room," she explained. "And the old coal bin."

"We don't use coal," Mama said, momentarily distracted. "Changed to natural gas fifteen years ago."

"Stand back," Cooley ordered, motioning everyone away from that area of the basement.

Cautiously, the three men approached the door. One of the federal officers laid his ear against it, listened, then motioned with his free hand for silence. He straightened, grim-faced, and whispered, "Heard something." He motioned to Cooley and his partner to cover him as he prepared to break open the door. Cooley, losing his machismo, managed to position himself off to one side.

"On the count of three," the agent whispered. He turned the knob cautiously and, with a swift jerk, flung open the door. Like everyone else, Vangie could only gape at what the open door revealed: a scrawny Hispanic-looking man attempting to pull his stout partner backwards into the room through the narrow basement window.

35.　"We're Coming In Loaded"

Lacey McLeod toasted herself with the can of Pepsi on her desk. Life was sweet. The publisher practically fawning his approval. TV anchormen calling to interview her for the six o'clock news. A byline, Page One, thank you very much, this time *above* the fold.

Star's Reporter Covers Capture of Dangerous Drug Dealers.

Actually, she'd done a great job on the piece about the capture, if she did say so herself. The whole thing had been so bizarre, such a comic opera quality to those Keystone Kops nabbing a dangerous drug dealer who was stuck halfway through a basement window, his butt exposed as his partner tugged frantically on his trousers trying to yank him free.

Of course, there was one vital detail she'd had to omit from the story: what had happened to Floyd O'Toole. For Vangie's sake that would remain a secret. But at least Vangie's brother wasn't going to be dealing any more drugs for a long, long time to come. Herb Polaris's revelation had eased her mind on that issue. His handling of Floyd had been a stroke of genius, that job on a guano freighter the absolute essence of poetic justice.

Lacey glanced at her watch. Eleven-thirty. Just time to freshen up her makeup before her lunch date with Tim. Getting it together with a guy who worked nights wasn't a snap, but somehow it felt as if they were going to work things out this time. After all, as Tim had said after their date last Sunday, "There's no law says you can't make love with the sun shining."

***

From the deck of the guano freighter, Floyd O'Toole stared forlornly toward the coastline of Mexico sliding past, a hazy layer of green against the distant horizon. Hadn't been for his damned rotten luck, he and Angelina would be loafing on some Mexican beach right now, sipping Margueritas, snorting a few lines.

"By the time you get back, things will have cooled down," Herb Polaris had promised him. Oh, sure…by the time he got back. Sonuvabitch hadn't bothered to mention that this tub was heading first for Chile, then New Zealand, and back by way of Zanzibar. Guano all the way.

If Polaris thought one Floyd O'Toole was going to bust his ass shoveling bird shit for three years the boss had another think coming. So his luck had run out temporarily—big deal. Matter of fact, he was already hatching a plan: Pick up a load of dope in one of those Spic countries. Stash it inside those stinking bags of guano. This time make a killing for sure.

***

The limo glided down Gwynnbrook's elm-lined drive. India Marlowe glanced back over her shoulder at the hulking mansion perched on the hilltop behind. The last she'd ever see of this dump, thank God.

Even if this new role wasn't the lead, it was her ticket out of Greenspring Valley. She was still India Marlowe. She was still a star.

***

The club members milled around the Greyhound station, waiting for luggage to be tagged, saying goodbye to families and friends. Vangie had taken an early lunch hour to come see them off. She was trying hard to look cheerful and upbeat, not let anyone see her disappointment at being left behind. No reason to dampen everyone else's pleasure just because she couldn't go.

Brenda Sue promised Vangie she'd take lots of pictures. Pearl patted her shoulder and vowed to bring her a memento from the mansion. "Even if it's only a leaf or a blade of grass, you'll have something from there," she said.

Right up to the time the announcer called out "Graceland Express now boarding," Aarona kept insisting Vangie ought to just come ahead and go with them. "Call your Mama when you get there and tell her we hijacked you," she giggled.

All the women promised they'd be thinking of her during the candlelight vigil.

Through the glass doors of the bus terminal Vangie watched the big charter coach pull into the loading area. The women gathered their carry-on luggage, and she followed them out to the platform. Sylvia, who had stationed herself at the bus's door, handed out tickets as the members boarded.

The platform finally emptied, and the driver signaled for Sylvia to climb aboard. Brenda Sue tapped on the bus window and held up the candle Vangie had given her to light during the vigil by Elvis's grave. Vangie waved a last good-bye, then turned away quickly. All during the farewells she'd kept a smile plastered on her face, but now that the bus was preparing to pull away she was afraid her expression would betray her.

She shoved open the door to re-enter the terminal building, but just then she heard Sylvia screech, "Wait!"

Turning, Vangie saw the bus door re-open. Sylvia disembarked, still clutching tickets in her hand. "There's somebody missing," Vera called over her shoulder to the bus driver. "I've still got three tickets left. One's mine. One would have been Vangie's, but she's not going. But there's a third."

From inside the bus someone called, "Where's Darla?"

"Oh, damn," Sylvia snapped," that's it. Last I saw Darla she was flirting with that soldier who was waiting for his bus to Aberdeen Proving Grounds. Hold a minute while I run back in the terminal to take a look."

Vangie started to follow Sylvia through the glass door to the terminal building, when suddenly the air was split by a tremendous blast, an air horn blaring loud enough to make her eardrums ring. Startled, she turned and saw a huge tractor-trailer pull into the loading area.

36. "Memphis, Tennessee"

Herb eased the rig into the flow of traffic on the Interstate, right behind the Greyhound with the huge Elvis poster taped to the back and the sound of "All Shook Up" blaring out of the open windows. He glanced over at his passengers. Lotte O'Toole and Konstanze were sharing the seat like long-time traveling companions, the two of them staring straight ahead through the windshield, surveying the passing scenery, a pair of queens looking down upon the peasantry. Feeling his glance, Lotte turned ever so briefly to give him a thumbs-up sign accompanied by a triumphant grin.

You just couldn't figure women, especially Lotte O'Toole. Here he'd thought the hardest part of the whole business would be convincing Vangie's mother to go along with his scheme. Was he ever wrong. The old girl seemed as pleased as he was at the stunt they'd just pulled off.

All in all it had been quite a day. First persuading the guy from the temporary labor agency to round up six of his biggest, strongest workers on a moment's notice. Then arriving at the O'Toole house with the truck and crew only to find that Vangie had already left for work. "She's taking an early lunch hour and going directly to the bus station to see the others off," Lotte O'Toole informed him.

Actually, it had turned out to be best that way. Lotte O'Toole was the one he had to persuade and, as he'd guessed, it had been easier without Vangie there. "I've got a plan, Lotte," he told her. "I need your help."

At first he'd thought she was going to balk when he told her they were all going to Graceland. But she'd seen the light when he explained that none of her possessions would be left behind for the Gypsies to steal. "These men are going to load all your furniture into the van, every single thing in the house."

"You mean everything?"

"Right down to the sugar in the sugar bowl," he told her.

"And then we'll all go to Graceland?"

"Right. Vangie on the bus. You, me, and Konstanze in my truck."

"Can we stop at one of those Stuckey's places on the way? Mabel McWhirter always says they've got the best pecan candy."

"Stop any place you want," he assured her.

"So what are we waiting for. Tell those fellows to get busy. I'll go pack Vangie's suitcase."

No problem getting the crew he'd hired to pitch into the job. The promise of an extra hundred apiece if they finished in two hours flat had worked miracles. It had been close, but they'd pulled it off. By 10:20 they'd loaded the trailer with every last stick of furniture, every knickknack from the O'Toole house right down to the goldfish bowl and Lotte's TV Guide.

By 10:21, he, Mama and Konstanze were in the van and ready to roll. He'd begun to worry a bit when downtown traffic had proved heavier than he would have liked. By the time they arrived at the bus station he was sweating bullets for fear the chartered bus would have gone.

Thinking back on that scene at the bus station, Herb laughed out loud. That stunned look on Vangie's face when she saw the truck with him and Mama and Konstanze pull into the parking lot was one he'd long remember. He'd practically had to lift her onto the bus, and how those women had cheered. But it was Vangie's mile-wide grin that made it all worthwhile.

Just for kicks, Herb stepped on the gas and pulled up alongside the Greyhound. Vangie, seated next to the third window from the rear, spotted the truck immediately. An ecstatic grin lit her face as her lips formed the word Graceland.

Herb eased back into the line of traffic. For just a minute there he could have sworn the huge Elvis poster that decorated the rear of the bus had given him a sly wink. Herb grinned, the strains of "That's All Right, Mama!" running through his head as they rolled on south toward Memphis.